The Honey Jam Murder

by

Meg Benjamin

Luscious Delights, Book Four

Copyright Notice
This is a work of fiction. Names, characters, places, and incidents are either the product of the author's imagination or are used fictitiously, and any resemblance to actual persons living or dead, business establishments, events, or locales, is entirely coincidental.

The Honey Jam Murder

COPYRIGHT © 2024 by Margaret Batschelet

All rights reserved. No part of this book may be used or reproduced in any manner whatsoever without written permission of the author or The Wild Rose Press, Inc. except in the case of brief quotations embodied in critical articles or reviews.
Contact Information: info@thewildrosepress.com

Cover Art by *Tina Lynn Stout*

The Wild Rose Press, Inc.
PO Box 708
Adams Basin, NY 14410-0708
Visit us at www.thewildrosepress.com

Publishing History
First Edition, 2025
Trade Paperback ISBN 978-1-5092-5919-9
Digital ISBN 978-1-5092-5920-5

Luscious Delights, Book Four
Published in the United States of America

Dedication

To my hubs and my bestie Carol Ann. And to my editor, Dianne Rich, and the team at Wild Rose.

Prologue

Nate walked over to the service line, pausing to slide his arm around my waist. "How's it going?"

"Okay, I think. Although we may be close to done with the beans, and the slaw and potato salad are both starting their last pan."

He nodded. "Yeah, we're down toward the end of the meat, too."

I checked the grills. Dan had taken over Nate's hamburger grill, which made sense because I still had lots of plant-based burgers and sausages ready for anyone who wanted them. We'd given out a few— maybe a hotel pan's worth—but there hadn't been a big demand. If we ran out of full-strength hamburgers and sausage, we could always hand out the plant-based stuff.

Nate peered at the far end of the line. "Coco's still got half of her desserts, so that can hold people for another half hour or so."

"As long as the beer holds out, we should be fine."

Nate rapped his knuckles on the wooden tabletop. "Don't even joke about that. The only thing that would turn this evening into a disaster would be running out of beer."

It didn't look like the brewery guys were concerned about that. They went on pouring cups from the various spigots they had set up, and no one seemed even slightly nervous. It was, in fact, the mellowest crowd we'd ever served. "Got any feedback from Sawmill?"

Nate shrugged. "No problems so far as I know. Everybody was happy with their food. Didn't see much getting thrown away."

"I guess we go with the rest of the hamburgers and sausage, if anybody wants them. But you can probably stop cooking for now. Looks like everything worked out. Tim's a little beat, but the rest of us are doing okay."

"Yeah, if we ever do another one of these, I'll get two runners."

I felt like we'd had a good night. A good shakedown cruise for future large events. For the most part this had been a success. In fact, it had been close to a triumph.

Somewhere nearby someone screamed.

Chapter 1

Buzzzzzzzzzzzz!

I was having a dream about jam, not uncommon for me since I spend a lot of my time making jam and jelly and preserves. But this time I seemed to be in high school again, making jam in math class for some reason. And I had to finish, but then the class change buzzer sounded.

Buzzzzzzzzzzzz!

I couldn't leave class until I finished the jam, only it wasn't jelling, and somehow I'd gotten dirt into it, which I tried to brush off, only...

Buzzzzzzzzzzzz!

I finally surfaced enough to acknowledge my alarm was sounding. I reached up to slap the snooze alarm but hit the *off* button instead. Beside me, Nate mumbled something and turned over, sinking deeper into sleep.

I stifled a completely unjustified impulse to kick him and climbed out of bed. Nate could sleep late, having successfully catered a party the night before. He might have to help at lunch at Robicheaux's Café—I wasn't sure about that. But he had no demands on his morning.

I, on the other hand, had the farmers market. I'd also worked the Friday night party with Nate, but I couldn't snooze the morning away, given that I needed to transport several cases of jam to the market area and

3

set up my booth. Farmers market sales accounted for over half of the profits for my jam company, Luscious Delights, and I usually started selling as soon as the market opened at ten. That meant hauling myself out of bed and getting everything loaded up in my truck for the trip into town.

Normally, it wasn't a problem for me to get up and around early in the day. I'm a morning person, one of those annoying people who likes to get everything done right after breakfast. But like I said, I'd also worked the party last night with Nate. We hadn't gotten to bed until after midnight, what with cleanup and dragging all our dirty pots and pans and dishes to the catering kitchen so they could be loaded in the dishwasher. I was far from my usual bright-eyed and bushy-tailed self.

I tottered to the kitchen to get the coffee started, telling myself a heavy dose of caffeine would help. At least I'd gotten all the cases of jam ready the night before. All I'd need to do after breakfast would be to load everything into the truck and get going.

Of course, that meant loading the cases onto my hand truck, wheeling them outside, and then loading them into the pickup. Already I felt tired, and not just from sleep deprivation.

I'd known that when the farmers market season started, I might have to cut back on my work as sous chef for Nate's catering business. Most of our catering jobs were on weekends, most frequently Fridays or Saturdays. Since the farmers market ran from ten until two on Saturdays, I was limited in the amount of time I could devote to food prep since I'd either be getting ready for the market or running my booth.

But the full weight of the market work hadn't hit

me until today. I'd spent the week dividing my time between food prep at the catering kitchen and jam making at my place. The expression "There aren't enough hours in the day" had begun to take on new meaning for me. And now the event had collided with the farmers market at full speed. I'd been on my feet for five or six hours the night before, and now I'd be standing for most of the morning. My feet hurt. My knees hurt. My head hurt. And I was having trouble getting my eyes open. This was turning into the Week From Hell.

I'd just poured myself a large coffee when Uncle Mike swung through my front door. He'd be going to the market, too, to run the stand that sold his arugula and early strawberries. He also had a few spring onions and some spinach, but it was the strawberries that would move. "Hey," he said. "Ready to go?"

I shook my head. "I just got up. I need to swallow a couple of cups of coffee before I start loading." I also needed to put on some clothes other than my pajamas and brush my hair into something presentable. But the coffee came first.

"When did you get in last night?" Uncle Mike poured his own cup of coffee.

"Late," I said flatly. I didn't know exactly when we'd gotten in, but I knew it was later than we'd expected.

"Nate still asleep?" Uncle Mike raised an eyebrow.

"Yeah." I managed not to grit my teeth. There was no reason for Nate to get up just because I had to. No reason at all.

Uncle Mike took a swallow of his coffee, regarding me a little apprehensively. I wasn't looking my best. "I brought you some of Donnie's honey." He placed a mason jar full of amber liquid on the table.

Immediately, my day was a little brighter. "Cool. First of the season?"

Uncle Mike nodded. "Pretty much."

Donnie has been our farm manager for a lot of years. He and his wife Carmen have a few acres of their own a little way up the road from our place. They started raising bees a few years ago as a way to ensure we had pollinators around for our crops. Their honey production is still pretty small, but it's very tasty. "Maybe I'll try making some jam with honey this year," I said, or tried to say. A yawn interfered with the sentence.

Uncle Mike gave me another of those concerned looks. "Those the cases you're taking to the market?" He pointed toward the boxes stacked next to the door.

"That's it."

"Let me load some up for you before I take off," he said. "Give you a chance to get some breakfast."

I should probably have told him no. He's over sixty, and I'm not. Just then, however, I felt like any help would be welcome. "Thanks. I'll go take a shower." Maybe cold water would accomplish what caffeine hadn't yet.

I pushed myself to my feet and turned down the hall to the bathroom, with my uncle's worried gaze following my steps. I wished I could have reassured him, but at that point my main concern was working up enough energy to make it through the morning. I don't think I'd ever felt so tired in my life.

Three cups of coffee got my metabolism going, or as *going* as it was likely to get. Uncle Mike had loaded all the cases into my truck, which meant I'd just have to unload them at the market. I considered having some honey, but I wanted to save it for a time when I'd appreciate it more. So I ate some toast and jam—my breakfast whenever culinary inspiration fails me—and headed out a little after eight. The day was lovely: bright blue sky; sparkling sunshine; cheerful pansies, petunias, and marigolds in washtubs around the edge of the market grounds. If I hadn't still been fighting exhaustion, I'd have been a happy vendor. Nice weather brings out customers in droves.

Oh, guts up. I didn't have any choice, and if I spent the day thinking about how tired I was, I'd only feel worse. At the market, I assembled my booth, which I'd done so many times I could almost do it blindfolded, then loaded five cases of jam on the hand truck and got ready for my first sales of the day.

All around me my fellow vendors were also getting set up. I directed a few grins at my friends, and a couple of nods at newbies I'd met a few weeks ago at the season opening. The market had been expanding every year now that visiting the mountain town markets had become a major tourist attraction. Right now we were still in late May, so most of our customers were locals, but in another week or so, we'd start drawing big crowds of tourists.

Most of us were using the opening month to get a sense of how sales were going to go this year. My mail order business was taking off, and if market sales were up to their usual numbers, I'd need to increase my production by quite a bit. I was still sort of nervous about that. I was used to being a small business, selling mainly to people in Shavano. But I'd been featured on a national TV show, and the notoriety had brought me a lot of new customers who were becoming regulars. I was already thinking about hiring a full-time assistant along with the part-timer who helped me fill orders and cook jam. And I needed more jars, more fruit, more mailing boxes.

More time. A whole lot more time.

Which brought me squarely to the major speed bump in my current path: my job with Robicheaux Catering.

I loved working with Nate, but I didn't love giving up so many hours a week to do it. If the choice was between Luscious Delights and Robicheaux Catering, I'd go with Luscious Delights every time.

I sighed as I set up my sample bowls. Uncle Mike had raised the possibility of me selling jam at some of the other mountain farmers markets. If people had a chance to taste my jam at one, it would be a great way to increase interest in my mail order stuff. Crested Butte had a nice market. So did Steamboat Springs. Aspen had a sort of chi-chi one that probably already had enough jam. But if I started selling at the other markets, it would cut into my time even more. I'd have to hire someone to run the booth at Shavano while I traveled over the mountains to show off my jam in other cities.

Everything I did to increase my sales meant less time available to cook with Nate. Or help with the catering events.

I needed to talk to him. But I needed to be more awake when I did.

The market managers were pretty good about holding to the official opening time, but customers started flowing in promptly at ten o'clock. I had a new market assistant, a perennially sunny high school student named Beck who'd been recommended by my former assistant, Dolce.

Dolce was now my part-time kitchen helper, and she'd developed a real talent for strawberry jam. I was happy to have her four afternoons a week, and willing to let her take off on Saturdays. Beck kept the sample bowls filled and discouraged small children from raiding our cracker supplies, all the while radiating good cheer. I rang up sales and answered questions, of which there were blessedly few.

The locals mostly knew my stuff and knew what they liked. They'd pick up three or four jars of raspberry or peach or apricot and ask me when the strawberry basil would be in before turning toward Bianca Jordan's bakery stand. Simple and straightforward—about all I was capable of talking about right then.

My booth had been in the same spot for several years running. Which meant it was next door to the restaurant demonstration booth where the local chefs showed off their chops to the passing crowds. That was actually how I'd first met Nate; he'd been doing a demo for Robicheaux's Café, and he borrowed my extension cord.

And, like they say, one thing led to another.

Nate had run all the demos for the café last summer, but I wasn't sure what the arrangements would be this year since he had less time. He'd probably do some demos for the catering company, but I doubted it would be every week. Not this week, for sure.

I was vaguely aware of people setting up and then moving on in the restaurant booth as I sold jam.

Usually, the demos lasted fifteen minutes or so as the chefs produced their dishes and then put out samples for the passing crowds to try. Nate typically saved a couple of samples for me since I didn't get lunch until after two. That wouldn't happen today, but I didn't have much appetite anyway. Mainlining coffee will do that to you.

I'd just stuffed some twenties into my money pouch when someone leaned over the counter. "Hey, Rox, how's it going?"

I glanced up to see Coco, Nate's sister, tugging a shopping cart behind her. "Hey," I said. "Don't tell me they've got you doing demos."

Coco shrugged. "Nate had that big catering job last night, so he couldn't do it. And Bobby doesn't trust Marigold alone in the kitchen yet. He probably thinks she might change the chili recipe or something. So here I am, ready to hand out some pecan tassies."

Coco is the café's pastry chef and salad queen. Her pecan tassies are amazing, one of the most popular desserts on our catering menu.

"Save me one?" I was beginning to rethink my loss of appetite. Particularly when it came to Coco's desserts.

She grinned. "Oh, hell, Rox, you can have as many as you want. All I need to do is warm them up a little so people think I cooked them on site."

"Okay, I'll try to slip over and grab a couple." I might actually grab more than that, but two would be a good start.

Coco ambled over to the demo booth where a chef from Moretti's was handing out minuscule portions of lasagna. As she stepped into the back of the booth and began unloading her tassies on a tray, the Moretti's chef developed the same slightly stunned look I'd seen on a lot of male faces around her. Coco is tiny with dark hair feathered around her face and huge moss green eyes. A lot of men look sort of shell-shocked the first time they see her.

Coco appears not to notice, although I have a feeling she does that on purpose.

The Moretti's chef stepped close, as if he'd help her unload. Coco gave him a disinterested smile and shook her head. She might be small, but she doesn't need any help from anybody—something she'll let you know if you get into her space. The Moretti's guy backed off a little sadly and returned to his lasagna.

I returned to my jam. Sales were slowing down a little as we approached one o'clock. A lot of the crowd had taken off for lunch, which gave Beck and me a chance to catch our breaths and reconnoiter. Beck cast a longing glance toward the small arts and crafts fair being held across the street.

"Do you want to knock off?" I asked. "I can probably take it on my own for another hour."

"Oh, I don't want to leave you short-handed," Beck said dutifully. Her mother had clearly raised her right.

"That's okay. We're getting close to closing time. This early in the season, we probably won't have a rush." Which was my way of hinting she wouldn't be able to leave early every week.

"Okay, well, if you really don't need me." Beck gave me another of those sunny smiles, which only got sunnier when I opened my money pouch and gave her a few bills. "See you next week." She gave me a little wave and almost skipped over to the arts and crafts fair.

I told myself not to be a grouch. I'd once been fifteen and cheerful myself, although I doubt that I ever radiated as much delight with the world as Beck did.

Over in the demo booth, Coco's pecan tassies were flying off the tray—almost literally. She'd cut them in half so they'd last a little longer, but they were still disappearing at a great rate. My guess was she'd run out long before her fifteen minutes were up. No one was hanging around my booth just then, so I slipped over to her side.

Coco grinned. "I saved you a couple. Keep them to yourself." She handed me a paper plate covered with a napkin.

A couple of the market customers who were snarfing down the bite-size pieces stared at me with longing as I took a bite out of a full-size tassie, but I ignored them. "These are so good."

Coco sighed. "Marigold says I should make pecan pies for the café, but Bobby vetoed it. He still thinks frozen pies from the supplier are cheaper than homemade."

"Your homemade pies would sell out by closing."

"Damn straight."

"What did Marigold say?"

Coco shrugged. "Not much. She's got a great you're-an-idiot expression, though. I don't know if Bobby notices."

"How are they getting along anyway?" Marigold was the café's new cook, cousin of my friend Lauren and someone I'd recommended. I was pretty sure Marigold would be terrific, but I wasn't sure how long she'd be able to put up with Coco's ever-annoying big brother, Bobby.

"They're doing okay. She's a terrific cook, and even Bobby has to admit that. She's gotten to introduce a couple of new dishes, and they're hits with the customers so Mom's delighted. So far, she hasn't messed with any of Bobby's sacred recipes, so he hasn't lost his shit. You did good when you recommended her."

"Is Bobby actually working with her?" Bobby and Nate had clashed a lot in the kitchen, one of the reasons Nate was happy to shift over to the catering business. Bobby did not share his flattop happily.

"It's more like he's working around her," Coco said. "He doesn't pretend she isn't there. But he's careful to stay out of her way, and she does the same thing with him."

"I guess that's good." I picked up the second tassie and took a bite. I swear I heard a groan from the customers at the front of the booth.

Coco gave them a dry smile and set out her last plate of tassie bites. I figured they'd be gone within seconds. It took a little longer, but not much.

"Well, that's it for me." Coco started gathering her trays and storage containers to load them into her market cart. "I guess I'm done early, but I brought a couple dozen. Who knew they'd go that fast?"

I think anyone who'd tasted Coco's baking could have predicted just how fast they'd disappear. Another hit for Robicheaux's Café. "Are you going to be doing this every week?"

"Doubt it." Coco gave me a quick smile. "When Nate doesn't have a job on Friday night, I figure he'll be over here pushing the catering business. And maybe sometime Bobby will let Marigold take a turn. If nothing else, she should draw a crowd."

Marigold resembled a biker babe transformed into a chef, but she had the chops to go with her multiple tattoos and butcher's biceps. "I hope I'm around to see that."

"Wow, am I late?"

I turned to see Marcus Jordan wheeling his own market cart to the demo booth. He blinked at the empty paper plates at the front of the booth. There were usually a few samples left when the next chef arrived.

"No, I had a run on pecan tassies," Coco explained. She gave Marcus a warm smile. "I didn't know you'd be demoing today."

Marcus's smile was equally warm, transforming his good ol' guy face into something a lot closer to handsome. "Yeah, I didn't think to mention it the other day. Glad to see we're overlapping." He moved his market cart to the back and began unloading packs of sausages. Marcus has butcher's biceps of his own, along with a shock of red hair and blue-green eyes. I hadn't really noticed before, but he was a good-looking guy, particularly in low-slung jeans and a bright green Jordan's Meats T-shirt.

Coco gave him another quick smile. "Going by the Blue Spot later?"

Marcus paused, hefting a plastic bin of what appeared to be baguette slices. "Maybe. Most likely. I close down around four on weekends."

"Maybe I'll see you there, then." Coco turned to me. "Come by for brunch tomorrow, Roxy." She stuffed the last of her gear in her market cart and took off down the path with a spring in her step.

Marcus watched her until she was out of sight. The

Blue Spot was a kind of dive where a lot of the local chefs went after work. I hadn't realized Coco went there, too. But it made sense.

Now I had something to think about when I returned to my jam sales. Something other than how tired I was. Marcus and Coco would make an interesting couple, one I'd never considered before. They were both locals, born and bred in Shavano. And they both came from cooking families. Marcus's mom was Bianca Jordan, who owned her own bake shop and sold legendary bread and breakfast pastries.

I liked Marcus, and I respected his butcher shop. He'd had a rough year so far. His wife, Sara, had cheated on him in a very public way. Their divorce was in the works, but I'd heard Sara was making trouble about the financial settlement. Meanwhile, Marcus was running his butcher shop on his own. Not that Sara had provided much in the way of customer relations, but she'd been around to run the counter while Marcus was in the back doing his butchering. He'd probably value anything that got his mind off his current problems.

I figured Coco would be glad to do that. I only hoped she didn't leave Marcus in worse shape than when she'd found him.

Chapter 2

After I'd broken down the booth and put everything in the truck, I headed over to Robicheaux's Café for a late lunch. They'd finished service, but Nate was still in the kitchen, and I figured he could scrounge up something for me.

I found him in the kitchen with Marigold. Bobby was nowhere to be seen. "Hey, kid," Marigold called. "You bring me any apricot jam?"

I'd forgotten all about promising Marigold some apricot jam, but fortunately I hadn't sold out. "Out in the truck. Give me a minute."

She waved a dismissive hand. "No rush. Bring it in when you've got time." She returned to cleanup.

Nate put an arm around my shoulders and kissed my forehead. "You look tired. Are you hanging in?"

"Barely. I mainlined coffee before the market, but it's wearing off now." I dropped onto a stool at the side of the work area. "Any sandwiches lying around?"

Nate pulled off his apron. "Grill's off. I could make you a BLT with leftover bacon."

"Fine." Right then I would have eaten just about anything.

Nate put some bread into the toaster and pulled out tomatoes and bacon from the cooler. "Hey, Marigold, you want anything?"

She shook her head. "I've got plans. Thanks

anyway." She pulled off the ball cap she wore when she cooked and fluffed out her white-blonde hair. Her forelock was currently magenta. "Just drop the jam at my station, Rox. See you tomorrow."

"Is she already dating somebody?" I asked after Marigold left. She'd only been in town a couple of months.

Nate shrugged. "I don't know. She hasn't mentioned anybody. Not a whole lot of time for conversation during lunch." He took the bread out of the toaster and started assembling two large sandwiches. I stuffed a handful of potato chips into an aluminum bowl. Café kitchens always provide the basics.

Nate carried the sandwiches into the dining room and then poured a couple of glasses of iced tea at the counter. I joined him at the table. It was the first chance I'd had to see him clearly. "How are you?"

He gave me a quick smile. "Probably better than you. I got to sleep until nine. When did you get up?"

"Around six thirty. I had to get out the door by eight." I took a bite of my sandwich. It was, as anticipated, terrific.

Nate reached across the table to run his fingers along my cheekbone. "Not a good schedule, babe."

"Not great, that's for sure." I took a breath. Maybe now was actually the time to talk about this. "I don't know how much longer I can do this, Nate. I figured out I was on my feet for five hours last night and then five more today. And sure, other people have it worse, but it's a lot." I thought a little guiltily about the waitresses who worked full shifts at the café and then did catering. But they were picking up extra cash by doing it. With me it was my new normal.

Nate grimaced. "Last night wasn't typical—we don't usually stick around that long at an event. But I know it's been tough on you, getting all your jam ready for the market and cooking for us, too."

"It has been. I'm not sure how this is going to work out with both the market and the catering." Which was as close as I could come to saying I didn't think I could go on doing both. Except I was needed for both. And I liked doing both.

So either guts up or get smart.

Across from me, Nate picked up a potato chip. "I've been thinking a lot about this. We both knew the time was going to come when the market started and you were getting hammered, but I don't think either of us knew just how tough it was going to be."

"Not really," I admitted. I'd just figured I'd be a superhero and power through. Only my superpowers had fizzled out.

"So how about if I hired somebody part time to help with meal prep? That would free you up to get the jam done during the week, and then you could still help me with the parties. I figure most of them won't interfere as much with the market as the one did last night."

I stared at him. For some reason, it hadn't occurred to me that he might hire somebody to do the cooking with him. It was actually a good solution, but it wasn't one I'd ever thought about. And, against all logic, I felt a little hurt. Didn't he want me in the kitchen with him?

Don't be an idiot, Roxanne.

"That could work," I said slowly. "Do you have anybody lined up?"

"Not exactly. I thought I'd run it by you first to see how you felt. But if you're okay with it, I could put the word out on the grapevine, see if there's anybody around who'd like to pick up a few hours here and there."

Several of the restaurant cooks around town were part timers. They might welcome some cooking that didn't cut into meal prep times at the places where they worked.

"I think that sounds great. Then maybe we can reassess in the fall when the market ends." Because I wasn't ready to give up my sous chef status with Nate altogether. It was too much fun.

He nodded. "Okay, I'll get on it and see who's out there. I should probably clear it with Mom first, but I'm sure she won't have any problem with it. She knows how much business we're doing."

"You don't suppose Marigold would like to pick up some part-time stuff?"

"Nope. She's already full time. And Bobby would probably have a stroke if I started taking his crew to work for me." He gave me a dry smile. Bobby had made several loud complaints over Nate leaving the kitchen for the catering business. Marigold had been the solution to that problem. No doubt he'd be righteously outraged if we poached Marigold now that he'd gotten her for breakfast and lunch.

"So how was the market?" Nate asked, picking up a few more chips.

"Good. Lots of people. Still mostly local. I saw Coco when she came in to do her demo."

Nate sighed. "I guess I'll do that next week. Maybe. We've got that party Saturday night, so I might have to run back to the kitchen."

"Just demo whatever we're cooking for the party. Robicheaux Catering at your service." Actually, I couldn't remember what we were serving at the Saturday party. If it was prime rib, we probably weren't going to be sharing it with the market customers.

"It's heavy appetizers. I could mix up some extra meatballs."

"Absolutely. They're delicious." And cheap, which was one of the reasons we made lots.

"We'll do it." He leaned back in his chair. "Are you going home now?"

"Yeah. I could use a nap." Although I probably wouldn't get one since I was behind on my jam orders. "Are you staying in town?"

"A little while longer. I need to finish brunch prep."

"Okay, see you later." I kissed him. It started as a quick peck but morphed into something hotter and longer, as our kisses frequently did. "You want something special for dinner?" I managed after I got my breath back.

"Just you." He grinned.

A half hour later, I turned my truck toward the farm, a lot more energized than I'd felt before. As should be obvious by now, Nate and I are very much a couple. We met a little over a year ago. Dated, got serious, had our first major fight and thought about breaking up, got back together again, and were annoyingly happy. Annoying to other people, that is. I was more than delighted about our current situation.

Nate had moved in a couple of months ago, around the time Marigold had taken the job as the new cook at

Robicheaux's. She'd also taken over Nate's old apartment above his mom's garage and seemed to be settling in just fine.

Nate had settled in, too. When we were dating, we'd had to confine ourselves to only spending the weekends together because both of us had work during the week. Plus, Nate was cooking breakfast every day, which reduced possible late nights. Now that Marigold had taken over his breakfast slot, his hours in the kitchen were a lot more reasonable. He cooked lunch a few days a week as needed and helped with brunch on Sunday, which Marigold had off. When he had a big catering job that required a lot of prep time, he'd reduce his hours in the café, which worked out fine for everybody in spite of annoying the hell out of Bobby.

We were happy, and I figured we'd go on being happy as soon as we got my work situation smoothed out a little.

By the time I got to the farm, I'd decided to make jam instead of napping. I could get ahead of the orders if I put in a little time now, and then Nate and I could have Sunday afternoon to kick back and have a good time.

I was elbows-deep in early strawberries when Uncle Mike came in my front door. "Hey," he said, leaning on my counter. "Nate not here yet?"

"Still doing brunch prep." I wielded my potato masher on the pile of strawberries, getting them into an agreeable state of semi-mush before I added the lemon juice and sugar. We hadn't yet gotten the main part of the strawberry crop. Uncle Mike had raised these in cold frames. But they were perfect for a little jam. "How were your sales?"

He shrugged. "Decent. Strawberries sold out in a heartbeat. Sold out of spinach and the early arugula, too. Donnie had a few jars of honey for sale, and those went fast." He wandered over to my cupboard, searching for cups.

I emptied the smashed berries into my jam pot. "I didn't realize he harvested enough honey to be able to sell it."

"He's got around a dozen or so hives now. Figure maybe twenty thousand bees per hive. That's a lot of bees."

I adjusted the heat under the jam pot. "That's cool. I really do want to try some jam sweetened with honey. Maybe raspberry. That always sells, regardless. And the flavor's strong enough to blend with the honey easily."

"Didn't know you could make jam with honey. Is it sweet enough to make the fruit gel?"

"Yeah, but I may need to add pectin. Honey's actually sweeter than sugar. If I make jam with honey alone, I'll have to use less than the amount of sugar I'd use for the same mixture. But it changes the flavor, which sugar doesn't do. Still, I could advertise it as made with Shavano honey. Does Donnie enjoy being a beekeeper?"

Uncle Mike poured himself a cup of coffee, then resumed wandering around my kitchen. "He's not the one doing it. Carmen collects the honey. No bee would dare sting her."

Carmen had been Uncle Mike's housekeeper for a lot of years, and she'd been the major female presence in my life when I was a teenager. She was a very formidable lady, as I had reason to know. "If anybody can make a go of the honey operation, it's Carmen."

Uncle Mike nodded. "She should, with Donnie and Lulabelle on patrol."

"On patrol where? For what?" We didn't have too much trouble with interlopers on the farm, but it was always possible. Although Donnie's hound dog, Lulabelle, didn't strike me as much of a threat to anybody but the squirrels.

"Guarding the bee hives. Aram Pergosian had three hives stolen last week."

I turned to stare at him. "Stolen? Who would steal bees? And why?"

"Bees are worth a lot of money. People steal them to sell or to rent out for pollination. Hives can go for a couple of hundred dollars apiece." He was pacing again.

I gave the jam a stir. "I had no idea." Although stealing a beehive still struck me as a tough way to earn extra cash.

Uncle Mike isn't usually a fidgeter, but as he circled my kitchen, he was fidgeting like crazy. And making me a little nuts in the process. "Is anything wrong?" I asked finally.

"I'm fine." He paused. "Could you take care of Herman this weekend?"

Herman was the gentle giant pooch currently curled up in my living room. He sort of belonged to both of us, but he'd been living mostly at the main house since Nate had moved in. "Sure, I guess. Has he been a problem?"

"Who, Herman?" Uncle Mike shook his head. "He's fine. It's just...I might be going out of town for a couple of days."

"Oh?" I tried to keep my tone noncommittal. This

was new. Normally, if Uncle Mike went out of town for something to do with the business, he treated it as nothing special. This was clearly something different.

"Madge wanted to check out that new winery in Paonia. Thought we'd stay over for a day or so." Uncle Mike's voice sounded deceptively bland, as if this was no big thing. However, it clearly was a big thing, judging from the way my uncle was carefully not looking at me.

I gave him a bland smile of my own. "That sounds like fun. I'll be glad to take care of Herman while you're gone."

"Okay, fine. I guess I'll leave him here, then." He gave me a relieved grin.

"Sure, do that. When do you leave?"

"We thought this afternoon. Try to beat the tourist traffic."

That meant Madge would miss brunch at the café on Sunday. I hoped she'd let Bobby know in advance. Otherwise, tomorrow would be hell in the kitchen. I kept that bland smile in place. "Good plan."

"Okay, well, see you when we get back, I guess." The tips of his ears had turned pink, a sure sign that he was embarrassed and trying not to show it.

"See you then. Have a good time."

"Right, yeah, certainly." Uncle Mike escaped out my front door, leaving me with lots of interesting questions. So far as I knew, Uncle Mike had never gone out of town with Madge Robicheaux, certainly not for an entire weekend. Did that mean their relationship had moved to a new level? Or were they just being more open about the way they felt about each other?

Lots of interesting questions, like I said. And Nate

might be somebody I could ask, depending on whether he could wrap his head around the idea of his mom and my uncle traveling together to Colorado wine country for a couple of fun days.

Chapter 3

I was more anxious than usual for Nate to get to my place. Had Madge told all the kids she was going to Paonia for a couple of days? How would they feel about their mom getting serious with an arugula farmer who was also my surrogate father? Nate had been finishing culinary school when his dad died, then he'd worked in Las Vegas for a few years after that. After he'd returned to Shavano, he'd gotten involved with me, which included getting to know Uncle Mike. The two of them had a good relationship, or so I thought. This situation might put it to the test.

After Uncle Mike left, I went back to work on my strawberries. I'd just gotten the jars into the hot water bath when I heard Nate's SUV. A few minutes later, he walked in, looking a little shellshocked. "What kind of booze do we have on hand?"

"Beer and wine, mostly." I adjusted the heat under the pot, then paused. "Is this about Uncle Mike and your mom?"

He blew out a long breath as he pulled the bottle of sauvignon blanc out of the refrigerator. "Yeah. Pretty much."

"You're upset?"

"I don't know what I am." Nate poured himself a large glass of wine. "I mean, I like Mike. He's a great guy. But I hadn't really considered them getting serious about each other. Mom's never taken a day off that I can remember. Ever. And now she's skipping brunch so she can go off with Mike."

I decided I should go on record here. "I think it sounds great. I wish we could do something like that, too. Not during the summer, of course," I added hastily. "Too much is going on."

Nate stared down at his glass for a moment. "It does sound great, and I'm probably making too big a thing out of it. So what if my mom wants to take a couple of days off to kick up her heels in Paonia? Good for her." He took another swallow of his wine.

"They seem to enjoy each other," I said carefully. I had a feeling Madge having a new man in her life was probably a much more delicate subject with the Robicheaux kids than Uncle Mike's romance with Madge was with me.

I wondered what brunch would be like the next day. I usually helped out by pouring mimosas and Bloody Marys, although they could probably have gotten along without me. I considered begging off, but I didn't want anybody to think I wasn't happy about Madge and Uncle Mike stepping out.

"How did your mom seem when she talked to you?"

Nate shrugged as he took another swallow of his wine. "A little nervous. Maybe worried about what we'd think."

"She told all three of you?"

"Yeah. She wanted to make sure we knew what was going on with brunch tomorrow. Minka's going to fill in as hostess."

Minka was one of the senior waitresses at

Robicheaux's. Just like Madge to get everything lined up before she took off. "But aside from being nervous, how did she seem?"

Nate frowned. "Seem? Okay, I guess. She wasn't upset or anything." He looked a little confused, like he hadn't thought about it before.

Clearly, I was going to have to give him a shove. "Was she happy?"

Nate paused for a long moment, staring down at his wine. Then he looked up at me, his lips moving into a slightly startled smile. "She was. She was…really excited. And happy." He closed his eyes for a moment. "And the three of us just stood there like poleaxed goons, dammit."

I reached over to touch his hand. "What did Bobby say?" Bobby was the oldest son and the one who'd been closest to Robert senior. If any of the three was going to be upset, my money was on Bobby.

"I don't think he noticed. Or anyway, it didn't bother him much. He just said, 'Okay,' and took off."

That was weird. If nothing else, I'd have expected Bobby to be grumpy about the changes in their brunch routine.

Nate started frowning again. "To tell you the truth, I think Bobby's got something going on. He's been taking off faster than usual. And he hasn't had any problems with the size of my onion dice lately."

I tried not to goggle at him. "Bobby? Has a girlfriend?"

"Stranger things have happened." Nate sighed. "And by the way, I haven't forgotten about finding someone to help with meal prep in the catering kitchen. I'm working on it."

At that point certain smells reminded me of the fact I had a pot of strawberry jam getting close to scorching, and I spent the next half hour or so in frantic activity. But when I had a row of filled jars on the counter, I joined Nate in the living room with my own glass of wine.

"And you're okay with this weekend jaunt?" Nate said, as if the conversation had never stopped.

"I'm absolutely okay with it. Uncle Mike and Madge are great together, they deserve to have fun, and I wish them every bit of it they can grab." I took a fierce sip of my wine.

"You got that right." Nate took a sip of his own. "So you'll be at brunch?"

I'd been considering bowing out, but after my speech, I didn't think that was possible. "Of course."

"Great." Nate paused. "Keep in mind, Bobby may be a royal pain in the ass without Mom to keep him in check."

"Bobby's always a pain in the ass." I slid down to rest my head on his chest. "You really think you can find someone to help out with the catering?"

Nate smiled down at me. "Yeah. Yeah, I think I've got a lead. "

I should have knocked on wood then, but I didn't. Hindsight is always perfect.

Chapter 4

Things settled down a bit over the next few days. Neither Madge nor Uncle Mike said much about their trip to Paonia. Maybe they were both trying to cool things down with their respective families.

I was working in the catering kitchen again, trying to balance my time between there and my own jam-making. I'd tried turning more of the jam making over to Dolce, who had a talent for strawberries. But I felt guilty about putting too much of it in her hands. After all, Luscious Delights was my business, and I still felt like I needed to produce most of the jam or at least have a hand in producing it. And yes, I knew that attitude was a major roadblock on my way to becoming a jam kingpin. Sue me.

The party we were getting ready for at the catering kitchen was medium big: a bash for a local outdoors club to mark the start of the season. They estimated around seventy-five guests, and they wanted something healthy, but they weren't fanatical about it. We were doing heavy apps, one of our specialties. Most of them were the make-ahead type since I'd be at the farmers market on the day of the party. Nate was getting as much done as he could on the ones that had to be finished just before the event since Saturdays were always hectic even without a catering job.

By now, it was obvious to both of us we needed

another cook, even if that person only came in a couple of days a week. Between making jam and doing prep for the party, I was running on empty, even though Dolce was doing a lot of the jam scut work. Nate was doing as much of the catering prep as he could, but he had cooking of his own to finish up. He could do meatballs in advance, but our vegan filo pockets might get soggy if he tried to cook and reheat. We'd decided to do wings, which we'd never done before and might never do again, given how much trouble they were turning out to be. Nate had the sauce in hand, but the wings themselves needed to be fried up close to service so they wouldn't get greasy. Nate was breading them now and letting them chill so the breading would stay on a little better.

By Friday, after a four-hour sprint, I was more or less done with my part of the food prep. I could leave everything in the walk-in, and Nate could take care of the remaining apps during the day on Saturday. I was already beginning to feel played out and spent—time to go home and take a load off.

"Go," Nate said. "I can finish. Go home and rest for a while."

"Okay, I'll have dinner ready when you get back."

As I pulled into my parking space next to the cabin, however, I remembered what I'd mostly blocked out of my mind: I had the market tomorrow, and I needed to get the cases of jam lined up next to the door so I could load them in the morning.

I was at the point you reach when you're almost out of steam, but not quite. I knew if I sat down for even a minute, I'd probably never get on my feet again. So I started stacking cases on the hand truck as soon as

I stepped inside the door. The mail-order boxes ready for the package pickup were already taking up a lot of space in the living room, but I managed to push them farther to the side, then bring out the cases of peach, apricot, raspberry, pepper peach, and strawberry and stack them in a line behind the couch. Tomorrow I'd have to figure out how to get them out the door, but for now they'd be more accessible, and I'd be sure I had the right number of cases overall.

It took me around an hour to get everything done, and after that I collapsed into a rocking chair and sat very still for what seemed like a long time. Sooner or later, I was going to have to get up and make dinner. But right now *later* was definitely more appealing. I was still sitting there, sort of stupefied, when Uncle Mike strolled in with Herman.

Herman padded over to me and licked my face, which almost made me whimper. I put my arms around him and rested my forehead against his neck.

"Um…you okay?" Uncle Mike looked like he was sorry he'd come over.

"Just really, really, really, really, really tired." I slumped back in the chair again. "And I need to fix supper."

"Jade Garden does delivery," Uncle Mike said. "So does Moretti's."

"I can't face pizza." We'd been having it regularly whenever we were so tired neither of us felt up to cooking. "I've got some stuff in the freezer."

I pushed myself to my feet. My legs felt like they were full of feathers or glue or something so insubstantial that they wouldn't hold me up. *Guts up, Roxanne.* I grabbed hold of the wall and worked my way into the kitchen.

What I had in the freezer, as it turned out, was meatballs and marinara. Not even fancy meatballs and marinara, but I didn't care. I threw them into a pot and put it on the stove.

"You want a glass of wine?" Uncle Mike asked.

"Not until I've got this warming." If I had wine before then, I'd zone out. "Go ahead and have some if you want, though."

"I'm meeting Madge. We've got plans." Uncle Mike's cheeks flushed bright pink, which I found adorable, even in my impaired state.

"How was Paonia?" It had been a few days since they'd returned, but I hadn't had a chance to ask him. I'd been too busy cooking jam and making apps.

Uncle Mike shrugged. "Fine. A little crowded. They've got a farmers market, too. You might want to check them out some time."

"And the wine?"

He sighed. "Tasted good to me. Madge really liked it."

"You should invite her to dinner sometime. Or I guess actually I should do it. Nate and I can cook. It'll be fun." It should have been, although Uncle Mike looked slightly horrified.

"Fun. Sure. Well, you can check with Madge to see when she's free." That was about as far as he was willing to go in setting anything up. "Can you keep Herman tonight?"

"Sure. He likes curling up around the boxes. Like he's in the cave with his fellow wolves."

"Okay, then, see you tomorrow." He beat a quick exit, leaving Herman staring after him. Poor thing. He was used to being banished from the cabin to stay with Uncle Mike so I could be alone with Nate, and now he was being banished from the main house so Uncle Mike could be alone with Madge.

Maybe we needed to find Herman a girlfriend, although things would have to be strictly platonic, given Herman's lack of breeding equipment.

Nate arrived around six, looking as beat as I felt. "We're in good shape for tomorrow, but this has been a grind."

"It has. I wish I had something haute cuisine for you, but it's grocery store meatballs and a jar of marinara."

He waved a hand. "Anything. Right now, I'll eat anything. As long as there's booze to go with it."

Midway through dinner, and a bottle of chianti, I started to relax. Maybe too much. The third time I stifled a yawn, Nate reached across the table and took my hand. "I've got a line on a part-time cook. Joe Draper at Moretti's has a friend who needs something a couple of days a week."

"Praise the saints. Have you met him?"

Nate shook his head. "Not yet. Joe's going to bring him over for lunch tomorrow so we can talk. Maybe he can start next week. Knock wood."

"Knock wood."

We dragged ourselves through the process of loading the dishwasher and cleaning up the kitchen, but when we were done with that, I headed off for a shower. I figured I could read a couple of chapters of the book I was trying to finish before I went to sleep since it was only around eight thirty. But my eyes were drooping by nine, and I decided an early night was a good idea. Not that I'd have been able to keep my eyes open in any case.

Fortunately, having a child's bedtime meant that I felt a lot better at six thirty the next morning. I got out of bed without waking Nate, and I was on the road by eight, breakfasted and caffeinated and ready for the market.

I'd probably be dragging by the time the day was over, but I was starting with a positive attitude. But who knew how long that would last.

I actually got my booth set up early. For a few minutes, I watched the booths take shape around me. Then I grabbed my travel cup and went in search of a cinnamon bun.

Bianca Jordan was all set up in her booth, too, laying out the baked goods that would probably be gone by noon. Bianca is the town's best baker. Other people have tried to compete, but Bianca always comes out on top. Her breakfast rolls routinely have people lined up in front of her door at seven in the morning, and her fresh baked bread has them lined up around the block. We'd known each other since I was a child, and Bianca had been friends with my dad back in the day. She was one of the first people to sell my jam at her bakery. Now she also baked bread for Robicheaux Catering, so our connections were even tighter.

I studied her breakfast pastry offerings, trying to decide between a scone and a pecan roll. "Morning," I said. "I guess I'll go with the raspberry scone."

"Good choice," Bianca said. "Of course, there are no bad choices here."

Bianca has never been shy about her own baking prowess. Why should she be? She's the oven queen. I took my scone and prepared for a different kind of morning dish. After all, Bianca was not only the town's oven queen, she was also the gossip queen. "So what's new?"

Bianca put her hands on the small of her back and stretched. "Not much. Your uncle and Madge have become a hot topic, though. Any wedding plans?"

I managed not to choke on my coffee. That was moving a lot faster than I was ready for. "Not that I've heard. I think they're just enjoying themselves." I figured that was vague enough that it wouldn't lead to more speculation.

"Not ready to think about what happens next? They're looking really friendly these days."

I shrugged. "They're a cute couple. I think they have a good time together."

"How does Bobby feel about it?" Bianca raised her eyebrows. Bobby's glum nature was well known around town, along with his hatred of change.

"So far as I know, he's okay with it. I guess he's got his own social life to think about."

I was hoping Bianca might have a little more dish about Bobby's hypothetical girlfriend, but she resumed arranging scones. "That whole family's gotten a lot more active in that area. Coco's gone out with Marcus a couple of times. Did you know that?"

Technically, Coco and Bianca are in the same business. But Coco bakes exclusively for the café and the catering business, so her products don't compete with Bianca's stuff. I didn't know how Bianca felt about her son dating another baker, though.

"Hadn't heard." Although given Coco's conversation with Marcus at the market, I wasn't too surprised. And I wasn't surprised that Bianca was keeping track. She'd already seen Marcus through one disastrous relationship. "How's he doing with Sara?"

Bianca grimaced. "They're supposed to be working things out with the lawyers, but it's slow going. Sara thinks he should pay her for her part of the shop. Only she thinks the shop is worth a lot more than Marcus has on hand. He's trying to negotiate her down."

Marcus's divorce from Sara was bound to be nasty. Sara had cheated on him and then been caught in public. I'd have thought she'd want to get out of Shavano as soon as possible, but apparently, she wanted to take part of the butcher shop with her.

"Is Sara still around town?"

"Nope. She's working at that hoity-toity grocery over in Geary, Sylvano's. Giving them the benefit of her expertise in butchering." Bianca looked like she'd tasted something sour. So far as I could tell, Sara didn't have much to do with the professional side of Jordan's Meats. She'd mainly been counter help.

"I haven't been over there yet. Is the place any good?"

"Not so far as I can see. It's priced through the roof, and the produce isn't any better than what you get here at the farmers market for half the price. But the job keeps Sara out of Marcus's hair. And that's all to the good."

I sighed in a commiserating sort of way. "Okay. Guess I'll get back before they start letting the customers in. The scone was great."

"Thanks. Be sure to bring some of the strawberry jam to the shop next week. We ran out by Thursday."

I trotted up to my booth, feeling a rosy glow. *We*

ran out is always good to hear, as long as it makes them want more.

By the time I returned to the booth, Beck had arrived and was laying out the sample bowls and crackers. I got a few more jars out of the boxes and then filled the sample bowls. We were ready to rock.

And rock we did. The closer we got to Memorial Day, the more people showed up. The locals, my regulars, grabbed the jars of jam they already knew and took a quick sample of whatever new stuff I had out to try. The tourists sampled everything and then, with any luck, picked up two or three jars to take home. By noon, I knew we were going to sell out of almost everything I'd brought before we reached closing time, which meant I'd need to increase the number of cases next week.

That was good and bad. Good because it meant sales were up over last year. Bad because it meant I'd have to find a way to cook up even more jam during the week if I wanted to cover both the market and my mail orders.

I was very happy by the time I saw Coco walk by, pulling her market cart behind her. The restaurant demo booth was still next door, and I'd been watching a parade of chefs for most of the morning. I hadn't thought to ask Nate who was doing the Robicheaux demo—clearly, it wouldn't be him since he was getting ready for the party that night. Maybe Coco was the only one who could be spared from the kitchen.

Once I'd dealt with a momentary rush of customers, I slipped over to the demo booth to check things out.

A guy from one of the bars on Second Street was

just cleaning things up. Apparently, he'd served something like nachos because a scattering of melted cheese and a few fragments of tomato littered the prep table. Coco was watching him, arms folded. I was pretty sure she'd let him know if he didn't clean it to her standards.

"Hey," I said. "What have you got today?"

Coco shrugged. "Cinnamon rolls. Some of the ones I baked up for brunch tomorrow. I didn't know I was going to be doing this until this morning." She narrowed her eyes at the nacho cook. I had a feeling she was not in the mood to be crossed, even by accident.

"Bobby backed out?"

"Sort of. Marigold offered to pass out grilled cheese, but Bobby didn't want to do lunch by himself. To tell the truth, I think he just didn't want Marigold on her own." Coco started hastily cutting the cinnamon rolls into quarters, and I put them on the paper plates she'd brought, ready to set them out for the passing customers.

"He still doesn't trust her?"

Coco paused. "He trusts her. Weirdly enough, I think he trusts her more than he trusts Nate or me. They're a lot alike in some ways."

That was a little surprising. Marigold with her tattoos and multi-color hair seemed a far cry from buttoned-up Bobby. But maybe he had hidden dimensions.

Coco put the sections of cinnamon buns out on the sample table, along with the placard for Robicheaux's Café, and I left her to deal with the descending hordes of customers. Fifteen minutes later I glanced up and saw Marcus helping Coco load her stuff. She gazed up at him and smiled a more genuine smile than I'd seen from her since she'd watched the nacho cook mess up the prep area.

Maybe a romance with Marcus would be good for everybody involved, particularly if he got Coco to take a little time for herself.

I was supposed to meet Nate for lunch, but I got a text saying he was off interviewing a potential part-time cook. Since that was all to the good, I packed and went home so I could get cleaned up and changed for the catering job that night.

By three thirty I was headed to the catering kitchen. We had all the apps done for the event, but I figured Nate might like some help with any last-minute warming, plus we might need my truck to carry some of the food to the event site.

Nate's SUV was parked out front when I got there, so I breezed right in, ready to warm up meatballs and finish any last-minute prep with crudités and filo packets. But when I opened the door, I saw two people in the kitchen where I normally expected to see one. It was Nate and an unfamiliar guy.

Well, sort of unfamiliar. The face reminded me of someone, but I wasn't sure who. It wasn't a particularly pleasant memory, whoever it was.

"Hey, babe." Nate stepped around the counter and kissed me, sliding his arm around my shoulders. "Come meet the new guy. Except he's not exactly new."

The new guy was wearing an apron over his jeans and T-shirt, sort of chef fatigues. But I didn't think I'd seen him in a kitchen around Shavano before. Still, I'd seen him somewhere.

"Hey, Dan," Nate called. "Come out and meet

Roxy. Unless you already know each other."

The new guy straightened, directing a slightly smoldering smile in my direction. "Oh, we've met," he said. "It's been a while, but we've met. How are you, Roxy?"

And then it hit me. Dan Griffin. "Well, hi, Dan," I said, making sure my lips stayed flexed in a sort of smile. "Long time, no see."

Dan Griffin of Shavano High School. The smooth-talking son of a bitch who'd relieved me of my illusions concerning romantic love, along with my virginity, back in the day. Nate could probably have hired somebody worse, but at the moment it was hard to think of whom that somebody might be.

Chapter 5

To understand about me and Dan, you need a little background. It was the summer after my dad died. I'd just turned seventeen, going into my senior year, and I was still trying to figure out how my world would function without my father in it. Plus, of course, I was experiencing the typical seventeen-year-old restlessness, that feeling of "is my life ever going to get started?"

Into my life came Dan Griffin. He'd just graduated high school, and he had a job in town, although I can't remember what he was doing. He was also a high school dreamboat: darkly handsome, a babe magnet, and a Bad Boy with a capital B. I couldn't believe he'd be interested in me, but he was. At least for a while.

We went out for a month or so—movies, fast food burgers, bad ice cream at the local drive-in. He gave me my first beer, which I didn't like much as I recall. Even then I had certain standards as far as food goes.

And because he had a car—a crummy one, true, but a car—we parked out in one of the fields near the farm and did what you usually do in parked cars. At first it was heavy petting, which I'd never really done before. But we soon moved on to more serious stuff. I was pretty naïve about sex, but not so naïve I didn't know where we were heading. I didn't have anybody to talk to about it. My friend Susa didn't like Dan much, and I was pretty sure she'd tell me to kick him out. I was scared of going all the way and scared not to. I figured Dan would walk out if I didn't do it, and right then I wanted to hold onto him.

And, if I'm honest, I have to admit a certain part of me was curious. I wanted to know what it was like, and here I had someone who was obviously experienced and who could probably show me how to do it right. Everybody else thought it was so exciting. I wanted to see what all the fuss was about.

To say I was disappointed would be an understatement. Dan was nobody's idea of a thoughtful lover. He was, in fact, a horny eighteen-year-old boy who mainly wanted to get his rocks off with any available female. After having sex with him, I decided the whole thing was overrated. When Dan wanted to have sex again, I made excuses. He put up with me for a couple of dates, and then he disappeared.

From my lofty current position, I could say that was predictable. But seventeen-year-old me was devastated. I spent a few days moping and being sorry for myself until Susa told me to pull myself together and Uncle Mike put me to work picking arugula. But my broken heart didn't entirely mend until Dan took off for Denver for some kind of work. Once he was gone, I forgot him, more or less.

But now here he was again, front and center, in Nate's catering kitchen. I had a whole new set of questions to deal with. What should I tell Nate, as in how much of my past history with Dan was relevant? How was I supposed to work with Dan, who might or might not remember just what we'd done in the back seat of his rattletrap of a car? I was in danger of being returned to my seventeen-year-old self unless I made a very concerted effort to Put It Behind Me.

I suspect Dan had had a lot of dates like the ones he had with me. He certainly worked his way through the female population of Shavano High. I don't remember him ever settling down with anyone for long, maybe because he had more fun playing the field. The month or so he spent with me was pretty much par for the course.

With any luck, maybe for him I'd just blend into the masses of girls he dated. With any luck, he might have forgotten all about our time together. I'd done my best to forget about it myself once I'd had the good sense to understand that Dan was definitely not the love of my life.

"Are you going to be cooking with us tonight?" I asked him, using my blandest tone. I hoped he wasn't. I needed time to adjust to him being around.

"Dan's just checking out the kitchen," Nate explained. "He'll get going on food prep later."

"I start cooking next week. So you can get back to your jams and such." Dan gave me a bland smile of his own.

There was nothing openly snarky about what he'd said, but I still felt a little annoyed. My *jams and such* had turned into a flourishing business. And yes, I did need more time to get them ready for my customers. "Great," I said through my teeth. I turned to Nate. "I'll go get changed. Back in a few."

I turned down the hall to the café, ignoring Nate's confused expression. My getting changed didn't involve much more than putting on my chef's coat, but I figured I could stretch the process out until Dan had left for the day.

I spent around fifteen minutes pretending to check my makeup. When I came out, I found Coco in the kitchen loading up the pecan tassies and chocolate chip cookies that were going to be our desserts. She gave me a quick smile. "Meet the new prep cook?"

"Dan?" I nodded. "I remember him from high school." And I still hoped he didn't remember me too well.

"Me, too. Who doesn't, right? Everybody female at Shavano High knew about Dan."

I stretched my suddenly tense shoulders. "He had a rep."

"He did at that. I was a few years behind him, but even I heard about it. He was supposed to be irresistible or something." She paused to tear off some plastic wrap. "I guess he seemed that way at the time. Not so much now."

I hadn't focused much on Dan's current incarnation while I was recovering from the shock of seeing him in the catering kitchen. But now that I thought about it, I had to agree. He was no longer Mr. Tall, Dark, and Handsome. In fact, he looked like he'd lived a few rough years. "That's the chef's life, I guess. It can run you down if you're not careful."

"Tell me about it. I've seen him at the Blue Spot. He's one of those guys who likes to knock back a few after work." She paused. "Which is better than doing it before work I guess." She smoothed the last piece of plastic wrap into place. "He'll probably do a decent job for the catering, but I'm glad Nate's got you to rely on for doing the events. God knows how he'd function in the event kitchen."

Of course, Nate might not be able to rely on me for all of them, given my own schedule, but we'd cross that bridge when we came to it. "You want some help carrying those to the catering kitchen?"

"Sure, I've got to get going myself. Hot date tonight." She grinned, and I wondered if she was meeting Marcus. Still, Coco's love life was her own business, and I didn't feel like asking her about him.

Dan had taken off by the time we arrived with the desserts, thank God. Nate, Coco, and I got all the food into the SUV, so I left my truck in the parking lot at Robicheaux's. I still wasn't sure what to say to Nate about Dan. I knew for a fact I didn't want to discuss my dating history with him. But as it happened, Nate took the lead.

"Did you know Dan in high school?" he asked.

I gave him a wary look. "He was ahead of me by a year or so, but everybody knew him." I took a deep breath—if I couldn't be frank with Nate, who could I be frank with? "We dated for a while back in the day. A short while."

"Yeah?" Nate raised an eyebrow. "Anything serious?"

"Nope," I said flatly. "I'm guessing Dan dated most of the girls in my class. And his."

"I remember he was supposed to be a hound with the ladies." Nate blew out a long breath. "High school feels like a lifetime ago."

Nate had been a year ahead of me in school, which meant he'd been in Dan's class. I'd been vaguely aware of him, but only as one of the Robicheaux kids. "Was Dan a friend of yours?" *And did he pass on information about the girls he dated?*

"He hung with a different group of kids. And in high school, that was like an uncrossable line. I think he played football—I ran track. He might have been friends with Bobby. He was on the football team, too, but a couple of years older than Dan and me. I'll check tomorrow at brunch."

Terrific. I hoped Bobby didn't know anything about my past with Dan. But that probably wasn't the kind of thing Bobby would remember. At least I didn't think it was. I couldn't picture Dan and Bobby hanging out together.

"Where's Dan working now?"

"He's cooking on the line at The Hungry Farmer, over in Geary."

The Hungry Farmer had been around forever. It was a huge family restaurant that featured burgers and fried chicken and catfish—whatever was cheap and plentiful. Food there was fast and reliable, if not particularly gourmet. If Dan was a line cook there, he had some chops. The line at The Hungry Farmer kept moving. "What kind of experience does he have besides that?"

Nate shrugged. "I guess he got his training in the army. After that he worked in Colorado Springs at a couple of the big hotels. I figure he can handle apps and sides. I'll keep doing the mains and anything tricky."

"Right." Dan would probably be fine. Plus he might have a reason to stick around Shavano. "Does his family still live here?"

"Don't know—he didn't mention it." Nate pulled the SUV into the parking lot next to the event center where the Mountaineers were holding their bash. We watched a guy wheel a hand cart loaded with a keg of beer into the side entrance. "So much for clean living," I muttered.

"Hey, babe, grain, hops, and water. Healthy as it gets."

Nate was clearly in a great mood. I decided I'd join him. After all, Dan was going to take up the slack so I wouldn't have to divide my time between cooking for Robicheaux's Catering and making jam for Luscious Delights. One major problem solved.

It remained to be seen if there'd be any other major or minor problems along the way.

The evening went off without a hitch for once. Our busboy and waitress both showed up. The event center kitchen was adequate if not particularly spacious. We managed to keep up with demand as far as the food was concerned, and all the apps were a success, including the vegan filo packets, which people sometimes regarded with suspicion. I even had enough time to run some of our pans and serving dishes through the dishwasher, which meant they wouldn't have to be dropped off at the café tonight.

Coco's tassies and cookies disappeared as quickly as we could get them out on the tables, although I wondered just how well they'd go with the beer everybody seemed to be drinking.

Not my problem, as they say.

At the end of the evening, the Mountaineers' program chair found Nate and pumped his hand enthusiastically, so I guess they were pleased with everything. He gave us a bonus, not a big one, but I didn't expect that from a group of clean-living climbers whose spare money probably went for equipment purchases. But the bonus was enough to give the boy and waitress a nice tip on top of their more than generous salaries for the evening.

And there was even a little left over for us so we didn't feel like we'd worked all that time for peanuts ourselves.

"You want to go to the café and pick up your truck?" Nate asked.

I shook my head. "I can drive it home tomorrow after brunch. Right now, all I want to do is go back to the cabin and put my feet up."

"If that includes a beer and some of the chili I brought home last night, I'm in. We only have a few platters that haven't been cleaned and no leftover food for once. We can drop everything off tomorrow."

One of the advantages of living with an owner of Robicheaux's Café was the leftovers that frequently came home with him. Friday there had actually been leftover chili, a very rare occurrence, given the popularity of Robicheaux's version. But the day's special had been Marigold's fried catfish, and even the chili regulars had been won over.

"What did Bobby say about having too much chili?" Bobby was normally a stickler for cooking the right sized portions.

"He was too busy chowing down on Marigold's catfish." Nate grinned at me. "I think she's winning him over."

The idea of Bobby actually liking somebody else's catfish was mind boggling. He revered the café's original recipe as if it were written in stone. Maybe Marigold practiced sorcery along with her undeniable cooking skills.

The fact that chili was waiting for us at the cabin

was enough to make me overlook the slight shiver down my spine I got every time we rolled down the drive from the county road to the farm. We'd had a couple of narrow escapes on that drive, and sometimes the memory was a little unnerving.

Even more unnerving was the fact that all the yard lights were on and Uncle Mike was standing near the barn with Donnie. It was a little late for him to be out taking the evening air.

"What the hell?" Nate murmured.

"Don't know," I said.

Uncle Mike started toward us as Nate parked, but Herman beat him to it. As soon as I stepped out of the car, he was all over me, whimpering and batting his head against my hand for pets.

"Okay, okay, pup, calm down." I scratched his ears. "What are you doing out so late anyway?"

"He's being a watchdog," Uncle Mike said. "Sort of."

I stared down at Herman again. He's big—there's some Great Dane in his lineage. But he's also a creampuff. He barks a good game, but I don't think he'd take on an intruder. "Who or what is he watching for?"

Donnie caught up then, holding the collar of his dog Lulabelle. Lulabelle is largely hound and she's as good-natured as Herman, although she spends more time outdoors roaming the yard around Donnie and Carmen's place. "We're going to see if they can watch the hives," he explained.

"Has something happened?"

"Not to me. But Fred Hutchinson lost five hives last night. That's four different bee farmers who've been hit." Donnie paused to rub Lulabelle's forehead. "I thought I'd let her out in the yard at night. It's fenced, so she can't wander too far or run into a lot of unfriendly critters. But if anybody comes around, she'll make a racket for sure."

"I figured Herman could be out in the run behind the house," Uncle Mike said. "He'll bark if he hears a car coming down the drive."

Herm would definitely do that, but he'd also do it inside the house or inside the cabin. Herman was one of those dogs who was constantly going on alert, whether the thing he was alerting about was worth it or not. "He won't like being outside all night," I said. "He's likely to raise a racket to get you to let him in."

Uncle Mike shrugged. "He's got his doghouse and his chew toys. And I'll make sure he's got plenty of food and water. He'll adjust."

I wasn't so sure about that. The dog run behind the house wasn't all that big, since it had been built originally for my dad's beagle. But I wasn't going to have to put up with whatever noise Herman made. "Do the police have any idea about who's stealing the bees?"

Donnie shook his head. "Whoever it is has been coming at night, working fast. Fred heard a truck, but by the time he pulled on his pants and got out there, they were gone. His hives are a good fifty feet from his house. They took five hives and knocked over two others. Fred's fit to be tied."

"You'd think they'd get stung in the process," Nate said. "Picking up a beehive isn't like grabbing some cash."

"They probably wear protective gear," Uncle Mike

said. "Gauntlets and hats. But sooner or later, the bees will get them. Bees are smart critters. And they don't like being disturbed."

"We'll all just have to keep our eyes open," I said. "If you see anybody with suspicious swelling, you tell Fowler." Frankly, I doubted Chief Fowler would appreciate being kept informed of iffy skin conditions, but it would give him something to snarl about.

Nate and I went inside as Donnie and Uncle Mike went back to dog wrangling. "You think Herman has watchdog potential?" Nate asked.

"Are you kidding? He barks at everything that makes him nervous, including chipmunks and raccoons. I figure he'll drive Uncle Mike nuts in short order. Lulabelle's a much better bet."

I set about warming up the chili while Nate grabbed some cornbread from the freezer. It was left over from last winter, but I figured it would still work. "You're okay with Dan, aren't you?" He set the cornbread in the microwave. "I didn't know the two of you'd been involved."

I paused. "I wouldn't call it 'involved.' And it was in high school. I'm okay with him. If he can handle the cooking, he should be fine." And if he could handle the cooking, I'd make it a point to handle my own reaction to him. *Time to be a grownup, Roxanne.*

"I think he can handle it. I guess we'll find out over the next couple of weeks." Nate found the soup bowls as I gave the chili a stir. "We've got a new event order, did I tell you?"

"No. What for?" Now that I was less likely to be stuck in the kitchen stirring up apps and sides, I was glad to hear about new possibilities for Robicheaux

Catering.

"Sawmill Brewing's going to throw a big party for their new release. It's some kind of summer lager, and they want to do something outdoors with grilling and summer sides. They've got that big outdoor dining space behind the brewery. It could end up being the biggest thing we've done—they're anticipating two hundred or so guests." Nate picked up the kettle of chili. He was suddenly very interested in ladling it into the bowls.

I dropped into a chair. We'd never done an entire dinner for more than a hundred guests, and even the event where we'd just done soup for two hundred had been a real stretch. "Wow."

He nodded. "Wow is right. We'll have to pull in extra people so we can cook for a crowd. Plus hire extra servers to handle the buffet line. And I'll have to find some grills to rent. I don't think our kettle grill is going to be enough."

I sighed. "Probably not. Have you ever done grilling for a group like this?" We hadn't done any catered grilling so far, but it wasn't surprising that a customer would want it.

"When I was in Vegas, I worked a few. I've never put one together, though." He dropped into a chair beside me. "If we can do it right, it'll give us a new kind of meal to offer, particularly in summer."

"I'd say only in summer. No way am I standing over a grill in December." Although there were Coloradans crazy enough to do it. "When is it supposed to happen?"

"Next month. We've got a couple of weeks to get ready."

"And meanwhile…"

"Meanwhile we go with the usual corporate stuff, along with birthday parties and anniversaries and the rest of it." He grinned. "Good times, babe. Good times."

"Yeah. Good times for sure." Assuming I got over my nerves about Dan Griffin. And assuming Dan Griffin turned out to be the kind of cook we needed. Both question marks at the moment.

Chapter 6

Susa called me a couple of days later. "Hey," she said, "I haven't talked to you in an age. I've been submerged in a big project, but I'm finally above water again. What's new?"

I stopped to think. "Well, we're doing the food at the Sawmill Brewery release party—our biggest event yet."

"Cool," said Susa. "I'll be there. Ethan's taking me."

Ethan was Chief Fowler. Susa and Fowler had an on-and-off relationship, maybe because they both had insane schedules. I was glad to hear it was currently *on*. Fowler seemed a lot less grouchy when he was going out with Susa.

"And Nate hired an assistant, so I don't have to do food prep for the catering events."

"Great. That should take some of the pressure off. Who did he hire? Anyone I know?"

I managed an ironic smile, which, of course, she couldn't see. "Oh, yeah. You knew him back in the day anyway. Nate hired Dan Griffin."

There was a bit of a pause on the other end. "Holy shit. We need to have lunch. Meet me at Dirty Pete's at noon today."

I didn't even try to resist. Susa was one of the few people I could vent to, and I seriously needed to vent.

Caroline, the waitress/hostess at Dirty Pete's, gestured me toward the back of the restaurant without even looking up. She knew both me and Susa and probably figured if one was there the other had to be coming soon. Susa was almost vibrating with impatience as I pulled out my chair. "Well?" she said as I sat down. "What did you tell Nate? Did he know about you and Dan before he hired him? What did Dan say?"

I considered which question to tackle first. "Nate knew Dan in high school, sort of. They were in the same year, but they weren't close so far as I know. And no, he didn't know I'd had anything going with Dan. I told him we'd dated, which is about as much as I felt like sharing."

"Yeah, 'dating' covers a pretty wide range. He shouldn't feel like you're concealing anything."

My shoulders tensed slightly. "You think I should have told him everything?"

"Lord, no." She shuddered. "Nobody should have to go into detail about what happened during your teenage years. I think 'dating' is just as much as anyone needs to know."

"That was my feeling." I waved Caroline down and gave her my order for a taco salad. It was hot outside and I thought a salad would be virtuous. Of course, a taco salad is probably not the most virtuous choice.

"What did Dan say to you?"

"Not much. He kind of sneered about my business, said he was working with Nate so that I could get back to my 'jams and such'."

"*Jams and such?*" Susa raised an eyebrow. "What the hell does that mean?"

"I thought it was kind of an insult. Like my jams were too unimportant to matter. But I don't know what he meant, to tell the truth." Now that I thought about it, I wondered if I'd overreacted to the phrase because it was Dan. I was sort of primed to think the worst of him, after all.

Susa *hmphed* as Caroline brought our lunches. My taco salad came in a king-size tortilla shell and was loaded with cheese and hamburger, so virtuous it wasn't. But virtuous and delicious don't always go together.

"How does he look?" Susa asked between bites of her chicken burger.

I paused. "He's not a dreamboat anymore. He looks like he's had some hard living at some point, but Nate said he learned to cook in the army, so maybe he was stationed in some tough places."

"I can't picture Dan Griffin in the army. Taking orders was never his thing."

"I don't know how long he served, maybe just a few years."

Susa leaned back in her chair, considering. "So you haven't really talked to him?"

I shook my head. "Not really. I haven't been to the kitchen since Nate hired him." Although now that I thought about it, I needed to go over to the catering kitchen to drop off some platters that had been left in my truck. That didn't mean I'd have a heart-to-heart with Dan, though.

"Everybody thought he was such a stud," Susa mused. "He never appealed to me much."

"Unfortunately, I can't say the same." I pulled off a piece of the tortilla shell. It maintained its crunch to the end—the mark of a primo taco salad.

"Oh, honey, every woman's got a Dan somewhere in her past. I had a huge crush on Lloyd Kravitz when we were sophomores. We went out exactly twice, and he managed to get to second base before I regained my senses. Fortunately, for me."

"Lloyd Kravitz? The guy at the hardware store?"

"With the thinning hair and the developing beer gut? Yeah, that Lloyd. The ways of the heart, you know? Who can say why it wants what it wants." Susa grinned. "Although we both know we're not really talking about the heart, right?"

"Right." I sighed. "I should just get over it. I mean, it was a long time ago and it's more than possible Dan has forgotten all about it. And even if he hasn't, there's no reason he'd talk to Nate about what we did together. Especially not if he wants to go on working for the catering company."

"No reason at all. I think you're very safe on that score. But…" She paused to run her last French fry through the puddle of ketchup on her plate.

"But?" I prompted.

"But if you think he's forgotten what you did together, you're kidding yourself." She grinned again. "Guys do not forget, trust me on this."

Guys certainly didn't forget Susa. I was willing to accept that absolutely. But I was still hoping Dan didn't remember the details of our one-month relationship.

I decided to drive by the catering kitchen and drop off the platters just to prove to myself that I was in control, that being around Dan wouldn't bother me. Besides, Nate would be there along with Dan, so it wasn't like we'd be having any intimate conversations.

The Honey Jam Murder

I pulled up in the parking lot that served both the café and the catering kitchen. There were still quite a few cars since the café was still serving lunch, but I found a spot near the kitchen and grabbed the box with the platters from behind the seat.

I pushed open the door to the catering building and paused. I could see movement in the kitchen, but I wasn't sure who it was. *Oh, grow up, Roxanne.* It didn't matter if it was Nate or Dan. I would be perfectly comfortable around either of them.

Or anyway, I should have been. I stepped into the kitchen and saw Dan at one of the counters chopping vegetables on a cutting board. I didn't want to startle him, since you never want to startle someone with a knife in his hand, but he seemed to sense that I was behind him. He half-turned, then smiled. "Hey, Roxy."

"Hey," I said. "Nate around?"

"He's over helping with lunch. Said he'd be back by one thirty."

I should have known that, and I would have known it if I'd stopped to think. But so what? Even if Nate wasn't there, I was fine. Perfectly fine. I carried the box with the platters to the pantry and put them on the shelf.

Dan was leaning against the counter when I came out, wiping his hands on a towel. "You want me to tell Nate anything?"

For a moment I wasn't sure what he was asking, then I figured he meant did I want him to tell Nate about the platters. *Not about us. Definitely not about us.* "That's okay. I'll tell him tonight."

Dan's lips slipped into a faintly sardonic smile. "So I guess you and Nate live together?"

I nodded. "At the farm." Which was all I was going

to say about it. I couldn't see any reason why Dan needed to know about our personal lives.

"I was going to look you up when I first got here. Guess I missed my chance." His smile had edged closer to a smirk, but I decided to ignore it.

"Nate and I have been together for a year now." *And you never had a chance anyway.*

Dan decided to change the subject. "How's your uncle?"

"He's fine. He's dating Nate's mom." I wasn't sure why I added that detail. Maybe to let Dan know just how tight the Constantines and the Robicheauxs were.

"Oh, yeah?" Dan raised an eyebrow. "She's a good-looking woman."

I wasn't sure how I felt about Dan rating Madge. What I mainly felt was that I needed to get out of there. "Guess I'll go back. You can let Nate know I dropped by." Just in case he thought he needed to keep quiet about my being in his kitchen.

"I'll do that. Drive safe." He returned to his cutting board and vegetables.

I found myself reviewing the entire encounter on the way home. Maybe I was making way too much out of my former relationship with Dan, but he still made me uncomfortable. And I still hoped he didn't say anything about our past to Nate.

But Susa was obviously right: Dan Griffin hadn't forgotten about me. Not nearly as much as I'd hoped he had.

Chapter 7

On Monday morning, I decided to use my newly freed-up time to decide on this month's featured jam. I'd started doing a sort of "jam of the month" thing after I'd appeared on a national TV show. My mail orders had really picked up then, and the marketing expert I'd consulted had recommended doing a featured jam. I wasn't as regular about it as I should have been; sometimes I didn't get around to setting up a new featured jam until a couple of months had gone by. But they'd proven to be very popular, and I now had a sort of repertoire of unusual jams I only offered online.

This month, I was bound and determined to do a jam sweetened with honey, especially if I could use honey from Donnie's hives, so that I could say it was from the farm. Since I usually only made thirty or so jars of the featured jam, I might be able to make it work, depending on how much honey it took to make the jam sweet enough without making it cloying.

That was the real question: how much honey would I need?

I decided to try doing my regular raspberry jam using honey instead of sugar. Raspberry anything was dependably among my best sellers, so I figured a honey version wouldn't go down in flames. The real question was how much honey I'd need to add. My regular recipe called for three cups of sugar for two pounds of raspberries. Three cups of honey would produce a jam that would leave you gagging from the fumes alone. But would one cup be enough? The only way to find out was to try it.

I weighed out two pounds of raspberries from the flat I'd bought the week before. They weren't Colorado berries, which wouldn't be around until late June at the earliest, but I figured I could make them work. After I located the jar of honey Uncle Mike had given me last week, I poured a cup of it into my adjustable measuring cup. Cook's note: an adjustable measuring cup is the absolute best way to measure something thick and viscous without tearing your hair out, believe me. Then I measured the pectin and lemon juice and stirred it all together in my jam pot.

If the jam worked, I'd have to make a lot of it. I'd want the thirty jars for the featured jam and then probably another fifty or so for the farmers market. And when you're making jam in quantity, there's a real temptation to double the recipe and get it all done in one fell swoop. Unfortunately, that way lies disaster, as I'd found out early in my jam-making career. Jam requires a lot of surface area to get rid of the water in your fruit so that it cooks down evenly, which is why you use a big jam pot. If you double a recipe, you get more jam with less surface area, which means you can get more rubbery jam, more scorching, more jam that just doesn't set, more jam disasters than you can imagine. Jam has a mind of its own. It knows what it wants, and you'd better supply it. If I needed a lot of jam, I'd have to make two batches simultaneously, doubling my output but keeping the amount of jam in the pot at the optimum for surface area.

The Honey Jam Murder

In short, there'd be a lot of jampots going more or less at the same time, with new possibilities for disaster. I'd either be working fast, or I'd have to have someone like Dolce at my elbow.

Assuming my single pot worked out, I'd have to do more than one pot at a time from now on, crossing my fingers that the honey I was working with would have the same sugar content, the same consistency, the same mojo as the honey I was basing the recipe on. But since honey is a natural product, you can't guarantee that, which meant each batch might be a crap shoot.

Yes, I could have avoided all those problems by using commercial honey that had been stabilized with corn syrup. But you can guess how I felt about doing that. Honey adulterated with corn syrup does not fit my definition of a Luscious Delight.

Uncle Mike strolled in after I'd gotten the jam pot boiling, sniffing the air appreciatively. "That smells great. Raspberry?"

"And honey. Donnie's honey. If this recipe works out, do you think his honey production is big enough to cover fifty jars? That would be…" I paused, grabbing my phone to use the calculator. "…around three quarts."

Uncle Mike frowned. "Depends on how fast you want it. If you had two or three months to spare, he could do it. If you want it sooner, it might be tougher. Donnie says it takes around two or three weeks to get a pound of honey from one of the hives."

I closed my eyes, trying to do calculations. "A pint's a pound the world around, right?"

Uncle Mike sighed. "Nope. Three pounds in a quart. Roughly. So you're talking around nine or ten pounds of honey. A bigger producer could sell you that without batting an eye. The guys around here might not have as much on hand."

I bit my lip. "Actually, it would be more than that if I make honey jam for the farmers market, too. It might be closer to twenty pounds."

Uncle Mike grimaced. "Stick with ten for now. See how it goes. If you want ten pounds of honey to work with in the next couple of weeks, you'll probably need to branch out. Buy some at the farmers market to go along with Donnie's."

"Yeah. I wonder who Donnie would recommend? It would probably be easier to standardize things if I could get all the honey from around this area."

"Lots of people have a few hives. Aram Pergosian has a dozen or so. Lynn Bridger has a few. Hutchinson probably had the most hives earlier, but he lost seven of them when they robbed him."

Speaking of the bee robbery, Uncle Mike was looking a little peaked himself. "How's Herman doing as a watchdog?"

"Dog never shuts up," he grumbled. "I can't leave him out all night. Maybe just during the day or early evening."

Herman already spent a lot of his time outside during the day, but he usually stayed in our yard rather than hanging around Donnie and Carmen's place. The real question was whether he'd be willing to stick around the hives or go wandering off to follow Uncle Mike when he headed into the fields. "Surely they won't try anything during the day. We've got people all around."

Uncle Mike sighed. "Likely not. But who knows?

Donnie's hives are away from the house, toward the pine grove. It's hard to see them from some of the fields."

I could understand why Donnie and, more likely, Carmen didn't want beehives close to the house, but Uncle Mike had a point. "I'll be around most days, and so will Carmen. If Lulabelle's out in the yard barking, we'll both hear her."

"Right. I might leave Herman with you anyway. Just in case."

I kept my enthusiasm within bounds. Herman could get in the way when my assistants, Bridget and Dolce, were here. My cabin wasn't all that big to begin with, and these days it was frequently full of cases of jam. "I might be able to handle him. Particularly if he's outside."

I got the honey raspberry jam into the jars a little after that. I couldn't taste it because it was the consistency and temperature of lava. But after I processed the jars and let them sit on the counter for a while, I figured Nate and I could try a taste after supper. Technically I should have let them sit overnight, but since I had more than one jar, I figured we could try one right off the bat and then let the others sit to see if the flavor changed at all.

Nate got home a little after six. He was doing a birthday luncheon on Friday afternoon plus a dinner party Saturday night, so the week promised to involve a lot of cooking. Dan would probably get a good workout.

Nate grabbed a beer from the fridge and set about stir-frying some chicken while I put the finishing touches on a salad. "How'd the prep go?" I tried to sound neutral, but I was interested in finding out whether Dan was going to be an asset or a liability.

Nate shrugged. "We're getting there. I've got Dan doing the filling for the lettuce wraps—it'll get better the longer it sits."

The birthday luncheon was all female, one sister giving a party for another, along with various friends and relations. Granny was supposedly coming, too. I'd initially thought they'd want to go with something like chicken salad—classic ladies lunch food. But these ladies weren't into classic. So we were doing lettuce wraps with a spicy beef filling, some vegetarian fried rice for the non-meat-eaters in the crowd, lots of apps, including Nate's take on egg rolls, and a major cake, courtesy of Coco. The sisters were providing their own bar and bartender, which relieved Nate of any duties.

"What about the rice?" Fried rice works best with rice that's had some time sitting in the refrigerator to dry out before you fry it, preferably overnight.

"Dan's going to do it tomorrow. And I've got him chopping up veggies for it now."

"And the apps?"

"In hand. For both the lunch and the dinner." Nate gave me a quick smile over his shoulder. "It's working, babe. I miss you, but it's still working."

My cheeks heated briefly. Of course, it was working. I didn't have to be in the kitchen for Nate to get an order going, and Dan could easily do what I'd been doing. Or anyway, I thought he could.

"How's Dan working out?"

"He's okay. Got good knife skills. Pays attention to the recipes. Works fast and gets stuff done."

"Is he going to be there all week?"

Nate shook his head. "All day Monday and Wednesday, and Thursday morning. He's got to be at The Hungry Farmer the other days."

"Does that mean you'll need me to help with the luncheon on Friday?"

"Yeah, if you can be there." Nate carried the chicken to the table and divided it between our plates. "And lord knows I'll need you Saturday night. I can get the last-minute prep done on Saturday, but I'll need you in the kitchen for the dinner."

So you need me. It was pretty dumb to feel good about that, but I did. I was still part of the team, even if I wasn't a starting pitcher anymore.

After dinner, we loaded the dishwasher, and I picked up one of the jars of raspberry/honey jam. It glowed a lovely scarlet color as I placed it on the table.

Nate picked it up, studying it. "So this is it?"

"First version," I said quickly. "Using a cup of honey, which is a third of what I use with sugar. I can go down or up from here, depending on how it tastes."

"Do you want to try it on ice cream?"

"Let's try it straight first. Then maybe on a cracker. Then on ice cream if it works out."

Jam on ice cream is delicious, but the cream affects the flavor. On the other hand, if it was lousy, we could use it up on ice cream or maybe shortcake. I sold some of my failures to Bianca to fill kolaches, but if this was a loser, it might not be up to those admittedly low standards.

I handed Nate a tasting spoon, then opened the jar. The first taste of a new jam is no big deal, usually. You hope for the best, but half the time it needs work so you just dive in again. But I always feel a little nervous when I pick up my spoon for the first time.

I took a very small spoonful and passed the jar to Nate. Then I nibbled at the jam on the end of the spoon. It had that unmistakable raspberry flavor: tart and sweet and overwhelmingly fruity. Also seedy, but that's another story. I paused, trying to analyze the taste.

"Not too sweet," Nate said.

"Nope." I tasted again. "Is it too tart?"

We both sat in silence, nibbling on jam. If anyone had been watching, they'd probably have concluded we needed a long rest somewhere.

"I don't think it's too tart," Nate said. "But I like tart. I may not be the best judge here."

"I like it, too. Maybe I'll try Uncle Mike. He's got a big sweet tooth."

"Can I have a cracker now?"

"Oh, hell, let's go for ice cream." The jam had made it through the first hurdle, but that didn't mean it was going to make it much farther. Still, I was happy with this beginning. It meant I wasn't much off the mark.

The next morning, I gave Uncle Mike some jam on a slice of toast. He took a bite, his forehead crinkling slightly. "Great raspberry taste. Maybe stronger than the regular version."

"That's because it's not as sweet. Is it too tart?"

He took another bite, staring off into space as he chewed. "Borderline," he said finally. "I like the strong raspberry taste, but it's almost too strong. It could stand to be just a touch more sweet."

Which would mean more honey. When I was already going to be scrambling to get nine pounds. Oh, well, make it an even ten for this first round. "Okay, thanks. I'll try another batch this morning with just a touch more. Maybe a couple of tablespoons." Whatever I ended up with as a final measure, it would have to be something exact. No way was I making fifty jars without a very precise amount of honey.

Dolce and Bridget, my assistants, showed up at nine and nine thirty, respectively. Dolce's a high school student with a full range of activities to fill her time and a couple of teenage boys worshipping at her feet. She's also Donnie and Carmen's daughter, so she knows her way around cooking with honey. She tried a spoonful of the jam, closing her eyes as she tasted. "That's really…intense," she said. "I like it. Really raspberry. It would be super in a doughnut."

"Uncle Mike thinks it's too tart," I said. "He wants a little more sweetness."

Dolce nibbled a little more. "I can see how he'd say that if he likes sweet things," she said slowly. "I like it, but it could be a little sweeter without losing its character altogether."

Which I figured was a diplomatic way of saying Uncle Mike had a point. Bridget is in her forties, a single mom with a couple of kids who also waited tables at High Country, a very upscale restaurant in downtown Shavano. I keep hoping I'll start making enough money to hire her on full time, but given the kind of tips she got at High Country, that might not have been a realistic hope. Bridget took her own spoonful of jam, then squinted as she savored. "Needs sugar," she said.

"It's sweetened with honey. I'm trying to figure out how much to use."

"More than this," Bridget said flatly. "I mean, it's

very fruity, pure raspberry, but too tart for me."

If it was too tart for Bridget, it would undoubtedly be too tart for a lot of other people. I sighed and set up another test pot, while Dolce got to work on a batch of pepper peach. "How much honey do your folks usually sell at the farmers market?" I asked her.

"It varies. Mom's started making creamed honey, some with flavors. It's a big hit." She paused. "I don't guess you could use that for jam, though. It has a different kind of sweetness, and it melts differently. Plus it's more expensive than the regular."

"I thought you could only use crystallized honey for creamed honey?" Or anyway that's what the YouTube video had said.

"It's a good way to use up crystallized honey, but you can also use some of the creamed honey from the last batch as a seed. You just whip it up and go from there. Sort of like sourdough bread. Mom's getting into the flavored stuff."

Terrific. If Carmen was whipping up most of their honey, that would mean even less for me. "I'll talk to your mom when I figure out how much honey I need. Probably after this next batch."

We worked for the rest of the morning and into the afternoon, Bridget bringing the orders up to date and getting the cases ready for pickup and Dolce making pepper peach and strawberry. Once I had the honey raspberry in hand, I started helping her, but I paused to nibble a little of the new batch from one of the mixing spoons. I thought it tasted great, but I'd thought that with the last batch, too. And the jam in the jar might well taste different from the jam on the mixing spoon.

That night we had another tasting party, this time

with Uncle Mike and Madge dropping by to sample. It was sweeter, but still on the less sweet side. I loved it, but I watched Uncle Mike with some trepidation.

"Pretty good," he said after a moment. "Let me try it on a cracker."

"It's wonderful," Madge declared. "Just sweet enough. Don't let anyone tell you to change it."

Uncle Mike cast a concerned look her way, but then he spread a spoonful of jam on a saltine and took a bite. "Yeah," he said after he'd chewed for a bit. "Yeah. This'll do."

"I'd say so." Nate spread jam on his own cracker. "You've got it. You kept track of the amount you used, right?"

I nodded. "Now I'll have to scale it up for a hundred jars or so to take care of mail orders and the market."

"Talk to Carmen," Uncle Mike said. "Even if she can't sell you all the honey you need, she can tell you who to go to for more."

"I figured I would." Because I needed around twenty pounds of honey, and I hadn't even considered how much money that was going to cost me yet. But that would come next. I gritted my teeth at the prospect.

Chapter 8

Dolce's mom, Carmen, had a professional kitchen in the farmhouse she shared with her family. Since the last time I'd dropped by, she'd added a large-size mixer, maybe to take care of the whipped honey. The more heavy-duty equipment, like the centrifuge that spun the honey out of the honeycombs, was kept in a separate workroom she and Donnie had added on a couple of years ago.

Everybody agreed that Donnie was a sweetheart. But they also agreed that Carmen was a hard ass, which made sense since somebody in the family had to keep things on track. Carmen had been Uncle Mike's housekeeper for most of the years I was growing up, which meant she was the main female authority figure I had to ask questions of. She wasn't what I'd call a motherly type—at least, not with me—but she was fair and straightforward, and she helped me when she could. We had a kind of grudging affection for each other, particularly now that Dolce was working for me and picking up some jam-making skills.

Carmen was pouring whipped honey into containers when I walked in, so she only spared me a glance as she kept on working. "What's up?" she asked.

"I need some honey," I said. "I'm going to make a special raspberry honey jam, for mail order and probably for the farmers market, too."

Carmen paused, brushing a lock of hair with the back of her hand. "How much do you need?"

I took a breath, steeling myself. "Around twenty pounds."

Carmen snorted. "Dream on. I can let you have a couple of pounds, wholesale, but we're whipping and flavoring most of our output now. Moves better at the market. Plus it uses up crystallized honey."

"Okay, I sort of figured as much." I picked up one of Carmen's tasting spoons from the jar next to the stove. "Can I taste?"

She stepped back. "Have at it."

I nipped a small taste out of the container she was filling: sweet, creamy, luscious. The stuff would be great on warm toast in the morning. But that wouldn't get me any closer to my twenty pounds. "Who else around here would you recommend? I want to get as much honey from the neighborhood as I can so it'll have the same level of sweetness."

"It won't," Carmen said flatly. "Even hives that are a few miles apart can produce different types of honey depending on what plants the bees are visiting."

I felt like sighing. Carmen was being Carmen, which was predictable but didn't make it any easier to work with her. "I'd still like to use locals. Anybody you guys can vouch for?"

She paused, narrowing her eyes. "Aram, of course. Don't know how many hives he's got now, but I know he's upped his production. Lynn Bridger's got a couple dozen hives, and he sells at his farm stand. And there's Hutchinson." Carmen's lips tightened.

"Hutchinson was the one who got hit by the thieves last week, wasn't he?"

"Yeah, but he's got a fair number of hives. Losing seven won't break him. Probably just annoy him." Carmen shrugged. "His honey's okay. If you're using it as an ingredient, the flavor won't matter much anyway."

"Okay. I'll check with Aram. Could I take the two pounds with me now?" I figured I needed to remind Carmen or she'd probably go on filling containers and forget all about me.

She rolled her eyes, lowering the can of honey she'd been pouring from. "Sure. Wait here."

Twenty minutes later I was at the cabin with my first two pounds of honey. I could probably do a dozen or more jars of jam with that, but I figured as long as I was on a honey expedition, I might as well keep going.

I'd never been to Lynn Bridger's farm, but I knew where it was. He was an orchard man, with several acres of apples and pears, along with a small cherry orchard, which made him one of the few people in the neighborhood who grew cherries. His acres of fruit trees explained why he had beehives, since he'd have a lot of pollinating needs.

Lynn had a farm stand, but no one was there, and it was pretty empty. I walked toward the yard in back, hoping someone would turn up. I didn't see Lynn, but his wife, Patsy, was weeding the vegetable garden behind the house.

She paused when she saw me, resting her hands on her thighs. "Hey, Roxy, what's up?"

"I need some honey," I said. "Carmen thought you guys might have some for sale."

Patsy pushed herself to her feet. "We've got some. Not as much as we should have since those bastards swiped two hives last week."

"Oh, no. I'm sorry, Patsy. I didn't know you'd been hit, too."

"Well, it wasn't as bad as it could have been," she said. "The dogs started barking around ten, and Lynn ran outside. He got there in time to see them drive off, but they didn't have time to do more than grab a couple of hives. And they didn't knock any over. So we're ahead of some other people, like Hutchinson." She walked into the barn, rummaging around some boxes at the side. "Here you go. Is this what you need?" She placed a couple of pint jars on a slightly rickety table.

I thought about telling her how much I needed, but I was still a little sore from Carmen's reaction. "I can take a couple more if you can spare them. I'm making some jam sweetened with honey, and I'm trying to stay local."

Patty frowned. "I could maybe let you have another pint, but we're running low right now. We're doing creamed honey, like everybody else, although if everybody else does it, we might switch to raw. Just to be competitive."

"I'll take the third pint," I said. "And thanks."

"No problem. When are you going to be selling the honey-sweetened stuff? I'll put it in the farm newsletter."

I had no idea the Bridgers had a newsletter, but why not? "I'm doing it for my mail orders first, but I hope I'll have some for the farmers market by next month." Although given how hard it was turning out to be to get local honey, I might need to stretch that calendar a bit.

"Good enough. We're always looking for news to

pass on." Patsy grinned. "People are getting tired of hearing about cherries, and we won't have much to say about the apples and pears until late summer. A little bit about the honey goes a long way."

I figured I'd hit Aram Pergosian's farm stand next. It wasn't that far away, just a few miles from our farm.

I've known Aram almost as long as I've known Uncle Mike. I met them at roughly the same time, when my dad brought me to Shavano as a three-year-old. Aram has the farm down the road from ours and is famous for his tomatoes, and that's no exaggeration. The entire county waits with crossed fingers and bated breath until Aram's tomato crop is out there—it's that good. He also does some other things that are just as tasty. He and Uncle Mike have a sort of gentleman's agreement about what they plant. Uncle Mike has a peach orchard, and Aram has an apricot orchard. Aram does legendary tomatoes and Uncle Mike does legendary arugula. They both do strawberries and raspberries, but it's not like there aren't enough customers for the two of them.

Aram has a farm stand on the county road, although he sells most of his retail stuff at the farmers market. During the week, he usually has his teenage son, Barry, running the stand. But today, I saw Aram himself behind the counter as I hiked up from where I'd parked my truck. He's not very tall, but he's very solid, like most farmers I know. His black hair is shot through with silver now, and he still has a great moustache.

"Hey, Roxanne," he called. "If I'd known you were coming, I'd have ordered some strawberry jam. Just ran out this morning."

"I'll send you some," I said. "I'm actually here for

some of your honey, if you've got any to spare. I'm trying some honey-sweetened jam."

"Sure, I can sell you some. Or we can work out a trade for jam. If you've got honey-sweetened stuff, maybe I can sell it here."

"That'd be great." I took another of those deep breaths. "I need a lot of honey. Upwards of fifteen pounds." After Carmen snorted at the very idea of selling me twenty pounds of jam, I decided to scale back a little on my requests.

Aram looked disappointed. "I don't have that much I can sell you. I can do maybe three or four pounds."

"I'll take it. I'm trying to put together fifty jars for my mail orders and the farmers market, and that'll help a lot."

Aram found four one-pound jars for me, and I dug out my money rather than try and figure out how many jars of jam equaled a pound of honey in barter. "I heard you had some hives stolen," I said as I packed away my liquid gold.

Aram's sunny smile turned cloudy. "Three hives. And the bastards knocked over another hive on their way out. Stealing hives is one thing, but destroying them is something else."

"I'm sorry that happened," I said. "We need all the bees we can get."

"We do at that," he said.

A car door slammed nearby and we both swiveled toward the parking lot. Sara Jordan, whom I hadn't seen since she and Marcus had broken up, strode toward the counter, her chin held high.

Being single hadn't improved Sara's disposition much. She glared at me and Aram, pretty much equally, although so far as I knew she had no reason to be pissed at him. She might have had more reason to be mad at me, but in my opinion, Sara had created her own problems.

"I'm here to pick up the produce for Sylvano's," she said to Aram, still without a smile.

"I'll get it for you." Aram wasn't smiling either. Maybe this was routine. He disappeared into a shed nearby.

I considered heading to my truck, but I was curious to see if Sara would even acknowledge my presence. "Hi, Sara," I said. "How's it going?"

Sara gave me a seething look, but then she stared straight out in front again. "I'm all right. As you can see."

"Glad to hear it. I heard you were working for Sylvano's."

"Yes." She kept her gaze on the farm stand's rear wall. "It's a real treat to work for a first-class grocery. One where they know what they're doing and sell quality stuff. It's been a real change."

Oh, grow up. Marcus's butcher shop was a specialty place that produced the best sausage in the county. Not that Sara had appreciated what Marcus did. "Glad it's working out." I gathered my honey and turned toward my truck. "Enjoy the produce."

"Oh, I will. You enjoy your little market stand. And your little town. So much going on."

I willed myself not to turn after her because I figured that was what she wanted me to do. I didn't know why she was mad at me, given that she was the one who'd cheated on Marcus. Maybe she was mad because he hadn't taken her back. Maybe she was mad because the guy she'd cheated with hadn't left his wife for her. Maybe she was just mad about life.

Knowing Sara, that possibility seemed most likely. At any rate I wasn't going to let her upset me. Sara could sulk all she wanted. She was no longer anyone I was concerned about.

I took Aram's honey to the cabin to reassess. I had enough honey now to make around half of what I needed for the mail orders. But I didn't have any raspberries, which were, let's face it, even more necessary than the honey. Stiegel's is my grocery of choice for produce. They get a better grade of stuff than the big chain stores. Of course, you pay for that quality, but I don't mind. If I've got to use out-of-state berries, they might as well be the best I can get.

I'd rather have used stuff from our farm or from Aram's place or from anybody else around Shavano, but the Colorado berries wouldn't be in for another few weeks, and I didn't want to use frozen fruit for this. I was already dealing with a lot of variables. I didn't want to add the problems that came with extra moisture from frozen berries.

I talked to the produce manager at Stiegel's and scored two flats of raspberries. I figured that would give me enough fruit and honey to make a dent in the mail order supplies. As I wheeled my flats to the checkout stands, I saw Bianca with a tray of cinnamon rolls. "Hey," I said.

"Hey, yourself. Those raspberries going into jam?" she asked.

I nodded. "Something new. Raspberry jam with honey."

"Sounds tasty. Bring me some jars when you can."

She placed the cinnamon rolls on top of the bakery counter for one of the bakery workers to pick up.

"I didn't know you were selling at Stiegel's."

Bianca grimaced. "One of Sara's deals. I'll keep doing it through the end of the month, but then I think I'll go back to selling exclusively at the shop. It's a pain to schlepp this stuff over here every day."

"I saw her at Pergosian's today," I said. "Sara, that is."

"She going after Aram for something? Maybe I should warn Carine."

Carine was Aram's wife of many, many years. My guess was she had absolutely nothing to worry about. "She was picking up some produce for Sylvano's."

"At least she's got a job over there so Marcus doesn't have to support her. Although to hear her tell it, she's on the verge of poverty."

My guess was Sara might have a point—her job at Sylvano's probably didn't pay that much unless she'd moved up to management. I started pushing my cart again and Bianca fell into step beside mt.

"You and Nate doing that Sawmill Brewing thing?"

"Yeah, I think so." I'd sort of lost track of the Sawmill Brewing gig since we had more immediate things to get ready for.

"Going to be a big bash, I hear. If you need rolls for it, give me some warning."

I sighed. "More likely to be buns. They want barbecue and they'll probably want supermarket buns to go with it."

"At least it won't be white sandwich bread like they use in Texas." Bianca shook her head. "Never understood that idea myself."

"No commercial white bread," I said firmly. "Not from Robicheaux's."

But as I turned home, I wondered what we were going to be doing for the Sawmill bash. Nate had said we'd need more people to help out, particularly if Dan wasn't available that weekend. Were we going to do hotdogs and burgers or were we going more upscale? How much was Sawmill willing to kick in for something unique?

They'd probably pay a bit more since this wasn't going to be an entirely free event. There was an entry fee, and they'd charge for the beer. Given that income, I figured they'd be interested in more than supermarket franks. Maybe we could even get franks and burgers from Marcus. Or maybe we could go for his sausage.

But whatever we were doing, we needed to nail it down soon. News about the party had already leaked out, which meant anticipation was building.

We needed to make sure Robicheaux Catering made it worth the wait.

Chapter 9

The ladies' luncheon was a hoot—ten spirited guests, *spirited* in more ways than one, given the number of bottles of champagne they went through. They also went through the apps like locusts in a wheat field, and the lettuce wraps and fried rice were popular, too. The real winner was an ice cream cake Coco had put together. I decided then and there that if I had a birthday catered by Robicheaux's, that's absolutely what I'd want.

Saturday's market was huge, with lots of people buying jam and jelly, along with produce and everything else that was out for sale. The strawberry crop was finally in, and people had lots of options for sampling. Everywhere I saw strawberry shortcake and strawberry pie, along with Bianca's strawberry Danishes. My strawberry jam flew off the shelves, along with some strawberry preserves Dolce had done. I was glad I'd reserved several more flats of berries from Uncle Mike's crop because we'd undoubtedly sell out again and again as long as strawberry fever was around.

That night Robicheaux Catering was working a dinner party taking place in one of the grand houses in the historical section of Shavano. As befit the address, it was a formal dinner, which we rarely did. In turn, this meant upping our game in terms of visuals. For a lot of the dinners we catered, I wore a black T-shirt and jeans, along with a Constantine Farms baseball cap. Since I rarely got out of the kitchen (except to sometimes take a bow at the end of the evening), I didn't figure I needed to dress up all the much. But for this one, I wore my chef's coat and beanie. I even put on eyeshadow. I figured if they wanted classy, I could absolutely oblige. Nate matched me—except for the eye shadow—but then he wore his chef's coat more often than I did.

Our waitress was a vet—Rachel, who'd been with Robicheaux's for close to twenty years. She wore a black skirt and a white blouse that looked a little like a tuxedo shirt, and she worked with the kind of quiet efficiency you expect at a top tier restaurant. We were one classy bunch.

The food was classy, too, of course. Nate had gotten a sumptuous pork roast from Marcus's shop that he served with duchess potatoes mashed and mixed in advance, then piped and finished at the house. We also had fresh asparagus from the Western Slope. I provided some Luscious Delights apple-cranberry chutney left over from last winter that worked well as a side dish. Coco had put together a beautiful salad and a beautiful galette for dessert, and we'd gotten fresh dinner rolls from Bianca that smelled like heaven when we warmed them up.

The apps were some of our regulars: crudités with a yogurt dip, cream cheese pinwheels, a blue cheese spread with water crackers, and our Asian meatballs. We'd served those meatballs so many times that Nate and I both had the recipe memorized by now. But this was the first time Dan had made them. I took one off the tray before Nate carried it out to the table.

It was okay. I wanted to find them less than terrific, but I didn't. But then it was an easy recipe, and any halfway decent cook could pull it off. Or so I told myself.

Stop trying to find reasons for Dan to fail.

It hurt to admit it, but that was what I was trying to do. Some of it was that I wanted to be seen as a better cook than Dan. But some of it was that, no matter how hard I tried to deny it, I was still uneasy about having Dan around. Except for our brief conversation when I dropped off the platters, we hadn't done more than exchange a few greetings, but I still felt like he was watching me and leering. I had no basis for that belief—hadn't seen a single actual leer that I could point to—but I still felt that way. I should probably just have confronted him and let him know I didn't appreciate leers. But I wasn't about to do that either.

Dinner went well. The hosts and guests were all on the twilight side of sixty, which was maybe why they'd gone for formal. But despite their age (or maybe because of it), the classy folks appreciated classy food and a classy staff. The host, who must have been upward of eighty, came to the kitchen wearing a maroon dinner jacket with tuxedo pants and, honest to God, dancing pumps. He shook Nate's hand, bowed in my direction, and gave us a nice, fat bonus. We went home happy. And exhausted.

Needless to say, we had nothing left over from the dinner. And even if we had, it belonged to the clients, not us. Nate grabbed a pizza from Moretti's on the way home, despite our vow to stop having pizza every time we were too tired to cook. I found a bottle of red tucked away in the wine rack, and we settled down to bask in our success.

"Are you going to give Dan part of the bonus?" I asked.

Nate nodded. "Yeah, some of it. I don't know how much. I've always given Coco a cut when she does the dessert. I figure Dan's no different."

Except that Coco devised and executed the dessert (and this time the salad, too), while Dan only followed the recipes. But then so had I when I was cooking for Robicheaux's, even though I was usually in the kitchen at the event as well. And Nate had always given me part of any bonus we got.

Stop trying to think of reasons to push Dan out.

I closed my eyes. It was time for me to grow up and move on. "So now we start working on the Sawmill Brewing thing?"

Nate slid down in his chair, sipping his wine. "Oh, Lord, yes. We've got to get to work on that. I sent them a couple of sample menus, and they're supposed to get back to me ASAP. I've also got a line on the grills—Spence set me up with a place where High Country rents grills when they do outside stuff. We should be able to get as much equipment as we need from them."

"How many grills will we use?"

"Depends on the menu they choose. I've been pushing for burgers and sausage. To do that, we'll need around three grills, including one for plant-based stuff." Shavano wasn't quite as crunchy as places like Telluride and Aspen, but we still had a steady demand for vegetarian and vegan stuff.

"Who's working the grills?" I could grill like I could run a flat-top. Prejudices aside, there's nothing mystical about grilling, and women can grill just as well as men. On the other hand, I knew some people were sort of superstitious about having a woman working with fire.

"You can if you want to," Nate said. "But I need someone to make sure the line with the sides keeps going—I figure we'll do beans and slaw and maybe potato salad. And we'll need servers and a runner to make sure we don't run out."

I'd rather have been grilling, but clearly he was going to need someone who knew her way around a buffet line. "Okay, I can do that. What about dessert?"

"Coco's coming up with something. Probably cookies or brownies along with ice cream cups that we'll buy from somebody else. I figure she can handle the dessert table, maybe get someone to help her."

"So we'll need a wagonload of servers. You want to see if Dolce can rustle up some hungry high schoolers?"

Nate sighed. "I don't know if we can use them. It's going to be strictly over twenty-one for attendees, but maybe we could squeak by if we have them serving food and not adjacent to the booze."

"If we have to hire pros, it'll cost us."

"I know. We may be able to use some of the brewery people since they'll be there anyway, but I'll check at the café and see if anyone's interested."

Our rate for servers at the catering events was generous, which was why the waitresses at the café were glad to pick up the occasional dinner. But when they worked the events, they were usually being waitresses, more or less. Dumping spoonsful of potato salad on paper plates wasn't exactly up their alley.

"Let me check with my contact at Sawmill," Nate

said. "They know the liquor laws better than I do. Dolce's friends would probably like to earn some extra cash. Hell, if worse comes to worst, Mom could help serve. Maybe Mike, too."

"Definitely yes on the teenagers and the cash," I said. "I'd hate to make Madge dish beans, but needs must, I guess. But if I'm not cooking, who's going to be on the grills along with you. Dan?"

"If he's free that night, yeah. I thought I'd check to see if Marcus could run the one for the sausage. If anyone's a grilling pro, it would be him."

Plus Coco would be there, which might make the proposition more attractive from Marcus's point of view. "The three of you ought to be able to handle the grills. Who puts together the sandwiches?"

Nate closed his eyes. "Shit. I hadn't gotten that far. Maybe we could skip the plant-based stuff and Dan could assemble the sandwiches. I'll see what the brewery people say."

"Or maybe the three of you could assemble sandwiches as the meat gets done and a runner could bring them over to the serving line. Or you could send the meat to the serving line, and we could have another server who puts sandwiches together. Hell, we could even put out the meat and the buns and let the customers serve themselves." I shrugged. "We've got alternatives. It shouldn't be that tough to figure out."

Nate reached for my hand. "You're right. I'm overcomplicating stuff. It's not rocket science."

"Not exactly. But it's bigger than anything we've done before. I mean, you've got a right to be worried about logistics." Among other things. We were used to cooking for smaller groups, where we had better quality control. Cooking potato salad for two hundred plus people was going to be a new experience. I hoped Nate had some ideas for how we could do it since he had more experience cooking for crowds than I did.

"Everything about this is something to be worried about. If it works, we'll have a lot of people who might be inclined to hire us for whatever they've got going on. If it doesn't work, we'll slide down in people's estimation behind the barbecue places and Gordita's, the places that usually handle something this big." Nate set his empty glass on the table.

"It'll work," I said loyally. "Monday you can talk to the people at the brewery, get the info on whether we can use teenagers or whether we'll have to find pros. And get the menu. After that we'll have a little over a week to get it in gear. And we can do that."

"We can. But right now I want to go to bed and sleep and then wake up and make love to you before we have to go serve brunch." Nate gave me a sweltering look that made my pulse speed up a bit.

"That can be arranged," I said. "That can definitely be arranged." Sawmill Brewing could take a backseat for a while.

On Monday I was doing raspberry jam again. Dolce had shown up after some kind of summer school project she was involved with and helped out with the strawberry jam that still needed to be processed for this week's farmers market. She was also interested in the raspberry stuff since it involved her family's honey.

"Did you go with the tart version or did you sweeten it up?" she asked.

"I sweetened it a little. I figured more people like sweet than tart. But it's not sugary. You can still taste the raspberries."

Dolce scraped a little jam out of the pot I'd placed on the counter with a tasting spoon. "It's good," she said finally. "But I want to make some with your original recipe sometime so Mom can taste it. She doesn't like sweet."

It figured that Carmen would be more into sour than sweet, but that was fine with me. "I'll write down the proportions for you so you can make it for her." Dolce could whip up some jam in her home kitchen, using some of the honey that Carmen was saving for the market.

I still needed to track down another twenty pounds or so of honey for the rest of the jam, but I'd exhausted my local sources for now. Except for Fred Hutchinson, of course, the local honey magnate.

I decided to try Hutchinson that afternoon since I had several jars of the raspberry jam special cooling on the racks in the kitchen. Dolce had gotten a good start on the strawberry we needed for the weekend, and I figured I could do peach and pepper peach later in the week. If I could get more honey from Hutchinson, I could also do another round of raspberry in a few days, hopefully before Bridget posted the new special on the website and the orders started pouring in. Assuming they *did* pour in.

Fred Hutchinson's place wasn't on the county road like the rest of us. He had a fair-sized spread on the other side of Shavano where he grew peaches and apples along with the usual tomatoes and arugula and cucumbers and eggplant and everything that got stocked at the farmers markets around the mountains. Hutchinson had a farmers market deal where he provided his customers with paper bags they could fill with whatever produce he had piled around his stand. He charged them a set amount per bag, and it varied depending on the time of year and how much produce he had out.

It was a good deal, and a lot of people took him up on it. But I'd heard rumors that not all the produce he offered came from his farm. He always seemed to have lots of product, no matter what the other farmers were selling. Some of the other farmers grumbled that he was bringing in stuff from the Grand Valley, or even from New Mexico or, horrors, California. If it was true, he was violating the market rules that required farmers to sell only the vegetables they'd harvested on their own acreage. I don't know that anybody ever checked up on him, though. How do you tell if an eggplant comes from a particular farm, unless it's something exotic that isn't grown around here?

I'd never heard anybody openly accuse Hutchinson of cheating, and I'd never heard Hutchinson say anything about it himself. He'd probably say it was just sour grapes from other farms whose acreage wasn't as productive as his. And he could have been right for all I knew.

Still, I'd never had much contact with Hutchinson before, and I had to admit I was curious. His farm was pretty much like everybody else's as I turned up the gravel road to his farm stand. Some close-in fields under production. Some people working those fields. Uncle Mike's farm, which was also partly mine, was successful, and we had the same crews of farm workers planting and harvesting the fields every year. I couldn't tell whether Hutchinson's production was bigger than ours or about the same size. Land prices around Shavano had increased a lot over the last few years. I figured it had cost Hutchinson a fair amount of money to get started here since he hadn't been around that long. Unlike my dad and Uncle Mike, he hadn't gotten in before the market began to expand.

I parked near his stand, which appeared deserted. If no one was around, I could always go up to the house and check, but I felt uneasy about doing that. We didn't like people coming to our outbuildings at Constantine Farms, and I wouldn't blame Hutchinson if he felt the same way. There was a building set away from the stand, and I figured I could start there if I needed to find someone to help.

When I got close to the stand, though, I could see inside the building where someone was working. I took my place next to the counter. "Hello?" I called.

Fred Hutchinson himself backed out of the building. He was a big man, sunburned like most farmers I knew. His jeans strained around a sizeable gut, and his John Deere T-shirt was well worn. He didn't look like a prosperous farmer. He also didn't look happy to see me. "Yeah?"

"I need some honey if you've got any," I said. "Twenty pounds total, but I'll take whatever you can spare."

Hutchinson narrowed his eyes. "You're Constantine's kid, right?"

"Mike is my uncle," I said, a little stiffly. Hutchinson had gotten to Shavano long after my dad had died.

"You make that jam at the market. The stuff Bianca Jordan sells."

"That's right. I'm trying some jam made with honey now." I wasn't sure why I had to provide my bona fides to buy honey from Hutchinson, assuming he had any to sell me.

He paused, wiping his hands on a grease rag. "I could maybe let you have ten pounds or so. Production's down this week. Bees are still stirred up because of those assholes ripping me off."

"I heard about that. Did they knock any hives over or just take some?"

Hutchinson grimaced. "Yeah, they knocked a few over. Why?"

"Aram Pergosian had a couple of hives knocked over, too. He said the hives were destroyed when they stole two others. He was upset about it."

"Imagine he was," Hutchinson said. "What about Bridger?"

I shook my head. "Stole some hives, but Lynn got out there quick enough to drive them off."

"Bastards," Hutchinson growled. "Better hope I don't find out who they are. I don't take kindly to people who screw up my business."

"I'm sure you don't." Hutchinson and I stared at each other for a moment, and my neck began to prickle uncomfortably.

I really wanted my ten pounds of honey, but I wasn't sure how to get him to find them for me. "Well, if I could get that honey from you…"

After another moment, he leaned down and pulled some jars of honey from beneath the counter. When he had ten stacked on the counter, he cleared his throat. "That'll be a hundred and fifty."

I managed not to gasp. That was the price I'd

expect for single source wildflower honey, which this was not. In fact, based on the label, this was regular garden-variety raw honey. On the other hand, he had me over a barrel, and he probably knew it. I needed the honey, and he was the only one who could supply it in quantity. I pulled my credit card out of my purse. "Do you take plastic?"

He shrugged. "Sure."

A few minutes later I was in my truck, traveling down the road to town. I was running numbers in my head, trying to figure out if I could possibly make any money on this raspberry jam. I hadn't been paying anywhere near what I'd just paid Hutchinson for the other honey. I'd have to be very careful with measurements to make these jars last as long as I could.

Dolce was still working on the strawberry preserves when I got there with my cardboard box of honey jars. Bridget was working on the orders that needed to go out that afternoon. We were a busy bunch.

"Whose is that?" Dolce asked as I unloaded the honey jars on the counter.

"Hutchinson's." I picked up a jar to show her the label. Hutchinson had gone more upscale with his labeling than the other producers. In fact, it looked like he'd used someone with graphic design skills to put it together.

Dolce grimaced. "Mom doesn't think much of his stuff." She picked up one of the jars, holding it to the light so that I could see it was a little cloudy. "This one's beginning to crystallize. You might want to use it first."

Terrific. Apparently, I'd paid top dollar for some second-rate product. "I'll do that. And I'll be sure to taste it to make sure it tastes like the others."

"It should if he's selling honey from the hives he's got around here."

"You're talking about Fred Hutchinson?" Bridget asked.

I nodded. "Yeah. This is from his farm."

"Which one? I've heard he brings in produce from out of state. Could do the same thing with his honey." Bridget wiped her hands on her jeans. "I wouldn't trust that man any farther than I can throw him. And you know I've got a lousy arm."

"I'll taste his honey before I use it," I repeated. Although I had no idea what I'd do if his honey wasn't up to snuff. Try to find a way to make it work, I guess.

"It'll be fine," Dolce gave me a sunny smile. "It's hard to screw up honey. The bees always know what they're doing."

I hoped so. Now if I was only sure I knew what I was doing, I'd be ahead on this project.

Chapter 10

As the Sawmill Brewing event approached, things began to fall into place. The owners of the brewery approved the menu: burgers, sausage, buns for the sandwiches, baked beans, potato salad, coleslaw, chips, chocolate chip cookies, and ice cream. And, of course, beer. Lots and lots of beer.

We were also doing a plant-based alternative version of both burgers and sausages, although the vegan sausages would be a lot closer to hotdogs. The ice cream would need to be dipped since the brewery guys had vetoed cups. That meant we'd need two people at the dessert table.

Actually, the server problem was looming even larger. It turned out the servers had to be eighteen and supervised by someone over twenty-one. The supervisor part was not a problem, obviously, since I was a good deal past twenty-one myself. But Dolce was only sixteen, and so were most of her friends. Madge volunteered without being asked, and so did Uncle Mike, although I was guessing Madge had prodded him to. But we still needed two more people.

I considered asking Marigold and Bobby but dismissed the idea almost as soon as it occurred to me. Bobby had made a point of avoiding the catering part of the business since he considered it Nate's project. Finally, we asked one of the veteran waitresses,

Donnell, if she'd be willing to dish potato salad for two or three hours on a Thursday night. If I were her, I'd probably have said no, but Donnell was a trooper and agreed. Nate hired one of the café's busboys, Tim, to be our runner. We needed at least one more person, but that would be for the dessert table and Coco said she'd find her own helper.

Marcus and Dan had both agreed to work the grills along with Nate, which left us trying to decide on the recipes for potato salad, beans, and slaw.

"I'm inclined to go with German-style salad," Nate said. "Less chance of it going bad without mayonnaise."

"Works for me. You got a recipe?"

Nate sighed. "Yeah. Dad used to make it at the café. I dug it out this afternoon. I thought maybe we could whip some up and see what we think."

"If we do German potato salad, how do you want to handle the slaw? You won't want two vinegar salads in a row." And I personally hated boiled dressing for coleslaw, which also had a sizeable glug of vinegar.

"Well, creamy coleslaw has the same problems as creamy potato salad. Yeah, we're going to need to test some alternatives."

It's safe to say that after a few days, I was thoroughly sick of tasting both potato salad and coleslaw. The café's version of German potato salad was sturdy and serviceable, but it involved bacon, and Nate worried that we might have vegans to feed. He found a vegetarian recipe that used smoked salt to replace the bacon flavoring. It was good, but I secretly missed the bacon.

We worked through a lot of coleslaw recipes, some

with exotics like grapefruit or raisins, but we landed on a Mexican version that had jalapenos and cilantro and that I liked a lot. I also liked the fact that I wouldn't have to eat any more coleslaw once we'd settled on it for sure.

The baked beans recipe was a classic, and Nate had already decided to use canned beans for the base rather than soak a hundred pounds or so of dried beans. The recipe did include meat, but this time Nate decided to go with it anyway. Baked beans without pork just didn't work on any level.

Once the menu was nailed down, Dan and Nate got to work. Hundreds of pounds of potatoes were boiled. There were mountains of cabbage and onions and carrots to be chopped and processed, more than any one person could handle. I offered to come in one day to chop cabbage, and Nate gratefully accepted.

I headed over that afternoon after I'd finished another batch of raspberry honey jam. Bridget had posted it on the website as our summer feature, and the orders were already beginning to come in. It was too early to say how big a success it was going to be, but I was close to my goal of fifty jars for mail order and market. Hutchinson's honey wasn't as flavorful as Carmen's, but it worked. I adjusted for its sweetness and used up most of what I'd gotten at the farm stand.

Grateful to be ahead in terms of jam production, I parked my truck in front of the catering kitchen and breezed in. And paused.

Once again Dan was there, and Nate wasn't.

I took a deep breath and pasted a patently phony smile on my face. "Hi. Where's Nate?"

Dan stopped chopping onions for a moment. He

had a large pile at his elbow already. "He had to go meet with the people at Sawmill to work out some of the logistics. He said if you showed up, to point you to the cabbage and give you your weapon of choice."

"Right." The catering kitchen had a professional-size food processor, but it was almost easier to chop the cabbage by hand, particularly since the processor reduced the cabbage to shreds rather than the sturdier ribbons we needed. And yes, we could have bought pre-sliced coleslaw mix, but it would inevitably be stale. I grabbed one of the chef's knives off the knife rack and a wooden cutting board. I had my own chef's knife at the house, but I wasn't going to bring it along for this job.

"They're in the walk-in," Dan said. "Come on, I'll show you."

I followed him into the walk-in cooler, where the boxes of cabbage were stacked on one of the shelves. We were using a combination of red and green cabbage for color and the heads were equally distributed in the boxes. I reached up and pulled one off the shelf.

It was heavier than I expected and I staggered backward. Dan stepped forward, his arms on either side of me, to help me regain my balance. For a moment, I was very aware of a very warm male body very close to mine. Then I stepped away. "I've got it," I said flatly.

Dan stepped away, giving me another of those meaningful half smiles, as if he knew just what was going on in my mind.

Maybe he did. I didn't. I'd felt uncomfortable when he'd stood so close, but I wasn't sure how I felt now. Mostly I just wanted to get out of the walk-in. I'd had a bad experience in my Denver line-cook days when a chef had attacked me in a walk-in pantry. I really, *really* didn't like being in a small space with another cook, particularly a male one. Particularly *this* male one.

I pushed past Dan and walked to the kitchen with my box of cabbages. There was room on the counter behind where Dan was working, and I set up my cutting board. After another few moments, we both began chopping on our respective piles of veggies.

It took several minutes, but I finally settled down into a routine, coring, slicing, chopping, and dumping the resultant pile of ribbons into a large stainless-steel bowl. Eventually, I'd need to find out where we were keeping the prepped veggies, but I wasn't ready to ask yet.

After a half-hour or so, I decided it was once again time to be a grown-up. "Where are we storing this stuff after it's cut up?"

Dan stepped back so we were side-by-side again. "Storage bags are on the shelf on your right. Stuff them full, then put them in the walk-in."

I wasn't sure why he'd felt the need to step close to me, but I decided I wouldn't be rattled. "Okay," I said, without looking up.

Dan picked up a handful of the cabbage I'd just chopped. "Seems okay. Should work."

"Thanks. I do know how to chop coleslaw." There was a little more acid in my voice than I'd intended, but I was slightly pissed. Dan wasn't in charge. Nate was.

"Never thought you didn't." Dan stepped to his counter as I started stuffing sliced cabbage into a storage bag.

We worked in silence for another twenty minutes

or so, and I was beginning to feel a little embarrassed. I didn't have any good reason to snarl at Dan, and I knew I was coming across as a lousy co-worker at best and a queen bitch at worst.

"Any particular reason you don't like me anymore, or is it just my winning personality?" Dan said finally without turning around.

I thought about brushing the question off but decided not to. If Dan went on working for Robicheaux's, we'd inevitably be sharing a kitchen now and then. "I don't dislike you," I said. "But I remember you from when we were both in high school. Being around you sort of sends me back there, and I don't enjoy it that much. High school wasn't my finest hour."

That produced another of those long silences from Dan. "I was sort of a shit in high school," he said finally. "Took me a while to grow out of it. If I told you I wasn't that guy anymore, would it help?"

I gave him a flat smile. "It's not your fault. We're neither of us in high school anymore, thank God. I just need to remind myself I'm a big girl now."

That wasn't a great choice of words. In fact, I was a very big girl now, over six feet and built in proportion. But I'd been a big girl then, too, which Dan had reason to remember. My cheeks flushed and I kept my gaze resolutely on the cabbage I was chopping into ribbons.

Dan chuckled softly, and I resolved not to turn around no matter what. I'd gotten myself into this mess, and I'd get myself out by pretending it hadn't happened.

"We're both grown," Dan said. "Good thing, I'd say."

"Very good." I continued chopping, keeping my eyes resolutely on my work. Gradually the kitchen became silent again except for the sound of our knives on our respective cutting boards, a sort of soothing series of *whacks* as we concentrated on getting our work done.

"You ever tell Nate about us?" Dan's voice sounded unnaturally loud in the silence of the kitchen, and my stomach clenched tight.

"There is no *us*," I pronounced. "Nate knows we dated in high school. That doesn't constitute an *us*." I wanted to be adamant on that point. I wasn't going to acknowledge that we were ever anything approaching a couple, no matter what we'd done in the back of Dan's old car.

"Whatever you say." Dan sounded like he had another one of those smirks, and I gritted my teeth.

Nate showed up a half hour or so later, looking harassed. He nodded at Dan, gave me a quick kiss on the cheek, and grabbed an apron. "How far along are we?"

"I've done around seven cabbages. Three bags and a bit."

"Great. That's about halfway through." He turned to Dan. "How are the onions coming?"

"I've done three or four pounds. We're on top of it."

I told myself there was nothing risqué about saying we were *on top of it*. We'd need to chop up around ten pounds of onions before we were through since they went into everything except for the chocolate chip cookies.

"Okay, I'll work on the onions for a while," Nate

said. "Why don't you run some carrots through the Buffalo chopper? Nobody's using it in the café right now."

"Got it." Dan grabbed a large sack of carrots and turned through the door that led to the café kitchen.

The tension in my shoulders relaxed for the first time since I'd walked into the catering kitchen. Nate took Dan's place behind me and started chopping onions. "How'd the meeting go?" I asked a few minutes later.

"Great. They're taking care of the grills. They said there's one at the brewery, and the other two are property of the owners."

"Will they be big enough?"

"Probably. I checked the one at the brewery and it's good sized."

By five, I was ready to stop. And I was more than glad that I had fried chicken in the refrigerator at the cabin. I didn't think I could chop anything else for at least ten hours or so. It was enough to make me happy that I wasn't working at the catering kitchen regularly anymore. Let Dan get carpal tunnel damage. Chopping strawberries was nothing like chopping cabbage. And you didn't even have to chop raspberries—you just dumped them in the pot and did a quick mash.

Nate was less wiped out than I was since he hadn't spent his entire afternoon chopping, so when we got to the cabin, he went to work on some mashed potatoes and peas to serve as sides for the fried chicken. I grabbed us a couple of beers from the refrigerator and went to the living room to veg out. Outside, I could hear Herman and Lulabelle yipping with delight as they played. They were supposedly working as watchdogs, but they hadn't gotten the memo. For them it was all play.

At night, Uncle Mike kept Herman inside, so he didn't drive everybody nuts with his barking. But Lulabelle was sleeping in her backyard, alert for whoever might try to come around the beehives.

Nate dropped down on the couch beside me, grabbing his beer. "How's the raspberry honey jam coming along?"

"I'm almost finished with the jam for the mail orders, but if I want to do any for the farmers market, I'll need to find more honey." Which I wasn't happy about. Hutchinson would probably sell me more of his overpriced stuff, but I hated to buy from him. His quality control wasn't great, and I honestly thought his honey wasn't as tasty as the other jars. But nobody else would have enough to spare me more than a couple of pounds, and if I was going to sell the honey jam at the farmers market, I had to have enough to make it worth my while.

Nate massaged my shoulder, which felt wonderful. "You could ask around. See who's selling honey around Geary. You could even take a field trip to Palisade and pick up some honey there."

"Yeah, I know. I'll get on it after the brewery thing is over." That was an excuse, of course. I could go over to the Geary farmers market since it was held during the week rather than competing with the Shavano market on the weekend. But I figured if I went all the way over to Palisade, I'd want Nate to come along and make it a weekend out. And there was no way that was happening until we finished chopping stuff and running the grills.

Nate took a long swallow of beer. "Well, we're on

top of it, although the refrigerator and walk-in are both stuffed full of chopped veggies. I figure we can start making potato salad on Tuesday. Maybe slaw at the same time. I'll do the beans the day before so the pork will have time to sit and flavor everything."

"We'll serve it on cold trays?"

"Yeah. And a warming tray for the beans. And maybe another warming tray for the sandwiches. The brewery guys are responsible for making them. They wanted to be in charge of the meat."

"Let them do it. One less thing for us to worry about." And one less thing on Nate's shoulders. I knew he'd been obsessing about how the service line would work.

He sighed, resting his beer on his chest. "I've been dreaming about this. Trying to make sure I've got everything covered. How we serve everything. Where we keep it before we bring it out. What Tim's going to need to do to keep everything rolling."

"Tim knows what he's doing," I said. "He'll be okay." Being a runner didn't require a whole lot of skill, just stamina.

"Yeah, but will I?" He gave me a rueful smile. "What if somebody doesn't show up? What if we underestimated how much sausage they're going to want? What if we overestimated it? What if it rains?"

"Or snows? Or hails?"

Nate's eyes widened, and I shook my head. "Kidding. I think. It very rarely snows in June, and this has already been a hot, dry year."

"Right." He slid down in his chair. "I'm really glad we got this order, and I'll be really glad when we're done with it. I will never complain about a dinner party again."

"I will," I said. "I promise to bitch about stuff just so we can keep our hands in."

"Thanks, babe, I knew I could count on you." He put his arms around me, sliding me over against his chest. "What have I forgotten? Lord, there's got to be something that's going to bite us on the ass."

I put my hands over his. "You're fine. We're fine. Nothing's going to happen. It's going to be one of those routine deals, and when it's over, we'll wonder what the fuss was about."

Which just goes to show—when it comes to prophecy, I'm a much better cook than soothsayer.

Chapter 11

Uncle Mike usually let Herman out around six when he got up himself. Herm was a homebody—he never wandered far from the house and yard, but he did like to be outside in dry weather. He wasn't a great snow dog, and thunder made him cower.

I'm not usually up early myself, but I hadn't slept well the night before—some residual sore muscles from chopping cabbage and some worries about finding enough honey for the farmers market jam. I finally pulled myself out of bed very early and went in to make coffee.

I'd just pulled on some jeans and a T-shirt, along with my usual running shoes, when I heard Herman's howl.

Herman's not a hound. His howl isn't particularly impressive. But it is loud, and since he doesn't howl much, it's unexpected. I hurried to the front door, afraid he'd wake Nate. I couldn't see Herm, but I could definitely hear him. So could Uncle Mike, apparently, since he was just coming out the front door at the main house.

"What's gotten into that fool dog now?" He turned toward the sound, and I started trotting behind him.

We saw Herman finally when we rounded the corner of the barn. He was plastered up against the fence that separated our farm from Donnie's.

The Honey Jam Murder

"Herman," Uncle Mike called, "shut up. You'll wake everybody on the place."

Herman glanced at us and promptly resumed howling.

"Herm," I called. "Come on, pipe down."

The back door of the McCray's house opened, and Carmen stepped out in a bathrobe. "What's gotten into that dog?"

By then, I was next to Herman, ready to grab his collar and drag him to our place, when I saw something in the grass. "Carmen, look. Is that Lulabelle?"

Carmen was running down the stairs before I'd finished speaking. "Lulabelle," she cried. "Oh, my Lord, Lulabelle."

Lulabelle was lying very still in the grass next to the back steps. Uncle Mike grabbed hold of the gate, and the two of us hurried through. We dropped to our knees beside the dog as Herman began howling again.

Lulabelle's eyes were open, but she was lying very still. And her sides were going up and down at what seemed to be an abnormal rate.

"She's alive," Uncle Mike said. "But she's in a bad way. You call the vet. Carmen and I will get her into the truck."

Carmen gazed down at herself helplessly. "I have to put some clothes on first."

I didn't like the idea of Lulabelle waiting or Carmen trying to find clothes when she was so upset. "We'll take her. We'll use my truck. Call the vet, Dr. Fortas."

Uncle Mike had found a blanket somewhere, probably from Lulabelle's doghouse. We picked her up as gently as we could, then rolled her in the blanket and trotted across the yard toward my truck.

Herman galloped along at our side, whimpering. Clearly, he'd been worried about Lulabelle, and clearly, he still was.

I ran inside the cabin and grabbed my purse and keys, while Uncle Mike climbed into the passenger seat with Lulabelle's considerable bulk in his lap. Nate stepped out of the bedroom, staring at me sleepily. "What's going on?"

"Animal crisis. Go grab Herman, will you? I'll explain later." I ran outside and jumped into the driver's seat.

We weren't far from the vet's, but it felt like it took longer than usual to get there. Fortunately for us, Dr. Fortas actually lived in a house out behind his office. He was waiting for us at the front door of the clinic.

"I talked to Mrs. McCray," he said. "And I had her check the yard to see if there was anything Lulabelle could have eaten. She found some hamburger near the fence. She's going to get it into a baggy and bring it in to analyze, but let's see what we can do before she gets here."

It was the beginning of a very long morning. The hamburger was laced with ibuprofen and acetaminophen. Fortunately, Lulabelle hadn't eaten it all. Even more fortunately, she'd thrown up some of what she'd eaten. But she still needed to be treated for what she'd managed to keep down, and that involved a lot of stomach action.

I decided that since Lulabelle wasn't my dog and the exam room was already crowded, I'd sit in the waiting room. This meant I ended up having to describe what had happened to Mrs. Fortas, who was the office manager, and Lola Reyes, who was the vet tech on duty. Both of them were properly outraged.

"That's a mean trick," Lola said. "And it was obviously deliberate. Everybody knows painkillers are bad for dogs and cats. They meant to kill that poor dog or maybe make her very sick."

"Somebody meant to harm her," I said. A quick shiver went down my spine. If Herman had been out last night, he might have had the same treatment.

"Why would anyone do that?" Mrs. Fortas asked. "Lulabelle's a sweetheart."

I was beginning to have some ideas, although nothing I could share. "Hard to say."

"Some people are just mean, I guess." Mrs. Fortas looked sour.

I profoundly hoped things were that simple, but I had a feeling they weren't.

Uncle Mike came out after a half hour or so. "They've got her stabilized. Carmen's going to stay and talk to the doc, but we should go home. I need to tell Donnie what's happening."

I bit my lip as we walked to the truck. "Do you think we should call Fowler?"

"The chief?" He shook his head. "Carmen should probably file a police report just in case somebody's poisoning animals around town. But it's not something the chief would be interested in."

"Suppose it's related to the honey thefts."

Uncle Mike paused. "The honey thefts? Why would it be?"

"Because Lulabelle's out in the yard to guard the bee hives. I mean, maybe it's not obvious, but that's what she's doing. And if someone was planning on stealing some of Donnie's hives, the fact that he's got Lulabelle out there now could be an obstacle."

Uncle Mike's eyes widened. "Hell, I hadn't thought of that. And if that's what they were after, they may be back."

"I'd say there's a good chance of that. Now they've gotten rid of Lulabelle, they can get in and steal some hives."

"Not with us around they won't." Uncle Mike squared his shoulders. "Let's get on home. I need to talk to Donnie."

I didn't much like the sound of that. I was much more in favor of calling the Shavano cops and letting them search for clues. But Uncle Mike looked like this wasn't something he felt like discussing, so I turned the truck toward home.

Nate had made coffee when I stepped inside the cabin, for which I was immensely grateful. I hadn't had time to have any before we'd taken off for the vet. I filled him in on what was happening.

"Nasty," Nate said when I'd finished. "Poisoning the dog just because she was in the way. Seems like it would have been easier just to go steal hives from somebody else."

"Maybe they did. Maybe this was just for future reference."

Nate sipped his coffee. "I suppose there's no chance this was just kids? Nasty, vicious kids?"

"I doubt it. We're pretty far from town for kids to come out just to play a prank. There must be easier targets in Shavano."

"Yeah, probably." Nate sighed. "So what happens now?"

"Now I try to talk Donnie and Uncle Mike out of going on patrol tonight. But I may see if I can talk to Fowler before I do that."

"Donnie and Mike on patrol? I don't even know what that means."

"I wish I didn't." I massaged my suddenly tight shoulders. "After I suggested that Lulabelle might have been poisoned because she was guarding the bee hives, Uncle Mike started thinking the thieves might come back tonight or maybe tomorrow night. If they poisoned Lulabelle to get in, they might want to get in and out fast, before Donnie could come up with any other protective measures. That means Uncle Mike sitting out in the yard with his shotgun."

Nate rubbed his eyes. "Aw, geez."

Uncle Mike mostly uses his shotgun to scare wildlife away from his fields. If a deer gets inside the deer-proof fence, he'll fire a couple of shots in the air to get it to take off. Same with raccoons and coyotes. He doesn't waste shotgun shells on the rabbits, just yells and sends Herman after them. All of which is to say Uncle Mike is no marksman. He also doesn't hunt. So far as I know, he's never actually hit anything with his shotgun shells except beer cans and pop bottles.

So the thought of Uncle Mike patrolling the bee hives with his trusty shotgun did not make my heart light. Donnie hunts deer in the fall, so he's a little more acquainted with pointing his gun at something alive and moving. But needless to say, neither of them has ever shot a person.

I figured any bad guy who was ruthless enough to poison Lulabelle wouldn't be deterred by a couple of old farmers with shotguns, although a thief might slow down long enough to inflict some damage on one or both of them.

"I'm going to call the Shavano cops and tell them about Lulabelle. If I point out that it's possibly connected to the beehive thefts, it might be enough to get them out here."

I wanted to talk to Chief Fowler about the problem, since he knew both Uncle Mike and Donnie and was close to being a friend. But I doubted I'd be able to get through to him. Dog poisoning was nasty, like Nate said, but it wasn't the level of nasty that required the chief of police's attention. In the summer he had his hands full with traffic violations and drunken tourists and the occasional burglary of one of the vacation homes up toward Lost Horse Pass.

Nate went to the bedroom to get ready for work, and I tried my first call to the police station. I figured it would probably take me more than one to find the right person to talk to. I explained to the dispatcher that I wanted to report a dog poisoning but that I thought it was related to the beehive thefts. She didn't say much, but she didn't sound impressed. Eventually, I was routed to a cop I sort of knew—Trevor Albright.

He didn't sound particularly impressed either, but I hadn't really expected him to be. "So somebody threw some poisoned hamburger to the dog?" he said.

"Yeah. Last night. But that dog guards Donnie McCray's beehives. I thought it might be related to the thefts."

Trevor paused, and I figured he was writing everything down. "Have they had anybody around causing trouble at their hives?"

"Not that I know of." It would have been a lot

more convincing if they had, but maybe Lulabelle had been doing her job, such as it was.

"How many hives does Donnie have?"

"Around fifteen, I think. It's not a big operation." But neither was Lynn Bridger's or Aram's, and the thief had hit both of them.

"Right." Trevor sighed. "It's all a little thin, Roxy."

"I know, but I thought maybe it was worth telling you about." Although for all I knew, they were getting lots of fake beehive thief reports.

"Oh, it's worth telling us about, sure. It's information, and it may fit in with other information." Trevor was probably trying to make me feel okay about calling and at the same time let me down gently.

"Okay, well, thanks anyway." I refused to feel self-conscious about calling the cops. It still seemed logical to me that Lulabelle's poisoning was beehive related.

After Nate took off for the catering kitchen and doing lunch at the café, I got set up to make peach jam and pepper peach jam. I'd be using the same frozen peaches for both. They were peaches from our orchard that I'd put up last summer, the last of the frozen fruit before Uncle Mike started harvesting this year's crop in July. I leave the skins on both the fresh fruit and the frozen because the skins make for a pretty color in the jam. And if you chop the peaches finely, the skins don't cause any texture problems.

The peppers for the pepper peach were local jalapeños. Originally, I'd used Pueblo chilies, which are related to Hatch chilies but grown in Pueblo, Colorado (and yes, the people from Hatch and the people from Pueblo have very strong opinions about which chili is best). The problem with Pueblo chilies is that they're only available for a short time and it's not a huge crop. I'd learned to settle for jalapeños when I couldn't get Pueblos.

In a half hour or so, I was up to my elbows in frozen peaches. They weren't as wet as fresh peaches can get, but since I didn't bother to defrost them, I had to make sure I mashed them down enough in the pan so they'd cook up right. It figured that I was at a point where I really didn't want to leave the pan of peaches to fend for itself when someone knocked on my front door.

My cabin has a sort of open floor plan, meaning I can see from the kitchen to the living room, mostly, and hear when somebody knocks. "Come in," I yelled. "It's open." Because I absolutely was not leaving the peaches at that point in the process.

Chief Ethan Fowler stuck his head around the edge of the door. "Roxy?" he called.

"In here. I'm in the middle of something."

Fowler turned toward the kitchen at the point when I finally decided I could leave the mashed peaches to get nice and jammy on their own. "Hey, Chief," I said as I wiped off the masher. "What's up?"

"You tell me. You're the one who called the station."

Fowler and I have a kind of guarded relationship. We're sort of friends, and we've worked a few cases together, not willingly on his part. But he can be a mite testy, particularly when he suspects I'm pulling him into something he doesn't want to be pulled into. There's also some other tension between us, although I usually pretend there isn't. Back before Nate and I were a solid couple, Fowler made a couple tentative passes in my direction. And if it hadn't been for Nate and the fact we were very much together, I might have been tempted.

The chief is a good-looking guy, although he rarely smiles, so he comes across as severe a lot of the time. He also dates my best friend Susa off and on, which makes it a little easier to ignore any unacknowledged attraction between us.

Of course, I had no idea whether he and Susa were currently on or off, although the fact they were going to the Sawmill release party together probably meant they were on.

"I talked to Trevor about it. I didn't think he'd send you out here. It didn't sound like he was considering it."

"He didn't. But he mentioned you had some trouble that might be related to the beehive thefts." Fowler pulled out one of the chairs at my kitchen table, dropping his Stetson on the table. "Now what's going on out here?"

I returned to working on my jam as I told him about Lulabelle being poisoned and the possible connection to the beehive thefts, particularly since Lulabelle had been put outside to deter any possible thieves.

"So your theory is the thieves decided to get rid of the dog since she was standing between them and the bee hives?"

I couldn't tell if Fowler was being sarcastic or not. He has a kind of deadpan delivery sometimes.

"It occurred to me," I said carefully.

Fowler shrugged. "It's possible. There's no way to be sure, but you're kind of far out in the country for someone who just wanted to screw around with a dog."

"That's what I thought." I checked the temperature of the peaches, then turned off the burner and shoved the jampot to a cooler part of the stove. The jars that had been heating were ready to go, too, and I grabbed the lifter.

"You need any help?" Fowler narrowed his eyes.

I shook my head. "I could do this in my sleep. Although I'd prefer not to." I arranged the hot jars on the rack then pulled the jampot over to the trivet on the counter so I could start filling them. "The thing is, I told Uncle Mike about this, that I thought the people who poisoned Lulabelle might be after Donnie's hives, and now he and Donnie are planning to patrol tonight with shotguns, just in case the bad guys come around."

"Aw, geez," Fowler groaned.

I blinked. "That's what Nate said."

"Glad to know we're on the same page." Fowler rubbed a hand over his face. "The last thing I need is people wandering around in the dark with shotguns. They're liable to shoot each other. And if the bad guys happen to show up, they might get hurt."

I wasn't sure whether he meant the bad guys or Uncle Mike, but I figured neither outcome would be good. "So could you maybe send a patrol out here a few times during the evening? That might be enough to convince them not to start marching around themselves."

"I don't have that many patrols to spare." Fowler sighed, leaning back in his chair.

"Do you have any idea who's doing this? I mean, has anybody suddenly displayed a lot of bee hives they didn't have before?"

"That would be too easy. From what I hear, there's a big black market in bee hives. They're probably out of state by now."

"A black market in bee hives? Why?" I tried to picture a boutique beehive setup on a New York balcony, but it just didn't compute.

"Pollination," Fowler said flatly. "Big farms need a lot of bees, and hives rent for upwards of two hundred bucks apiece during the season. Supposedly, the almond farms in California rent around two-thirds of the country's bee hives during pollination. And they're not the only ones who rent them."

I stared down at my cooked peaches, which had required pollination before they became fruit. "I had no idea."

"Where's Mike? I can at least talk to him."

"He's probably out working by now. He's got crews to supervise."

"And Donnie?"

"He might be home. Particularly if Doc Fortas let him bring Lulabelle home." Although that had seemed unlikely, given how sick Lulabelle had appeared to be.

"Okay, I'll go talk to Donnie and see if he can find Mike." Fowler grabbed his Stetson and started for the door, pausing when he got there. "You think you'll have some of that peach jam ready to go later on?"

I shrugged. "This batch needs to sit, but I've got some from yesterday. And some strawberry."

"Okay, I'll check back with you on the way out." He gave me one of his half-smiles that were about as close to a happy expression as he ever got. "See you, Roxy."

I nodded. "See you, Chief." At least he was a fan

of my jam, even if he wasn't all that happy about my family at the moment.

Chapter 12

I wasn't sure how Fowler managed it, but he convinced Donnie and Uncle Mike not to go wandering around the yard with shotguns, to my great relief. He deserved the two jars of peach jam I gave him on his way out.

Instead, Uncle Mike rigged up an elaborate set of alarms around the hives, consisting of tin cans and other noisemakers strung on fishing line. The idea was that the noise would scare off the intruders or trip them up if they got too close. I only hoped it didn't ensnare either Donnie or Uncle Mike—it looked like a fairly lethal set of tripwires.

With help from Bridget and Dolce, I got all the jam ready for both the market and my mail orders. The honey raspberry was as popular as I thought it might be, but I was sticking to my fifty-jar limit. Given all my difficulties in locating honey, I didn't have much choice about that.

Once I had my orders taken care of and my farmers market cases ready to go, I was free to help Nate and Dan, which was good because they really needed it. I spent a day mixing cabbage and dressing to make slaw and getting the baked beans into hotel pans, while Dan took care of the potato salad and Nate checked the deliveries. Fortunately for us, the hamburger patties came pre-made, as did the plant-based stuff, although

Nate had to make sure we had enough of both. Marcus would take care of the sausages, and Coco had trays of cookies and brownies and blondies stacked in the walk-in. She'd decided against doing ice cream, which meant she could handle the dessert table on her own.

We were ready. Or as ready as we could be a day in advance.

The next day was as chaotic as I'd feared it would be. The release party was supposed to start at five, which meant we needed to be set up and ready to go no later than four. That meant we needed to be on site soon after lunch so that we could make sure all the necessary arrangements were complete before we brought over the food. Sawmill had roped off a beautiful meadow a few hundred yards behind their brewery. There were shade trees and long wooden picnic tables, along with a lot of smaller, temporary tables where people could stand and eat. The meadow ended in a small pine forest that extended around the edges, casting more shade and giving everything a lovely piney smell as the afternoon heated up.

The food tables were set up at the edge of a concrete slab behind the brewery building. More importantly from Sawmill's point of view, the beer table was set up a few feet away. Ideally, people would pick up some food and then get a beer, but my guess was the beer table would get a lot more early patronage than we would.

Sawmill had a lot of personnel on site—all young, all aspiring brewmasters, all wearing the most eclectic collection of brewery shirts and ball caps I'd ever seen. Theoretically, the attendees would have to show tickets to get in, and there were tables at the front door of the brewery where people got their hands stamped when they arrived. But in reality any determined party attender could probably sneak in through the pine grove if they knew where to slip through the trees. Sawmill management had posted a couple of their mellow kids at the edge of the grove, but I didn't have much faith in their ability to catch anyone determined to get by them.

All of which meant we might run out of food. Sawmill had kept us up to date on the number of tickets they'd sold, which currently hovered around two hundred fifty. We had food for around two hundred seventy, because Nate figured it was best to have a cushion.

If and when we ran out, we ran out. That, after all, was life.

It took us around an hour to get the food tables and the grills set up to our satisfaction. One of the grills was mammoth, the kind you use when you want to roast a half hog. The other two were more like backyard grills—decent sized but not huge. Nate decided to do the burgers on the big grill and leave the smaller grills for the sausages and the plant-based meat. I had to figure out the order in which people would want their sides so we could set up the serving pans to accommodate them. The beans would be in a warming pan, so I decided to put them last and put Uncle Mike in charge. Madge and Donnell could handle the slaw and the potato salad.

I'd been pressed into service making sandwiches. Apparently, none of the budding brewmasters wanted to sully their hands with food when they could be extolling the virtues of Sawmill's watermelon Kolsch. I had three warming pans for the meat, and a separate bin for the buns. We'd gotten them from a commercial bakery in Geary. They weren't as terrific as Bianca's would have been, but Bianca's would have been way too expensive for this gig.

I was also still in charge of the service line, which meant I'd have to be aware of what was happening on the line at the same time I was handing out hamburgers and sausage sandwiches. Multitasking. Fortunately, as a jam maker, I was more than acquainted with the idea.

Nate got his charcoal going early, then started grilling hamburgers around four thirty. We figured we needed to have some meat ready when people began to trail in, even if they went straight to the bar before considering our offerings. Marcus showed up around four and got his own grill ready. I had a feeling he was more of a grill fanatic than Nate was, if only because he wanted to show off his own products to best advantage. He seemed to spend a lot of time getting his charcoal briquets arranged in his version of the right way.

Dan was a little slower arriving and setting up. Nate had told him four, but he didn't actually show up until four thirty. He said he'd been stuck cleaning up at his restaurant gig, and he wasn't as spiffy and prepared as Nate and Marcus. In fact, he looked like he'd pulled on the first T-shirt he'd found that wasn't ready for the wash basket. Nate wasn't happy that he was late, but I figured Dan's grill was the most expendable of the three. We'd have some requests for plant-based hamburgers and sausage for sure, but based on past experience, the volume wouldn't be comparable.

The only thing we were missing was Coco's dessert table, but we were following tradition and setting up the dessert station only after everybody had a chance to get a meal and a beer. If they wanted to fill up on chocolate chip cookies after that, so be it, but we were giving everybody a fighting chance here.

Coco took up a position next to Marcus, beer in hand. I figured if she wanted to ferry his sausages to my sandwich station, I'd be more than happy to let her.

As five o'clock crept closer, lines began to take shape, both inside the brewery and outside. Donnell and Madge pulled on canvas aprons and took their stations at the slaw and potato salad stations, serving spoons in hand. Uncle Mike refused an apron of his own—a bad mistake, as I could have told him—and pulled his Constantine Farms ball cap down closer to his eyebrows. He had his spoon clenched in his fist, sort of like a ball peen hammer. Tim, our runner, stood beside the table, dressed in jeans, T-shirt, and a Robicheaux Café ball cap. A canvas apron would only slow him down, but I hoped he wasn't too fond of that outfit since it was most likely going to be splattered with food by the end of the evening.

I considered the small pile of hamburger patties and sausages on the hotel pans in front of me, along with the even smaller pile of plant-based burgers. Unlike the others, I had on nitrile gloves since I'd be touching the food. They were a pain in the neck, but they were absolutely necessary. I took a deep breath as the seconds counted down. This could be a triumph for Robicheaux Catering. It could also be a disaster.

There you go. Think positive.

The brewery back door opened, and the first people straggled out into the meadow. *Show time!*

The first hour we were running mostly on adrenaline. The crowds were large, but good natured and boisterous for the most part. As we'd all anticipated, they were a lot more interested in Sawmill's beer than they were in our food. But their interest in beer didn't prevent them from hitting the food line once they'd gotten their cups filled.

The burgers went fast. I wasn't surprised—they looked great. I had a couple of people ask for medium rare, and I had to tell them all the burgers were largely the same, which I'd qualify as somewhere between medium and medium well. A few adventurous souls tried the sausage sandwiches. Nobody wanted the plant-based burgers.

The demand for sausage began to pick up after a half hour or so, maybe because people were hearing how great they were. I tried to keep two or three completed burgers and sausage sandwiches ready to be picked up, but as the line started moving more quickly, I found that harder to do. Plus, I needed to make sure Tim was keeping up with the demand for sides. I was constantly checking to make sure we weren't running out of coleslaw or potato salad.

Tim was probably working harder than any of us, bringing out hotel pan after hotel pan and transferring pans of burgers and sausage from the table between Nate and Marcus to the table behind me. I thought about suggesting Dan give him a hand since the demand for plant-based meat was so far minimal, but I figured that was up to Nate. Dan appeared to be taking it easy. He had a beer cup resting on the table beside him.

After an hour, the crowd still clustered around the beer table. But they were also beginning to spread out across the meadow. Some people had brought blankets and they were reclining on the grass. The picnic tables were full, and the standup tables were mostly in use. I wondered what would happen if we ran out of places for people to sit, but that wasn't my problem. The grass was fairly dry, and people could always hunker down out there if they were tired of standing.

Around six thirty the pace began to slow down a bit. The initial surge was over, and the crowd was settling into beer-drinker mellow. I checked my fellow food line workers: "How's everybody doing?"

Uncle Mike looked a little dazed, but he'd never done food service before. "Okay, I guess. Do we still have more beans? There must have been five hundred people through here."

Donnell rolled her eyes, while Madge gave him an indulgent smile. "Not quite that many, hon."

I turned to Tim, who was taking a breather himself. "How are the sides holding up? Will we have enough for the next surge?"

He shrugged. "Slaw and potato salad should be okay. Beans are running a little low."

Which probably meant Uncle Mike had been giving generous servings despite what Madge and I had told him. "I guess you'll need to cut back a little on the baked beans servings," I told him. "We want them to last as long as the slaw and potato salad."

Uncle Mike blew out a breath. "I can do that."

Another group of ticket holders flowed through the entrance, and we went to our stations.

We didn't get another surge like the first one, but the traffic was fairly constant for the next hour or so. Plus, we had the inevitable people who wanted seconds. We had to accommodate them, of course, but we could tell them to get new plates. Frankly, I don't know how likely it is to contaminate serving utensils from used plates, but why take a chance? Particularly when it's a disposable plate anyway.

Around seven fifteen or so, I was on autopilot in terms of putting sandwiches on trays, when I heard someone say "Hi, Rox."

I looked up to see Susa, grinning as she took a sausage sandwich. "Are these Marcus's?"

I nodded. "He's over there cooking. From what I've heard, they're terrific."

"Got another one?"

I turned to see Chief Fowler with his own plate of slaw, potato salad, and a minuscule serving of beans. He was wearing jeans and a denim shirt, and I assumed he was off duty since he already had a beer. "Hey, Chief." I pulled a fresh sausage off the hotel pan and dropped it into a bun.

He let me put the sausage sandwich on his plate, then turned to Susa. "You see any place to sit?"

"Sure," she said. "Over there in the trees."

The two of them headed off toward one of the wooden picnic tables. I'm always pleased to see them out together since I think they make a perfect couple, plus I'd like to see Fowler off the market. So far, he and Susa have gotten together and then split apart more times than I can count, but I continued to hope.

By seven thirty, the evening had settled into a mellow haze. Lots of people stretched out on the grass, some on blankets but some not. Music played over loudspeakers on the brewery building, a mixture of rock and country, a sort of backcountry vibe. The beer table was still crowded, and Coco's dessert table was doing a booming business. She'd set out the cookies and brownies on individual plates, and inevitably people were walking off with multiples of both.

The young aspiring brewmasters had begun to empty the trash cans around the meadow, and not a moment too soon since they were close to overflowing.

Nate walked over to the service line, pausing to slide his arm around my waist. "How's it going?"

"Okay, I think. Although we may be close to done with the beans, and the slaw and potato salad are both starting their last pan."

"Yeah, we're down toward the end of the meat, too."

I checked the grills. Dan had taken over Nate's hamburger grill, which made sense because I still had lots of plant-based burgers and sausages ready for anyone who wanted them. We'd given out a few—maybe a hotel pan's worth—but there hadn't been a big demand. If we ran out of full-strength hamburger and sausage, we could always hand out the plant-based stuff.

Nate peered at the far end of the line. "Coco's still got half of her desserts, so that should hold people for another half hour or so."

"As long as the beer holds out, we should be fine."

Nate rapped his knuckles on the wooden tabletop. "Don't even joke about that. The only thing that would turn this evening into a disaster would be running out of beer."

The brewery guys didn't seem concerned about that. They went on pouring cups from the various spigots they had set up, and no one looked even slightly nervous. It was, in fact, the mellowest crowd we'd ever served. "Got any feedback from Sawmill?"

Nate shrugged. "No problems so far as I know. Everybody was happy with their food. Didn't see much getting thrown away."

A few more people came through the line, and I got rid of a plant-based sausage. Nate helped Uncle Mike move the empty pan of beans off the line. "One down. Two more to go."

I checked. Donnell's slaw might have three or four more servings. Madge's potato salad had a few more than that. "I guess we go with the rest of the hamburgers and sausage, if anybody wants them. But you can probably stop cooking them for now. Looks like everything worked out. Tim's a little beat, but the rest of us are doing okay."

"Yeah, if we ever do another one of these, I'll get two runners."

The thought that we might actually do another one of these sometime was a little daunting, but I wasn't exhausted yet. I felt like we'd had a good night. A good shakedown cruise for future large events. For the most part this had been a success. In fact, it had been close to a triumph.

Somewhere nearby someone screamed.

"What the hell?" Nate murmured.

It was still noisy in the meadow. Music still played through the loudspeakers and the sound of two hundred or so people laughing and talking could drown out a lot. But a scream tends to cut through most noise, particularly if it's not in a predictable place like an amusement park. The noise level in the meadow dropped quickly, and then the scream came again.

Several people turned toward the woods at the end

of the meadow, as if they weren't certain what to do. The screaming was coming from somewhere in the woods, and it wasn't stopping.

A moment later, I saw Fowler trotting toward the tree line. He shouted something to the people at the edge, which was probably along the lines of "Get back and stay there."

That was good advice, but it didn't have much effect on the crowd, which was inching toward the woods. Nate stepped away from me and began moving after Fowler, along with several of the aspiring brew masters. I recognized the Sawmill manager among them. They took up positions along the edge of the woods, trying to pretend that nothing much was happening although something clearly was.

I balanced for a moment, not sure whether to follow Nate or stay where I was. They might need somebody female to help calm the hysterical screamer. On the other hand, there were a lot of women between me and the edge of the wood, and I wasn't eager to be the designated comforter. At the grills, Dan had put down his spatula and stepped forward. Marcus stood next to Coco, his arm around her shoulders as they stared at the woods. Uncle Mike held Madge's hand, as if he was keeping her from entering the fray.

A moment later, Susa came running up the hill toward me. I hadn't seen whether she'd followed Fowler into the woods, but I was guessing she had. She stopped in front of Uncle Mike. "Ethan needs you," she said. "For crowd control. He said to try to keep these people back."

I could see the young brewmasters forming a more solid line along the edge of the woods. A couple of them were a little pale, but I might have been imagining it. Uncle Mike trotted toward the line, waving his hands to get them to move farther to the side and block anyone who tried to get through.

"Does he need more help?" I asked Susa. "Marcus and Dan could go down there."

Susa shook her head quickly. "Not Marcus. Definitely not Marcus."

"Why not?" Marcus wasn't a cop, but he was a solid guy with butcher's muscles. My guess was nobody would be getting around him if he took a stand.

Susa blew out a long breath, and for the first time I got a good look at her. Her face was pale, and she was biting her lip.

"Are you okay?" I asked.

"No," she said slowly. "No, I'm really not okay. And Marcus can't go down there because his ex-wife is dead in the woods."

"Sara?" I blinked at her. "Sara's dead?"

Susa nodded slowly. "Right. Somebody killed Sara Jordan."

Chapter 13

It was amazing how quickly our qualified triumph turned to crap. Fowler had obviously phoned for backup because a half-dozen Shavano cops showed up soon after Uncle Mike had taken his place at the tree line. They set about taking the names of everybody still around in the meadow. I say *still around* because I'd seen a lot of people sneak away before the cops arrived, probably only too aware of how long they'd be stuck at Sawmill while the cops gathered information.

The Sawmill manager started allowing free beer refills and we put out all the rest of Coco's desserts along with the remaining hamburgers and sausage sandwiches. Thanks to the delay, we finally got rid of the plant-based burgers and sausages—people were tired and bored and ready to eat anything they could get their hands on.

Madge and I started packing away the empty pans and cleaning up as much as we could without taking anything to the SUV that would ferry the stuff to the café. Since the police were trying to keep everyone corralled in the meadow, I figured they wouldn't be too excited about us trying to carry our pots and pans out to the SUV so that we could get them to the catering kitchen as soon as they were done with us.

I saw Coco a few minutes later as she set out the end of her desserts. She seemed a little shell-shocked, her eyes wide and her complexion paler than usual. Marcus had disappeared. After we'd packed away our pans, Madge went over to embrace her daughter, who looked very glad to have her mom's arms around her.

I wasn't sure if Marcus had been taken away or if he was still around. I hoped it was the latter, but I was a little worried about what might be happening. A few moments later Madge returned, her jaw firm and her eyes worried. Coco had gone back to packing up her sheet pans. "Where's Marcus?" I asked.

"They're questioning him," Madge said. "But he can't have been involved. He was out there cooking sausage all evening. I don't think he ever took a break. The demand was too constant."

Marcus certainly had a very solid alibi for this evening. But we didn't know when Sara had been killed. The thought that she might have been lying out there all the time the party was going on made me feel sort of nauseous, but it wasn't impossible.

I noticed the crowd was beginning to thin by then. Apparently, once the police had people's names and addresses, along with their assurance that they hadn't seen much of anything, they were allowed to go home. Nate and Uncle Mike were still missing, but I figured they probably weren't needed for crowd control now that the police were on site. I started down the meadow, passing by police officers taking statements. They didn't spare me a glance, but then, they knew me. Unfortunately.

Dan appeared at my side as I reached the edge of the meadow. "Are we done here?" he asked.

I paused. In reality, I had no idea what our status was. No one had asked me for a statement yet, and no one had said we could go. "I don't know. Ask Nate."

"I would if I knew where he was." Dan narrowed his eyes, surveying the meadow. "I need my pay."

The client usually paid Nate the balance of whatever the bill came to at the end of the evening, and then Nate paid the people who'd worked the gig. That way if we got a bonus, he could divide it between the people who'd been there.

I was pretty sure we wouldn't be getting a bonus tonight, given the way the manager was probably feeling right then. It wasn't our fault, but he wasn't likely to want to reward us for what was turning out to be a nightmare evening. And it went without saying that I couldn't pay Dan or anyone else. At least it went without saying as far as I was concerned. Dan looked like he'd take money from anyone he could convince to pay him.

"I'll see if I can find Nate," I said. "Stick around."

I found Nate talking to the Sawmill manager. Neither of them looked happy. He put his arm around my shoulders, as much for his comfort as for mine. "We're all cleaned up," I said. "Whenever we can get permission to load up our stuff, we're ready to go. Dan wants his pay." I kept my voice neutral on that last statement, although truth be told I was annoyed at Dan for causing yet another problem.

Nate sighed, rubbing his eyes. "Okay, I'll go find him. Fowler will probably let us load up the SUV, but he's going to want us to stick around and give him statements. He already said as much."

I tried not to feel unhappy about that. The truth was I hadn't seen squat, and taking my statement wouldn't require more than a couple of minutes. I'd been concentrating on getting the sandwiches ready and making sure the sides kept coming. I hadn't even been aware Sara was there.

I paused then. Had Sara been there? Had anyone seen her? I certainly hadn't. If she was at the party, she'd stayed well away from us, particularly from Marcus.

Nate and the Sawmill manager conferred again, probably about the final bill, and I walked back to what was left of the service line. Dan stood next to his grill. "Well?"

Once again, I tamped down my annoyance. Dan was acting as if this was Nate's fault. Couldn't he see this was a massive screw-up that had nothing to do with us and our business model? "He's working on it. This is a clusterfuck. If you're clear to take off, you can always pick up your pay tomorrow."

Dan's expression darkened. "And if I need it tonight?"

"If you need it tonight, you'll have to wait until Nate gets everything taken care of with the people here. Once he gets their final payment, he'll pass yours on to you." I pushed by him then. There'd been a murder here, for God's sake. Things were in chaos. Let him figure it out.

Madge and Donnell had found lawn chairs from somewhere. I dropped down on the grass beside them. "Is Coco okay?"

Madge waved a hand. "Probably not. But what do I know? I'm just her mom. She's over talking to the cops."

I glanced where she pointed. Coco stood with her hands on her hips, as she listened to a Shavano cop. She didn't look happy, but why should she?

"Has Marcus come back yet?"

Donnell shook her head. "He's still down there with the chief. Don't know what they're talking about."

I turned and gazed across the meadow. Fowler was standing next to Marcus at the edge of the woods. Marcus looked sort of dazed. He was staring down at his feet, and he didn't seem to be hearing much of what Fowler was asking him. I hoped Fowler wasn't drawing any conclusions based on a witness who was clearly in a state of shock over his wife's death.

Well, she wasn't exactly his wife, but she had been. Marcus and Sara weren't together anymore, and their divorce sounded bitter, but they'd been married for a few years. Finding out she was dead had to be a blow.

Susa broke free from one of the clumps of cops and beer drinkers and walked across the meadow toward us. "Fun evening. Up until a half hour ago, anyway. Sorry you guys got caught up in this mess." She dropped down on the grass beside us.

"I'm surprised you're still here," I said. "Surely, they've got your contact information."

Susa shrugged. "I came with Ethan."

"You need a ride home?" Madge said. "We can drop you off. Assuming they let us go sometime soon." She cast a baleful look at the cops taking statements.

Susa blew out a breath. "He got me here. He can get me home."

That didn't sound like the evening had done much for the future of their relationship. But I had other things to worry about just then. Marcus was still dazed, and Fowler was watching him, stone-faced. It was only too possible that Marcus might end up under arrest just because he wasn't thinking clearly.

All of a sudden I wanted someone to be there on his side, even if it couldn't be me. "Has anyone called Bianca?"

Madge had been watching Marcus, too. Her jaw firmed. "Probably not. I'd say this is something she needs to know."

"Yeah, I'd say so."

Madge pushed herself to her feet, pulling her cell phone out of her pocket as she walked toward the brewery building.

Susa watched her go. "We're calling in the cavalry?"

"Something like that."

A moment later, Donnell got up, too. "I'm gonna find a cop I can give my statement to. Tell Nate I'll get together with him tomorrow."

"Sounds fair." I wished Dan felt the same way. I also wished I could take off myself, but I was clearly here for the duration, or until Fowler decided to let us go home.

Speaking of which, I watched as the chief stalked across the meadow toward us, a patrolman following in his wake. When he reached Susa, he paused. "I'm going to be here for a while longer. Reyes is going to take you home."

Susa looked up at the patrolman then at Fowler. For a moment I thought she might make trouble, but then she sighed. "Okay. Give me a call sometime."

Fowler kept his deadpan expression in place. "I can do that."

"I know you can. I'm saying do it." Susa pushed

herself to her feet, turning to me with a wan smile. "Hang in there, kid. It can't be too much longer." She gave Fowler a quick smile, and then she followed the patrolman to the parking lot.

"Do you need us to stick around?" I asked Fowler before he could turn back to the meadow.

He nodded. "Just a while longer. You guys were here before most of the others. I need to know what you saw."

"Are you saying Sara was already dead when we got here?"

Fowler narrowed his eyes then trotted back to the meadow and his men.

It was a long evening, enlivened only by Bianca's arrival a short time later. She looked like she'd been ready for bed, her face scrubbed clean and her gray hair tied in a bandana. Bianca kept baker's hours, which meant she was normally up very early in the morning and in bed fairly early in the evening. But she was fully awake now. She marched across the meadow like a heat-seeking missile, going straight to her son. Marcus was standing by himself where he'd been most of the evening, but Fowler was nearby. I thought he was giving Marcus a breather before questioning him again. That particular intention was circumvented neatly by Bianca, who put her arms around Marcus, holding him tight for a long moment. Then she took her son by the arm and turned to Fowler with a few choice words.

I couldn't hear what she said, but I got the gist, which was that she was taking her son home and Fowler could talk to him in the morning if he still wanted to. They had a brief staring match, but Bianca won. She and Marcus disappeared around the edge of the brewery building.

Donnell was gone. Nate must have taken care of Dan, or else he'd gotten tired of waiting. He was gone, too. I'd lost track of Uncle Mike, but I knew he was still around because he wouldn't have left without Madge. She was still there, too, playing solitaire on her phone. Coco sat in Donnell's lawn chair, eyes closed. Maybe she was napping, or maybe she just didn't want to talk to anybody. I could sympathize with both possibilities.

Finally, after an hour and a half, Fowler walked across the meadow toward us. "Can we leave now?" I asked.

"Soon," he said. "Just a few questions." He extended his hand and helped me to my feet. I followed him across the cement slab to a relatively secluded spot, although I had no idea why he didn't want Madge to hear us. Maybe he wanted to make sure my recollections didn't interfere with hers. Not that that was likely. "What time did you get here?" he asked.

"Around four. We needed to make sure everything was set up before we brought the food over."

"Who all was with you?"

I gritted my teeth. He had to have asked Nate the same questions, but it was his job to make sure everything checked out. "Just Nate and me to begin with. Uncle Mike and Madge brought the food over around four thirty. Donnell and Dan and Tim came around five."

Fowler frowned. "Who are they?"

"Donnell helped serve, along with Madge and Uncle Mike. Tim was our runner, making sure we had food at all the stations. Dan was running one of the grills."

The Honey Jam Murder

"I thought Marcus and Nate did that."

"Nate did burgers. Marcus did sausage. Dan did the plant-based stuff."

Fowler's lips thinned, but he didn't express any opinion on plant-based meat. Just as well. "And you all stayed at your stations for the whole evening?"

"Once service started, yeah. We had a couple of slower spots where we could take a breather, but nobody had time to leave the serving area." Which was undoubtedly what he was really asking. No one had had time to go across the meadow, kill Sara, and come back to the line again. Of that, I was absolutely sure.

"And Marcus was grilling sausages all evening?"

"Absolutely. The sausages were a big hit. He kept turning them out all evening long." I raised my chin slightly, ready to go toe-to-toe if necessary.

Fowler made a final note, raising his eyebrows. "Anybody go off sightseeing before you started serving?"

I shook my head. "Not that I saw. We were all busy. We had to get set up and then get going. It wasn't like we were here for fun." Although the end of the evening was certainly turning into a laugh riot.

"Right." Fowler folded up his notebook. "Okay, you can go home. I've got your contact information."

Of course he did. "What about Madge and Coco and Uncle Mike? We need to take our stuff to the catering kitchen."

"You're all clear." He paused, then gave me dry smile. "Good food. Slaw and potato salad were outstanding. So were the sausage sandwiches."

"Thanks. Unfortunately, I don't know how many people are going to remember that." I only hoped

Fowler remembered Marcus and his sausage sandwiches. Surely, a man who was intent on making something that tasty couldn't also be murdering his wife.

Madge and Uncle Mike helped us load everything into the SUV. I wasn't sure where Coco was, but I figured she could take care of her own sheet pans. When we got to the catering kitchen, Nate and I unloaded all the pots and pans onto the worktable where Tres, the café's dishwasher and janitor, could find them tomorrow.

"You want something to eat?" Nate asked.

I paused to think about it. I hadn't had anything at the barbecue, and I was actually ravenous. "Yeah. What do we have at the cabin?"

"Not much. But I saw some leftover spaghetti sauce in the café refrigerator. I can grab it and then we can boil some pasta when we get back."

That was the good thing about living with a café owner (well, one of the good things, anyway), we had access to wonderful leftovers. Nate grabbed the sauce, and I took a couple of French rolls from the bread bin. It had been a hellish night, but maybe we could have a good meal.

At the cabin, we worked more or less in sync, both of us tired beyond belief but both of us hungry. And, I was guessing, both of us needing to talk about what had happened. I opened a bottle of wine and we collapsed at the kitchen table to eat silently for the first few minutes. Once my hunger was within bounds, I slowed down. "Good sauce. Tell Bobby my compliments to the chef."

"It's probably Marigold's," Nate said. "I don't recognize the recipe."

We stared at each other for a moment, then Nate sighed. "So. This was a hell of a night."

"It was at that." I paused, trying to figure out how to ask the things I was really curious about. "Did you...see her?"

Nate rubbed a hand across his face. "Just for a minute. That girl was still screaming when we got there, and it took Fowler a minute to figure out what was going on and clear us all out."

"Who found her?"

"Some couple trying to find a little privacy. She was in a sort of grove, a bunch of aspen. You couldn't see she was there until you were almost on top of her." He grimaced. "Which is not a great way to put it, but you know what I mean."

I nodded. "I know. I guess they're sure it's Sara?"

"It was Sara. Absolutely Sara. She even had on those high-top sneakers she liked to wear."

I'd been worried that maybe Sara had been naked, so that was weirdly reassuring. "Was she at the barbecue? I didn't see her, but I didn't notice who was there. I was too busy."

"I didn't see her. But if she was there, I'd guess she'd try to avoid Marcus, so she might not have been around the food line."

"Why would you come to a barbecue if you weren't going to eat?" Although I supposed some people might have come just to drink beer.

"I don't know." Nate rubbed his eyes again. "I don't know why Sara did a lot of the things she did. If she was there for the party, she was probably with someone. Fowler will check."

"He asked me about Marcus. If he ever left the

line. I told him no, not that I saw. But I wasn't next to him."

"Marcus stayed at the grill all evening long. We all did. You saw what it was like out there. Crowds of people coming in all night long. Marcus and I were both working the grills until the end. Dan took over for me when things died down a little, but Marcus stuck with it all the way through. He wanted to make sure the sausages were done right."

It made sense that he did. Marcus probably figured this would be great publicity for his butcher shop. Once people tasted his sausage, they'd want to see what else he had to sell. And it should have worked out just like that. It wasn't his fault that it hadn't.

"Until the screaming started, I thought it was a great evening. The food was popular, the beer was stellar. People were happy. I just hope they'll remember that when the shock wears off."

Nate sighed. "We can hope. But I've got a feeling it'll take quite a while for that to happen."

Sadly, I figured he was right. I couldn't blame Sara—she undoubtedly hadn't planned on being the centerpiece of a disaster—but it still felt just like her to leave a mess for someone else to clean up.

And with that singularly uncharitable reflection, I started clearing the table.

Chapter 14

Uncle Mike came down to the cabin for breakfast the next morning. He didn't do that too often anymore, in part because he was with Madge in the morning a lot of the time. But I figured last night they'd probably both gone off to get some rest after all the excitement. I decided to make blueberry pancakes because I had some berries to get rid of and because they were Uncle Mike's favorites. He poured himself a cup of coffee and took a seat at my kitchen table. "Any news?" he asked.

"About Sara? Nope." Of course, I didn't figure I'd be at the top of anybody's call list even if something major had happened.

"Fowler's barking up the wrong tree if he thinks Marcus had anything to do with it," Uncle Mike said flatly. "Boy came to the brewery with Coco last night, and he didn't leave that grill for more than five minutes."

"He and Coco came together? I didn't realize that." I added some buttermilk to the pancake batter just because I could. Not everybody likes the taste of buttermilk, but I'm a fan.

"The two of them have been hanging out together for a while," Uncle Mike said. "Marcus came over to the café in his van and helped Coco take those trays of cookies and brownies and what not to the barbecue."

"Oh, I didn't know she'd come in Marcus's van. I

didn't even think to ask. Did she get home okay?" I had a brief guilt attack because I hadn't even checked to make sure Coco was taken care of while we were getting ready to leave.

"Madge and I took her home and made sure she was okay. Or at least we got her home and her pans at the café. I don't know how okay she was after all that drama."

"What happened to Marcus's van?" Because I was betting Bianca had taken him to her place in her SUV. He hadn't looked like he was in shape to drive anywhere.

"Probably still in the parking lot unless he got someone to bring him back to pick it up." He paused and looked thoughtful.

I guessed he was thinking the same thing I was. If Sara had been killed somewhere else and dumped in the woods, chances were that the killer had used something like a van to bring her to Sawmill. I figured Fowler would need a search warrant or something before he could do anything to Marcus's van, even if it was sitting in the Sawmill parking lot. And I figured no judge in his right mind would give him a warrant based on the little evidence he had.

"Marcus is a good kid," Uncle Mike said slowly. "He didn't deserve to be treated the way Sara treated him. And he sure as hell doesn't deserve to be suspected of killing her when there's no way he could be involved."

I really hoped Uncle Mike was right, but I also knew people didn't always get the treatment they deserved. "When did he pick up Coco yesterday?" If they'd spent the afternoon together, that might give him the alibi he needed.

Uncle Mike shrugged. "No idea. Madge and I saw them when they pulled into the parking lot about ten minutes after we got there. Madge had been worrying that she should have checked on Coco before we came to the brewery. It was a relief when she saw them."

That didn't help much since we already knew when Marcus had arrived. Still, Coco could say when she and Marcus had gotten together, assuming Fowler was willing to believe her, given her relationship with Marcus.

"Don't know why Fowler's focusing so much on Marcus anyway," Uncle Mike grumbled. "He never left that grill, and we can all vouch for him."

He was right about that, anyway. If Sara had been killed while the party was going on, Marcus was in the clear. "I guess the question is, was Sara killed while the party was going on or before? And was she killed there or somewhere else?"

Uncle Mike chewed contemplatively. "You think somebody dumped her there?"

"I don't know. But I do know—or I assume, anyway—that nobody heard anything that sounded like a woman being murdered in the woods. I suppose she could have been murdered earlier in the day, before we all got there. But it just feels like a weird place to murder someone."

"Doesn't seem like all that great a place to dump someone either," Uncle Mike pointed out. "I mean, why not take the body up in the hills and leave it there? You'd have a much better chance of nobody finding it."

"That's true," I said slowly. Which made the choice of the woods behind the brewery as either the murder location or the place where the murderer chose to dump the body even more strange. "But it would be really dumb for Marcus to kill Sara and leave her there. I mean he was right across the meadow cooking sausages. He'd be a logical suspect."

"Which could be why somebody did that." Nate stood in the kitchen doorway pulling on a T-shirt. I'd been letting him sleep, given how exhausted he'd been when we finally got to bed the night before.

"Why somebody did what?" Uncle Mike sounded confused.

Nate speared a couple of blueberry pancakes off the serving platter and sat down at the kitchen table. "Why somebody killed Sara near where Marcus was working. It puts Marcus in the spotlight and maybe takes it off other people who might have wanted to hurt her."

I poured myself another half cup of coffee. "I guess that works if she was killed elsewhere and dumped there, too. Fowler will look long and hard at Marcus before he looks at anybody else."

"But why would Marcus kill Sara and leave her close to where he was working? He'd have to be an idiot, or maybe a nutjob. And the boy isn't either of those things. I've known him for most of his life, and I can vouch for him being as smart and sane as anybody in town." Uncle Mike gazed at us fiercely, as if he expected us to disagree.

"Absolutely true," I said. "And I'm sure Fowler knows that. Or if he doesn't, he'll find out soon enough."

"But what if it wasn't planned?" Nate said slowly. "What if Sara ambushed him before the barbecue, and they got into a fight? He might have killed her by accident and then left her there, maybe figuring he could come back later."

Uncle Mike gave him an outraged look, but I put a hand on his arm. "It's possible, I guess. But that would mean Marcus worked all evening long after he murdered his ex-wife and none of us noticed anything wrong. As far as I could tell, Marcus was having a great time cooking his sausages and flirting with Coco. And honestly, I don't think he could do that if he'd just killed someone."

Nate shook his head. "No, I don't either. I was just trying to see things the way Fowler probably will. He'll study all the possibilities."

"But that's not a possibility." Uncle Mike's jaw firmed. "Marcus and Coco were together before they came to the brewery. He couldn't have met Sara in the woods because he didn't have time to do that and pick Coco up and take her to Sawmill. I mean, he'd have to kill his ex at the brewery then turn around and pick up Coco at the café and go to the brewery again."

"Would Fowler think Coco might be his accomplice?" I mused.

Both men stared at me as if I'd just grown a second head.

I shrugged. "Not that I think she is. But would Fowler?"

"Madge would skin him alive," Uncle Mike said flatly. "If he even suggested such a thing, she'd go after him with a chainsaw."

"And I'd be right behind her." Nate sounded grim. "Coco and I don't always see eye to eye, but she's my sister. And I know damn well she's not a murderess. Or a murderer's accomplice."

I honestly hadn't been trying to stir up trouble, but I'd done that more easily than I thought I would. "Okay, wait. We've established that it's very unlikely Marcus could be a serious suspect, which is good. But Fowler's got more information than we do, and it's always possible we're missing something important."

"Maybe it's time we stopped thinking about it," Nate said. "It's not our problem, thank God. Let Fowler figure it out—he's usually good at it. If he makes a mistake, we can step in."

That was certainly true. Fowler had a good track record, although he and I occasionally butted heads. With any luck he'd arrive at all the conclusions we'd just arrived at ourselves.

I decided to follow Nate's advice and spend the day getting ready for the farmers market tomorrow rather than obsessing over Sara's murder.

Earlier in the week, I'd figured I'd be tired on Friday since it would be the day after the barbecue, but I hadn't figured on the extra exhaustion that would come from the murder investigation. I decided to concentrate on getting the cases of jam ready to take to the market rather than trying for anything fancy. I was pretty sure I had enough jam stockpiled in my storage shed so I wouldn't have to try any last-minute jam-making. Fortunately, since last minute stuff is always disastrous.

Bridget arrived full of questions, most of which I couldn't answer since I hadn't seen Sara's body (thank God). Like everybody else, she thought Marcus was the most logical suspect, but I quickly disabused her of that idea.

"He never left the grill. Believe me, the crowds were so big none of us could stop doing what we were doing. I don't know how long it would take to walk all the way across the meadow to the trees, find Sara, and kill her, but I can guarantee you Marcus was never gone that long."

"That's good to hear," Bridget said. "Bianca would be upset if anybody went after Marcus."

"To put it mildly." I confined myself to loading jars into cases, making sure I had ample supplies of all my most popular jams.

Bridget went to the computer, checking out the online orders and making up address labels so that we could get them loaded, too. "How did Sara die anyway?" she asked after a while.

I paused. "I don't know. Nobody said, and I didn't ask." Not that Fowler would have told me if I'd asked him. I wasn't sure whether Nate could tell me or not since he'd seen the body. I supposed that depended on how obvious the murder method had been.

Bridget sighed. "I didn't like Sara much. I don't know anybody who did. But I wouldn't wish this on her. Particularly when it's going to cause Marcus grief."

Marcus and, of course, his mom. Bianca and Sara had never gotten along, and now her son was in danger of being charged with Sara's murder. My guess was Bianca was suffering almost as much as Marcus was.

By the time Bridget had left for the day, I had my jam ready to go for the market and a stack of mail order boxes to be picked up by the delivery truck. Once again, I'd upped the number of cases I was taking to town because I'd been selling virtually everything I brought with me. Since I still hadn't found enough honey to do raspberry honey for the market, I'd fallen back on one of my perennials, blackberry and black pepper. It's a great combination of sweet and spicy, and it usually sells well, particularly if I put it out for people to sample. I had a case ready to go, and I'd probably make more during the following week because blackberries were in season.

I considered doing a blackberry honey jam, but discarded the idea. Blackberries are sweeter than raspberries, and they had less contrasting flavor. Blackberry jam needed something to spice it up, pepper or chili or even lemon verbena. Plus blackberry seeds are killers compared to raspberry seeds.

Besides, I still needed to make the rounds next week to see if I could pick up any more honey before I made any decisions.

I actually cooked dinner that night instead of relying on leftovers or takeout. It was just chicken Marengo, but even that was a step up from what we'd been eating for the previous week. Normally, we'd have had a catering job on Friday or Saturday night—or even Sunday on some weeks. But we hadn't taken any extra jobs this weekend because we assumed, correctly, that we wouldn't have had time to cook up any other dishes beyond those we were doing for the barbecue.

We had a Friday off for once. I wasn't sure what we'd do with it, though.

Nate got home early, or what seemed like early given that he was usually working in the catering kitchen. He flopped down on the couch. "This feels weird, being home on Friday night."

"It does," I agreed. "Let's just enjoy the weird, okay?" I brought him a beer and sank down beside him.

"When's our next gig?"

"Next weekend. Birthday party up in one of the houses on Wild Horse Road."

Wild Horse Road led to Wild Horse Pass, which was where most of the big fancy houses belonging to the newcomers to Shavano were located. We weren't in the same category as Aspen or Breckinridge, to be sure, but like a lot of mountain towns, we were attracting rich people who wanted impressive homes in the back country. And most of those homes were up toward Wild Horse Road. "Oh, Lord," I moaned. "What are we supposed to cook for them?"

"Heavy hors d'oeuvres, basically. Then a buffet with something like pasta Bolognese. I guess it's a cocktail party."

I narrowed my eyes. "Asian meatballs."

"Yep. And charcuterie. And filo packets. All the golden oldies." He rubbed a hand across his forehead. "We need to add some new hors d'oeuvres to the list of possibles. Even I'm getting sick of those."

"We could do something new this time—a different kind of dip for the crudités, say. Or maybe pigs in blankets like we did for the Blavatskys' birthday dinner."

Nate shook his head. "That would involve sausages from Marcus, and I don't know if he's up to that right now."

Which brought us right back to the ungainly elephant in the middle of the room. "Did you hear anything today? Any news from Fowler? Or Coco?"

"Coco came in, did her job, and left. I don't think she said more than 'Got it' when we called out an order. She's not sharing." Nate grimaced. "Not that I think she should."

"Maybe she's talking to your mom."

"I hope she is," Nate said slowly. "I think she needs to talk to somebody besides cops. Mom would be a very good choice."

"It's unfair. I mean, the more I think about what you said this morning, the more I think you're right. Somebody must have put Sara's body there to implicate Marcus."

"Maybe. But unless they can find out who killed her and where, Marcus stays under a cloud indefinitely."

That was brutal but accurate. People who knew Marcus and Bianca wouldn't jump to any conclusions about him, but the part of the town that didn't know either of them would figure that Marcus was the logical suspect. He was the ex-husband, and he was right there on site. QED.

Nate sighed. "On a lighter note…"

Lighter was good. "What?"

"Leila Fischer told Mom her daughter's getting married."

I blinked. "Okay. And this is important because…?" I barely knew who Leila Fischer was. She managed one of the recreational equipment stores downtown, but I'd never seen her daughter. In fact, I was pretty sure I'd never known she had a daughter.

"This is important because Leila's interested in wedding caterers. She wanted to know if we did weddings along with parties."

Nate gave me a cautious smile. Catering weddings would be a major step up for us, although it would also involve major hassles. Brides needed tasting menus and some tended to be insane. We'd had a few nutsy customers for birthday parties, but it was a single event and usually over quickly. Weddings stretched across months, considering all the advance planning that went into them. They'd also require us to get on the radar with wedding planners. We'd already had a couple of inquiries from women who were trying to start event planning companies, but nobody had followed through yet.

"I assume Madge told her we definitely did weddings."

Nate nodded. "Yeah. Leila's a friend. She said she'd pass the news on to her wedding planner. We'll see if they get back to us."

I blew out a long breath. Getting into the wedding business would push Robicheaux Catering up a notch. It would also mean we'd be doing the equivalent of the Sawmill barbecue regularly. I'd once heard someone describe a three-hundred-guest wedding as "intimate." If we dived into that pool, we'd need more help.

Thank God we had Dan.

I heard the timer *ding* in the kitchen. "Dinner's done," I said. "Let's eat."

Nate pushed himself to his feet, grabbing his beer. "Let's do that. Before anything else gets in the way."

I could definitely get behind that idea.

Chapter 15

The farmers market was as hectic as I'd thought it might be. I sold half of the blackberry black pepper jam within the first hour and it was entirely gone by noon. Pepper peach and plain peach were moving briskly because it was the beginning of peach season. Peach growers like Uncle Mike usually sold out early because they didn't yet have the bulk of their crop, which meant peach lovers had to canvass the other booths to find something to assuage their peach longing. Raspberry and apricot were flying off the shelves and I got rid of the last of last year's strawberry.

The market was full of tourists, God bless them. Tourists love to buy good jam, frequently lots of jars. It was the perfect souvenir in a way—they could put it in their pantries and then pull out a jar of peach preserves in the depths of winter and remember that lovely, sunny day in Shavano.

They kept Beck busy, too, asking her about places to go for lunch and what her favorite hike was. Fortunately for them, Beck was a fountain of information, having lived in Shavano all her life and hiked every trail in the area twice or more. Unfortunately for me, if Beck was busy being quizzed by the tourists, that meant I was the only one available to keep the sample bowls filled and ring up those sales. By noon, I was worn out from hopping from one task to another. By twelve thirty I was ready to start snarling at the tourists, no matter what that might do to my future sales. But Beck managed to cut her spiel down to a couple of minutes and pour jam into bowls while she delivered it.

The demo booth next door was also going great guns, judging from the crowds of people swooping in to grab the samples. I hadn't seen anybody from Robicheaux's, though; certainly not Coco. I hadn't actually spoken to her since the barbecue, and according to Nate she was keeping a very low profile. I wondered just what she was worried about—that Marcus was innocent and being persecuted or that he was guilty and getting away with murder.

I still didn't see how Marcus would have had time to kill Sara, but maybe the cops knew something I didn't. In fact, they probably knew a lot that I didn't. And in this case, I wasn't sure I wanted to know more.

We were close to sold out by one thirty. I had a few more jars of raspberry and even fewer of apricot, but everything else had been sold in the earlier tourist frenzy. I suppose the moral of that situation was that I needed to increase the number of cases I brought to the market. But at the moment, I was running at full tilt as far as jam production was concerned. I needed to see if I could increase Dolce's hours so we could make more jam. I could always store any excess to sell as mail orders.

Given that we were pretty much out of product to sell, I sent Beck off with her pay for the time she'd worked and put out the remaining jars in hopes I wouldn't have to carry them home. I was taking a breather, sitting in a lawn chair beside the sample table, when Bianca approached my booth.

"Done for the day?" I asked.

Bianca rarely left her booth, even though she had her own set of high schoolers helping with sales.

She nodded. "I didn't make as much product as I should have with these crowds. I got distracted."

She had a lot to be distracted about. I got a good look at her then. Bianca's around Uncle Mike's age, maybe a few years older, but she usually looks a lot younger than her years. Today, she looked every day of her age, and it also looked like every day had been a hard one. Her skin was washed out and pale; her gray hair curled limply around her face. Only her dark eyes still seemed sharp, although also vaguely haunted.

"Grab a chair," I said. "Have a seat. Would you like some cold water?" I always brought a few bottles with me, just in case somebody got hit by the heat, which can be surprisingly intense in a mountain summer.

"Sure." She took a long drink from the bottle I handed her. "Have a good day?"

"Pretty much. I've been selling out every week. I need to up my production, but that probably means hiring more help. Actually, it definitely means hiring more help." I felt like I was babbling, trying not to mention the thing that both of us were thinking about. But I couldn't come up with a decent way to introduce the subject, other than just blurting it out.

"Thought you had help already." Bianca didn't sound like she was all that interested.

"I've got Dolce. I may try to increase her hours if I can."

"And you got Dan Griffin in the kitchen, I hear."

I paused. "Yeah. Nate hired Dan to help with the catering kitchen since I'm not as available while the market's going on."

"Marcus said he was cooking at the Sawmill barbecue."

So there we were. I took a breath. "How's he holding up?"

"Marcus? He's okay. Considering."

"Considering?"

"Considering everybody in town thinks he killed Sara." Bianca was staring off at the few remaining customers wandering around the market.

"I don't think that," I said flatly. "Marcus was there all evening cooking sausages. There was no way he could have done it, even if she was just across the meadow from us."

"Yeah, if she'd been killed while the barbecue was going on, he'd have an air-tight alibi." Bianca sighed.

"She wasn't?" We'd all speculated about that, but nobody had any hard information.

"From what I hear, she was killed sometime earlier that afternoon somewhere other than Sawmill Brewing."

Well, damn. That pretty much shot down Marcus's alibi. Maybe. "How good is your information on this? I've heard all kinds of rumors."

"In this town, cops eat muffins instead of donuts. My sources are pretty solid." Bianca made the best muffins in town. I could believe the Shavano cops stopped by her place in the morning to grab some blueberry or maybe some cinnamon crisp.

"Marcus was with Coco part of the afternoon. Doesn't that clear him?"

"He picked her up late, around four. My sources say Sara died around two."

Damn again. Two hours was probably plenty of time to kill Sara and put her body in the woods. But that still made no sense.

"Marcus wouldn't kill her and then bring her where he was going to spend the rest of the afternoon and evening. He's not that dense. He would have left her somewhere that had no connection to him." I took a breath. "I mean he would have done that if he'd killed her, which he definitely did not."

Bianca gave me a dry smile. "Fortunately for us all, I think Fowler agrees with you. But Marcus is still one of his top suspects, given that he and Sara were fighting over the property settlement."

"Who are the others?"

"I haven't heard. But knowing Sara, there had to be some."

I figured Bianca was right about that. Sara was one of the most unpleasant women I'd ever met. And she'd cheated on Marcus with a real sleaze, which led to her helping somebody to almost kill me. She'd been blackmailed into it, but I didn't think she was particularly sorry she'd done it.

Bianca took another swallow of water. "And in case you're wondering if I killed her, no, I did not. And I'm well alibied since mid-afternoon is when we're clearing out as much of our product as we can and putting the rest of it into the Day Old bin or sending it to the soup kitchen. Lots of people were around, and lots of people saw me."

"I never considered it," I said. Although I probably should have since Sara and Bianca had a very rocky relationship. Still, Bianca had never struck me as the murderous type. She'd be more likely to call Sara something unprintable and have a high decibel argument on Main Street.

"How did she...I mean, do you know..." There is no polite way to ask how somebody was murdered, but I was trying my best.

"Blunt force trauma." Bianca stared out across the market again. "Somebody smacked her in the back of the head. Which sounds to me like she pushed the wrong person's buttons and got killed as a result."

"Yeah, sounds about right." It did, too. But unfortunately, that didn't let Marcus off the hook. "So was Marcus in his shop at two?"

Bianca shrugged. "He was there, but the shop was closed. He was getting the sausage ready for the barbecue. It's possible somebody saw him through the window, but nobody was in the shop except for him."

"And Fowler knows all of this."

She nodded. "Yep. And he hasn't arrested Marcus, which is a point in his favor. But that doesn't stop the people in town from coming to their own conclusions. Marcus was just beginning to build up a following. This has knocked him on his heels."

I knew only too well the way public opinion could swing against you. When a lot of people in town thought I'd killed a local chef I'd fought with, my business had taken a hit. Even after the real murderer had been found, it took a while before some locals started buying my jam again. They knew something unpleasant had been associated with me, but they couldn't exactly remember what. Consequently, they stopped buying my stuff, just to be on the safe side.

"I'm sorry, Bianca. I wish there was something I could do. I mean, Nate and I got Marcus into this when we offered him the barbecue job. It sounded like a great idea."

"It was a great idea. It got him a bunch of potential new customers. Until they found the body."

"Yeah," I said slowly. "That sort of put a damper on things."

"But if you want to help…" Bianca raised an eyebrow.

"Of course," I said. "Anything I can do. What does he need?"

"Marcus isn't asking for this. I am." Bianca gave me a steady look. "You've got a reputation for figuring things out. You and your friends. You figured out who killed Brett Holmes, and who poisoned Tera Bloomberg. Maybe you could investigate this. See what you can figure out about Sara."

I blinked at her. "I'm not exactly a pro at investigations."

"I know. But you've got your own point of view. And you've got a track record. If you could just try…"

I bit my lip. Fowler would hit the ceiling if he found out I was messing around in his investigation. And Nate wouldn't be happy. Neither would Uncle Mike. All of them preferred me to keep my nose out of places it didn't belong. But Bianca was one of my best friends. She'd stood by me when I'd had problems. She'd been a source of wisdom about being a foodie entrepreneur. And she needed my help. Really.

"Okay," I said. "I can do that. I can't promise anything, though. Fowler's a lot better at this than I am."

Bianca's jaw firmed. "My money's on you, kid. If Fowler decides Marcus is it, he may not feel like investigating much further than that, even if he can't prove Marcus did it. Which leaves Marcus in limbo, with a lot of people in town thinking he's a murderer."

Bianca left soon after that, and I broke down the booth and packed it away. I only had a few jars left to take back to the farm, which was good, but I knew now I needed to either get more hours for Dolce or find another assistant who could help on the days Dolce couldn't.

And I'd promised Bianca I'd find out who killed Sara. Well, I hadn't promised her I'd find out (I most likely wouldn't), but I'd given her reason to believe I'd find other possibilities beyond Marcus. I hoped I could do that, but I didn't know how likely it was.

Actually, I did know.

Very unlikely indeed.

Chapter 16

I decided I wouldn't mention Bianca's request to Nate or to Uncle Mike. They might find out what I was doing as I went along, particularly if Fowler got wind of it and got his knickers in a twist. But I figured they'd only try to talk me out of it, and I wasn't in the mood to be reasoned with. I most likely wouldn't find out anything, but Bianca mattered to me, and I was going to give it my best shot.

One person who probably wouldn't try to talk me out of it was Susa. We'd worked together on some other investigations, so I reasoned she'd be willing to serve as a sounding board for any theories I managed to come up with.

I called her that afternoon, although I didn't figure she'd be around since it was Saturday. Mainly, I just wanted to set up a time we could get together. Maybe lunch or something.

But Susa was answering her phone. "Hi," she said. "What's up? Are you and Nate going to Dirty Pete's tonight?"

"I don't know. I hadn't thought about it. Why? Is something going on there we need to know about?"

"No, but I'm meeting Ethan there. I thought maybe you and Nate could join us."

Crap. I'd forgotten all about the fact that Fowler and Susa were currently in one of the *on* phases of their relationship. That might make her reluctant to do any freelance investigating about a case Fowler was working on. "I don't know. Nate did breakfast and lunch today because Marigold went to Denver for the weekend. He'll probably be too beat to go out, particularly since he's also doing brunch tomorrow." That was Nate's schedule before the catering company had taken off and before Marigold had come to work for Robicheaux's. He was glad to fill in, but he said the work reminded him of why he'd wanted to do something different in the first place.

"Oh," Susa said. "Well, maybe next time. What did you want to know?"

"Know?"

"Why did you call? Or did you just want to dish, because I can also do that."

She sounded so chipper and upbeat. I didn't want to ruin that.

"Rox? What's going on?"

"I just had something…It's okay. We can talk some other time."

"Roxy." Susa's voice was sharp. "Don't you dare hang up. What's going on?"

It was probably better to let Susa know what I was up to and let her refuse to help. "I talked to Bianca this morning. She's worried about Marcus."

"Well, shit," Susa said. "Don't tell me she thinks he's guilty."

"No, no, nothing like that. But she's worried that Fowler might think he was guilty and give up searching for other possible suspects."

"Ethan wouldn't do that," Susa said staunchly. "He'll keep searching until he finds the person who did it."

Assuming that person was findable, Fowler would certainly give it his best shot. "She's worried that he may not be able to find the person who actually did it, and that Marcus will be in limbo, with everybody wondering if he killed Sara."

There was a beat of silence between us. Both of us had been suspected of murder in the past, and both of us had had to put up with the citizens of Shavano regarding us with suspicion. "That sucks," Susa said quietly. "Believe me, I know how it feels. What does Bianca want?"

I paused, but I figured I might as well dive in. "She asked me to do some digging, to see what I could find out. She seems to think I've got a track record." If we'd been in the same room, Susa could have seen me blush about that last bit. I was hoping my voice conveyed the message.

"And she wants me to help you out, too?" I couldn't tell anything from Susa's tone, whether she was annoyed or intrigued.

"She didn't say anything about you. I'm the one who thought you might be able to listen to me try theories out, assuming I come up with some. I forgot about Ethan and you—I'm sorry. I don't want to put you on the spot."

There was another moment of silence, then Susa sighed. "I won't tell you anything Ethan says to me about the case. Not that he's likely to say anything at all, but if he lets something slip, I can't take advantage of him."

"No," I said quickly, "of course not."

"But hell, Rox, Bianca's one of my favorite people.

And I like Marcus, too. It's not fair that somebody is screwing around with them like this."

"No, it's not. Do you think somebody's trying to set Marcus up?" I thought that myself, but I didn't want to influence Susa one way or the other. On the other hand, I intended to bring it up.

"I think it's possible. Don't you?"

"I do." I paused again. "Could we maybe get together for lunch next week and talk this through?"

"Let's do it Monday. I'm pretty much through with the project I'm working on, but I can tie things up with a few bow knots Monday morning and then have a margarita to celebrate."

I wished I could have a margarita myself, but cooking jam required concentration. Otherwise you risked dipping your fingers in something approximately as hot as lava. "Okay, Monday it is. I'll see how much information I can pick up before then." I didn't ask Susa to do the same because I didn't want to put her under any pressure where Fowler was concerned.

We said our goodbyes, and I headed for my kitchen, determined to start on next week's jam production. I had a bushel of peaches I'd just gotten from Uncle Mike, which worked out to roughly fifty pounds. I used around a pound of peaches per pint jar of jam. So I'd be making four cases of jam, give or take. I also had a flat of jalapenos, the peppers I used when I couldn't get my hands on either Pueblo or Hatch chilies. So the weekend would be an orgy of peach and pepper peach on repeat.

Nate limped in when I'd gotten just over half of my quota done. The cabin smelled like a combination of sweet peaches and fiery jalapenos. This time the peppers I'd gotten at the farm stand were on the spicy side. You could never predict whether you were getting mild or incendiary jalapenos just from appearance, but I always worked with rubber gloves just in case, so I wouldn't end up with fingers that left a trail of pain on my more tender parts. This time around, the capsaicin in the oils had been enough to irritate my eyes as my jam making went on, and I'd pretty much decided that I was done for the day.

"Wow." Nate waved a hand in front of his face. "The atmosphere in here is close to toxic."

"Open some windows," I suggested. "I'm done slicing. Maybe we can air things out."

By the time I finished what I was doing, the cabin had begun to return to its normal atmosphere, but Nate suggested taking a couple of beers onto the front porch while I let the exhaust fans finish their work.

"How was it being back at the café?" I asked after we'd dropped into the Adirondack chairs on the porch.

"About like it was before. Exhausting and sort of annoying and still an adrenaline high because that's the way it always is during the rush." He took a long pull on his beer. "But I'm glad I don't have to get up tomorrow. Bobby says he can take brunch on his own."

"Do we have any catering gigs next week?"

He nodded. "That birthday party up at the farm. Then we've got that corporate deal the Tuesday after that."

Corporate deals were our bread and butter since they usually involved a lot of people drinking cocktails and sucking down appetizers. Our appetizers tended to be relatively cheap, easy to scale, and delicious. Word of mouth was getting us a lot of business, which reminded me.

"Have we had any blowback from the barbecue?"

"Blowback?" Nate frowned. "Why would we get blowback? It wasn't our fault Sara got murdered nearby."

"No, but people aren't always logical about stuff like that. Something unpleasant happens, and all of a sudden everybody in the vicinity takes a hit, even if we had no connection with the unpleasantness."

"Yeah." Nate rubbed a hand across his neck. "Well, so far as I can tell, we're still okay. Sawmill paid their bills, and the manager talked about maybe doing something together in the fall. And none of the other customers has said anything to me. But a lot of these events had been scheduled before the barbecue happened. I guess we'll see if business slows down over the next month or something."

"It's happening to Marcus. That's what Bianca says, anyway." I glanced at him as I took a swallow of my beer.

Nate stared off at the mountains, turning deep blue as the sun began to dip down. "He's a little more directly affected than we are."

Which didn't make it right. "Will we go on ordering meat from him for events?"

"Of course." Nate looked puzzled. "Why wouldn't we? His stuff is the best in town. We'll go on ordering it whenever we can afford to."

"Just checking. Will customers have to okay the purchases?"

Now Nate looked confused. "I make up the budgets and give them an estimate of what the meal will cost. I don't usually tell them who the suppliers are."

"What would you do if they told you to avoid Marcus?"

"Order from the café's supplier. But nobody's going to do that, Rox. Nobody feels that strongly about Marcus from what I can tell. And besides, it isn't the commercial customers like me who are likely to be a problem for him. It's the walk-in business. That may well go down by a lot just because people are suspicious."

He was undoubtedly right about that. From what I understood, Marcus had a small but growing number of customers who came to his place to buy their meat rather than getting it at City Market like most people in town. That was the main reason he'd signed on for the barbecue in the first place—he wanted to pick up some more customers, people who hadn't thought about buying meats from him before but would be more likely to think about it after they'd had a couple of his sausage sandwiches. "That sucks. All of it sucks."

"I'm not arguing with you. But it should get better once Fowler arrests someone for Sara's murder. Someone other than Marcus." Nate slid his arm around my shoulders and took a last swallow of his beer.

"Yeah," I said. "Assuming that happens."

Because I wasn't all that certain that Fowler would find the real murderer any time soon.

I met Susa at the town's second-best coffee place on Monday morning. Bianca's bakery was without question the best coffee place in town, but we couldn't very well meet there if we were going to be hashing out the possibilities for Sara's murderer. Thus we met at Beans On the Rocks and satisfied ourselves with some decent coffee and slightly stale muffins.

"So what's new?" Susa asked.

"You mean about the case or about life? Doesn't matter. I guess the answer's the same, regardless. Not much."

I halfway hoped Susa would drop some tidbit about the investigation that would count as new information, but she only sighed. "How do we go about this?"

I took a sip of my coffee, considering. "I'd say we need to focus on Sara. I didn't like her much, so I never got to know much about her. But now we need to know as much as we can find out to see if we could figure out who might have had a grudge against her."

Susa grimaced. "I didn't know her at all. I mean I knew who she was, but I never spoke to her so far as I can remember. Who were her friends?"

"I only know two women who were close to her— one is dead and the other's in jail." My last run-in with Sara had ended badly for everybody except me. Fortunately, from my point of view.

"Great. So where do we begin?" Susa nibbled on her apple spice muffin and made a face. "Bianca's stuff is so much better than this it's a wonder they're still in business."

"They don't specialize in baked goods. And their coffee's good."

"Bianca's is better."

"Yeah." *No argument there.* "Okay, who can we ask about Sara?"

Susa shrugged. "Bianca's the logical person to go to. We both know it. Granted, she's got a king-sized bias, but she also knew Sara before we did. And she knew her better."

"Yeah," I said. "Okay. I'll call her and see if we

can talk to her. It'll probably be late in the day, after she's done baking and getting stuff set up for the next morning."

"That's all right. My hours are flexible. I do some of my best work at four in the morning." Susa gave me a quick grin. "Anything you need me to do before we talk to Bianca?"

"Talk to anybody you can think of who might have known Sara. We should both do that. She had to have had some friends."

"Not necessarily." Susa sounded glum. "What's the name of that grocery where she worked in Geary?"

"Sylvano's. I haven't been over there yet. Have you?"

"Nope. But I've got a couple of clients in Geary. Let me do a little nosing around."

On my way to my truck, I happened to think of someone who might know a little more about Sara. Coco might know what Marcus had said about her, although I doubted it would be what anyone would call objective, given that they were in the middle of a nasty divorce.

I parked outside the catering kitchen, then walked through, hoping Nate would be there. He wasn't, but Dan was. He was chopping up what was likely the filling for filo packets, our perennial vegan appetizer.

"Hey." He gave me a quick smile. "Nate's doing a market run if you need him."

"Not at the moment." I gave him an insincere smile. I still hadn't forgiven him for causing trouble during the chaos at the end of the barbecue.

Bobby and Marigold were standing side-by-side in the main kitchen, prep bowls arranged in front of them.

Neither of them were aware of me until I was halfway across the room. "You need something?" Bobby called when he finally noticed I was there.

"Need to talk to Coco," I explained. Bobby returned to chopping. He seemed to be standing unnecessarily close to Marigold.

Coco was in her corner of the kitchen doing her own salad prep. She glanced up when I got close. "Hi. If you want to know about the dessert, I haven't decided yet."

"I'm not here about the dessert. I'm on a sort of mission."

Coco slowed in her lettuce chopping. "That sounds interesting. Also somewhat ominous."

I blew out a long breath. "Bianca asked me to take a look at what happened to Sara. She's afraid for Marcus. I don't know that I'm going to be all that helpful, but I told her I'd try."

"Yeah, Marcus said she was freaking out. Not that she doesn't have a right." Coco took a particularly vicious swipe at her lettuce.

"Has Fowler been questioning him?"

Coco grimaced. "Off and on. Who else does he have to suspect?"

"I guess that's what I'm trying to find out. I didn't know much about Sara. I talked to her a few times at the shop, and I think it's safe to say she wasn't one of my biggest fans."

"Yeah, well, it's safe to say Sara didn't like anybody around here very much. She didn't like Shavano. She thought Marcus should have opened a shop in Denver or Colorado Springs or Ft. Collins, somewhere along the Front Range that was a lot bigger and more exciting."

The reasons Marcus hadn't done that were obvious. It would have been a lot more expensive to open a butcher shop there. And there probably would have been a lot more competition. "I think Marcus made the right call. He's got no serious competition in Shavano, and he's got all the good will Bianca has built up over the years."

"I agree, totally. But Sara wanted bright lights and big city. If she could have pressured Marcus into selling the shop and dividing the proceeds with her after the divorce, she'd have been on her way, and none of this would have happened. Or anyway, I doubt that it would have happened." Coco dumped her chopped lettuce into a storage container and jerked a tomato onto the cutting board.

"Did she have any friends you know of? I never saw her outside the shop." Except for the evening when she almost got me killed. But I wouldn't have called the people she was hanging out with then her friends.

Coco shook her head. "I don't know of anyone. She wasn't that much fun to be around. She and I worked on that project the restaurant association had with the library. We didn't talk much. What I mainly remember is how into gossip she was."

"Well, she'd get a lot of gossip at the restaurant association." In my experience, whenever the local cooks and suppliers got together, gossip was the most common kind of conversation.

"Yeah, but you know what chef gossip is like. Mostly it's about what goes on in the kitchen—who's moving into management, whose menu is going belly up, whose newest pièce de résistance is a dud. Sara was more into the personal stuff. Who Spence Carroll is currently boffing, that kind of thing. And if there wasn't much of that around, she'd start digging to see if she could unearth something." Coco pulled a storage container closer and began dumping chopped tomatoes into it. "It got so people would clam up whenever she came around. She was pretty transparent."

I frowned. I wasn't sure what that information meant for our investigation. Or even if it meant anything at all. But it was the first real picture I'd gotten of Sara. And it enlarged my own view. Sara was apparently both unpleasant to work with and sneaky.

"Does that help?" Coco asked.

"Maybe," I said. "I just started asking about things. Anybody you'd recommend I talk to?"

Coco paused, staring down at her tomato-juice-stained cutting board. "I didn't know her. Bianca's probably your best bet."

More and more I began to believe that was true.

Chapter 17

I tried calling Bianca the next day, but I got her voice mail. Not surprising—she was too busy to do much chatting during her prime baking hours. My prospects were good as far as this week's market was concerned. I had pepper peach and peach preserves ready to go in quantity, and Dolce was working on the strawberry jam, her favorite.

Now I needed to whip up some apricot and raspberry. The thought of raspberry made me think of the honey jam, which I still needed to get to work on. "How's your honey supply?" I asked Dolce as she gave her strawberry jam pot a stir.

She shrugged. "Fine so far as I know. Mom hasn't gotten around to whipping any for the next market yet. I know she'll be checking the hives today."

I resolved to go over to see if I could buy some more honey from Carmen later in the day. I'd decided I'd try to make do with supplies from her and Aram and Lynn Bridger rather than buying more of Hutchinson's overpriced lousy quality stuff. I didn't have any particular amount of honey jam I needed to make for the market, so if I didn't get much honey, I'd reduce the number of jars I produced.

Bridget showed up around nine, after Dolce and I had been working for an hour or so. She got to work on the mail orders and told me what I already knew—I was

The Honey Jam Murder

sold out of honey raspberry. "What are you doing for next month's special? More honey jam?"

"Nope. It's good stuff, but it's a hassle, and it's expensive. I'll probably do one of the regular exotics, like apricot thyme." Thyme grows like weeds up here, so aggressive that you have to cut it to the bone. I had enough thyme in my herb garden to make fifty jars of jam and then some.

"Probably sell out just as fast." Bridget started printing out address labels for the orders we'd need to mail out that day. "Heard anything new about the whole Sara Jordan thing?"

I paused. Bridget was a major-league gossip, and if anyone knew anything about Sara's activities since she separated from Marcus, it would probably be Bridget. On the other hand, I was supposed to be setting an example of proper adult behavior for Dolce. "I haven't heard anything, no."

"Heard her boyfriend was dating somebody else before she got killed. Maybe they broke up."

"She had a boyfriend?" Sara had certainly had a boyfriend when I was trying to figure out who'd killed my cousin Muriel. Of course, Sara was still married to Marcus at the time. The fact that she'd had said boyfriend and gotten caught was the main reason Marcus had been divorcing her.

"She was dating the manager at Sylvano's from what I heard. Be sort of typical of her to go for the person with the most power, I guess."

That did indeed sound like Sara, and I filed the information away to share with Susa. I knew nothing about the store where Sara worked in Geary, but maybe we could find out.

Bridget left to drop off the packages at the post office around twelve thirty, but Dolce kept on working. I knew what it was like to be in the groove with your jam, so I let her be. "Will you be okay if I leave for a little bit to buy honey from your mom?" I asked.

"Sure." She paused in the act of quartering strawberries. "You know we got a new dog, right?"

I blinked at her, suddenly afraid for Lulabelle. I hadn't kept up with her health, and maybe I should have. "Is Lulabelle…"

Dolce shook her head vigorously. "No, no. Lulabelle's fine. Mom just decided a second dog would be a good idea since Herman isn't out at night."

I felt a little guilty about that, but Herman was not a dog you wanted wandering the yard howling. "Okay, I'll check him out. Back in a few."

Carmen and Donnie's house was a brisk fifteen-minute walk from my cabin, but I needed the exercise after spending the morning sweating over a hot stove. The breeze from the mountains was welcome against my face. When I knocked on the front door, I heard a wild paroxysm of high-pitched barking inside. Definitely not Lulabelle, whose bay was a lot more like a bloodhound on the scent. Now I was curious about what kind of dog Carmen had found to be a Lulabelle supplement.

Carmen herself opened the door a moment later, turning over her shoulder as she did. "Hush, dog," she snapped. The barking subsided to a sort of low-level growling and whimpering, so he'd sort of complied. Carmen folded her arms. "What's up?"

"I need some more honey, if you've got any to sell."

"I can give you a few pounds. I haven't had time to whip any more this week. Might as well sell what I've got."

As I started to follow her inside, the dog began barking again. I looked down to see something that sort of resembled a footstool in a very fussy grandmother's living room. It was round and very fuzzy, a kind of grayish-white with black accents. After a moment, he lifted his coal black nose to stare up at me, and the barking subsided to growls again.

"Dog, you're a disgrace," Carmen muttered.

"Dolce said you had a new one. What's his name?" I thought about bending down to pet his ears, but the growling kind of put me off.

Carmen sighed. "Okay, he does have a name, but it's ridiculous. We got him from Martha Gonzalez. Belonged to her nephew who was moving someplace he couldn't take him. He's got a pedigree out to here and some damn-fool name like Duke of Earl. Donnie just calls him Duke, but he doesn't seem much like a Duke to me. Doesn't answer to much of anything, either. I just call him *dog*."

She gave the duke a baleful glare, and I reached down to scratch his ears without thinking about it. Duke was slightly anxious at my touch, but then let himself be scratched. He followed at our heels as we walked toward the honey shed.

Lulabelle glanced up at us from her shady spot near the back porch. She looked better than the last time I'd seen her, but since she'd been at death's door the last time I'd seen her, that wasn't saying much. "How's Lulabelle doing?"

"Almost up to speed, I guess. She's still a little

shaky on her feet now and then."

"How does she feel about Duke?"

"Tolerant. At least with him around nobody's going to sneak up on us again. He barks his head off whenever he hears a car." Carmen didn't seem to think that was a great argument in Duke's favor.

In the honey shed, she pulled down three jars of honey, which amounted to around three pounds. I could probably make half-dozen jars with that, which would be close to enough to keep the farmers market customers happy.

"Have you had any more trouble since Lulabelle came back?" I asked. I could still see the home-made burglar alarm on the trail to the hives, but I didn't think Donnie was patrolling anymore.

Carmen shook her head. "It's been quiet around here, but I heard they've had some thefts over around Geary. Maybe the thieves figured the farmers over there had more hives—we're pretty slim pickings around here."

"For once, I'm glad to let Geary get the advantage." Our competition with our smaller, richer neighbor was mostly friendly but sometimes not.

"Ain't it the truth." Carmen put the jars in a canvas tote. "Send the tote home with Dolce. She should be about done by now."

"She's bonding with the strawberries, but I'll tell her you're looking for her."

"Do that." Carmen raised an eyebrow. "I've got strawberries of my own she can bond with."

That afternoon, I checked with Aram Pergosian and Lynn Bridger to see how much honey they could sell me. They were both in better shape than they had been when I'd bought their honey before. I ended up with enough honey to make close to a case and a half of jam, plus a flat of raspberries from Aram that meant I could get some of the honey jam done tomorrow.

And Sara had had a boyfriend in Geary. Someone she'd broken up with, who might have a grudge.

All in all, a productive day.

I finally got hold of Bianca the next afternoon. I'd begun to wonder if I'd have to run her down at the farmers market on Saturday, which would be a pain since we had that birthday party to cater on Friday night. At least I hadn't had to spend any time getting ready for it, but I'd still have to drag myself out of bed early on Saturday morning after I'd worked two or three hours the night before.

"Hey," Bianca said. "What's up?"

"Susa and I want to get together with you to talk about Sara, whenever you've got a free minute." I figured I might as well be upfront about what we were doing. Besides, I couldn't see any reason to beat around the bush. It wasn't like Bianca was going to be too grief-stricken to talk about her former daughter-in-law.

"Why? I've got absolutely no information about her murder. If I did, I'd give it to Fowler."

"I know, but you knew her. We didn't really. And I figure Sara's character is the beginning of any investigation. We need to know what she was like to start thinking about who might have decided to kill her."

Bianca sighed. "You already know what she was like. Anybody who spent five minutes around her knew what she was like. But I take your point. I'll tell you what I can. Would tomorrow afternoon work for you?"

Tomorrow was Thursday, which would be a lot better than Friday or Saturday. "It's great with me. I'll check with Susa. What time?"

"Around four. I usually take a break then anyway."

Four worked for me, and I was pretty sure I could browbeat Susa into it if I had to. "See you then."

Susa didn't require any browbeating, fortunately. "Maybe she'll give us scones," she said wistfully.

"Maybe. I've got some minor news from Bridget—Sara may have been dating her boss at Sylvano's, and they may have broken up recently. Did you talk to your contacts in Geary?"

"Yeah, for what it's worth. Sara wasn't popular around town, but everybody knew her because everybody who's anybody in Geary buys their foie gras at Sylvano's and they saw her there."

"They saw her? Why would they see her? She said she was something like the buyer for the meat department."

"If she said that, she was exaggerating. Either that or Sylvano's is short on help. She checked people out, at least part of the time. I gather Sylvano's doesn't have anything as pedestrian as checkout aisles, but she ran one of the cash registers."

"We need to check Sylvano's out. Did you hear any gossip about Sara and the store manager?"

"Not exactly. People didn't have much to say about her, to tell the truth. Basically, no one knew her well, and no one wanted to. I've got a lead on someone who worked with her at Sylvano's, though. Maybe I can nail down the rumors about the manager."

"Let's get together before we go to Bianca's. You can tell me anything you find out, and I'll see if I can get Nate to go with me to Sylvano's to pick up dinner tonight."

Nate, as usual, was tired when he got home. But he was willing to make a dinner run to Sylvano's because it meant neither of us would have to cook. And he was always on the lookout for possible new suppliers.

The town of Geary had been a classic hangout for prospectors and miners, although they'd never had a rich strike in the area. That turned out to be a good thing for the town in the long run since the gorgeous scenery that surrounded it was unblemished by abandoned mines. At some point during the last decade it had become a fashionable hangout, probably because of the summer and winter recreation possibilities and because the property prices weren't as high as at Aspen or Vail. Of course, that was then. Now Geary was one of the pricier cities in the state.

I studied the new clusters of condos sprouting up around the edges of the city limits. "Every time we come here they've got new developments popping up."

"Like mushrooms," Nate said gloomily. "But I guess as long as they're over here, they're not popping up in Shavano."

I felt like knocking wood, except there wasn't any in Nate's SUV. Neither of us is big on development of mountain towns, although that wasn't something I'd pass along to the Shavano Chamber of Commerce.

Sylvano's was located in a block of stores in the newer section of Geary. As the town had developed, the more recent businesses had set up a few miles from the vintage main street. I didn't know if that was to escape possible restrictions on changing historic buildings or because stores like Sylvano's didn't want to be associated with the older and decidedly more funky parts of town.

Sylvano's building was one of those somewhat annoying conglomerations of "vintage" and new, sort of an ersatz antique. Inside there were several refrigerated display cases, along with shelves full of boutique pastas and chocolates. I saw canned fish from a variety of locations and some Calabrian chili paste that I might have bought if it had been a few dollars cheaper.

"No beer?" I murmured. Hard to believe a chichi grocery in Colorado didn't stock the most obscure IPA. Nate gestured toward the rear of the store, and I saw a separate entrance for their beer and wine store.

"Can I help you?" someone said brightly, and a very cheerful teenager stepped from behind the cash register. Her name tag read *Katie.*

"We're just looking," I said. "Trying to choose something for dinner."

"Oh, well, we've got our deli over there, with a selection of smoked meats and cheeses. And we've got prepared food on the other side. Lots of things to choose from." She gestured toward a couple of the refrigerated cases.

"Thanks," I said. "We'll check it out." She was probably a good person to ask about Sara, except I couldn't think of any way of introducing the subject without sounding ghoulish. Nate prowled the refrigerated cases, checking out the charcuterie. We served a lot of it for hors d'oeuvres, but we mostly bought it from the café's suppliers. And from Marcus. I hoped we didn't have to change that.

Sylvano's charcuterie wasn't particularly unique, maybe a step up from City Market, but not what I'd expect from a gourmet market. I switched to the prepared food shelves. Out of habit, I checked the jam selection. Mostly upscale national brands. I didn't see anybody local, which meant I should probably make a pitch to Sylvano's. I'd done it at a couple of gourmet stores in the area and they took a few jars a month. I figured every little bit helped.

They had a larger supply of honey, but local honey was something people appreciated. I saw a few jars from the big Colorado honey producers, along with a couple of jars that said *Mt. Oxford Honey*, along with a familiar mountain silhouette. Mt. Oxford is the mountain that looms over Shavano, but I'd never seen the label before. I picked up one of the jars, searching for a location. It had the bright red and blue "Made in Colorado" sticker, but no other location that I could see.

I turned back to Katie, who was watching me a little anxiously. "Where does this honey come from?"

She pointed to the sticker. "It's from here. Colorado."

I drew on my diminished stores of patience. "Right. What city, though?"

Katie took the jar from my hands and studied it carefully. Then she shrugged. "Doesn't say. But it's Colorado." She set the jar on the shelf. "It might be Shavano. It's over by Mt. Oxford."

"I'm from Shavano, and I've never seen this kind of honey before."

"Oh, well...I can't really tell you anything about it. My dad would know, but he's not here right now."

"Your dad?"

"Fred Sylvano." Katie gave me a polite smile. "This is our place. Anything else I can help with?"

"Actually, yes," I said. "Who's your meat supplier?" As a way into a discussion of Sara, it was pretty weak, but I decided to go for it anyway.

Katie stared at me. It was safe to say nobody had ever asked her that before. "Our supplier? Um…Swan? Swanson? Something like that."

"Swain?" I asked. Corey Swain sold meat to the café. His stuff was decent, good café quality, but not gourmet.

Katie nodded vigorously. "That's it. Swain's. Are you in the business?"

"Sort of. I work with Robicheaux Catering." Katie's expression was blank, but there was no reason she should know about us. I decided to go for it. "Have you ever tried Marcus Jordan's charcuterie? He's in Shavano. It's first-rate stuff. We use it." I tried my most innocent smile. I wasn't lying. Marcus's stuff was top of the line.

Katie's cheeks turned pink. "N–no," she stammered. "We…use Swain's. It's fine. We put it in the salads and the charcuterie trays. Everybody likes it." Her eyes darted back and forth, as if she was looking for escape.

I decided it was cards on the table time. "I know Sara Jordan worked here once. She probably didn't have a good thing to say about Marcus, but his charcuterie is excellent."

"She…she didn't have much to say about him period," Katie said slowly. "Only that she was divorcing him."

Marcus was divorcing her, but maybe that was too fine a point to bring up. "You knew Sara?"

"Oh, yeah." Katie's shoulders hunched. "I worked

with her."

"I knew her some. I'm sorry you lost a friend."

"She wasn't my friend. I just worked with her." Katie's shoulders stayed hunched, but her expression was fierce.

"Oh." I tried to think of something else to say and came up dry. Clearly, Sara hadn't endeared herself to her fellow employees.

Katie sighed. "She was okay, I guess. Just sort of know it all."

"Not the easiest person to get along with."

"Nope."

"Hey." Nate appeared at my elbow. "How about some cold pasta salad and a baguette? It looks delicious."

I glanced at him, then back at Katie. "This is Nate Robicheaux. He runs Robicheaux Catering in Shavano. Nate, this is Katie Sylvano. Her family owns the shop."

"Nice to meet you, Katie." Nate flashed her one of his more charming smiles, known to melt matrons at twenty paces.

Katie wasn't a matron, but she wasn't immune. "Likewise. How much pasta salad would you like? I can get it for you. You're right—it's really good."

"We need enough for the two of us with leftovers," Nate said. He and Katie headed over to the deli case to spoon up enough pasta salad to take care of us and possibly Herman, although I wasn't sure how pasta would fit into his diet.

As I watched Katie, though, I remembered what Bridget had said. Sara had dated the manager of Sylvano's, and he'd dropped her. I wondered if Katie's dad was the manager in question. If he was, that might explain Katie's lack of enthusiasm for Sara.

Or Sara might have earned that lack of enthusiasm all on her own. She definitely had the skills to do that.

Chapter 18

The pasta salad was indeed good—the dressing was light and didn't overwhelm the vegetables, and the salami and mozzarella had both been chopped fine enough that they blended rather than elbowing the other ingredients to the side. "Wonder who does their cooking?" Nate mused.

"Probably they do. Katie said they did the salads." I took another bite of my salad. "Have you ever heard of Mt. Oxford Honey?"

Nate frowned. "No. Is it local?"

"I don't know. They were selling some, but the jars didn't have any location. Just 'Made in Colorado.'"

"Could be anywhere, then. They don't have to actually be from Shavano. They probably just like the connection to the mountains. Hell, they could be made down on the flats somewhere."

"Maybe. Mt. Oxford isn't like Pikes Peak, though. I don't know how many people recognize it or know where it is."

"All the better if they're trying to cover up where they're really doing the harvesting. Just some mountain somewhere—the average person isn't going to check it out." Nate sighed, leaning back with his glass of wine. It had been a long day for both of us.

"How's the birthday party coming? Are we ready?"

"Oh, hell, yeah. They just wanted spaghetti

primavera and the fixings, salad, and garlic bread. That's dead easy—particularly at this time of year when everything's fresh. We'll do crudités and dip, along with charcuterie, for apps. Coco's doing the cake."

"Where are you getting the bread?"

"Baguettes from Bianca. We'll add the garlic."

Which reminded me Susa and I were having a conversation with Bianca about Sara tomorrow. "Charcuterie from Marcus?"

Nate nodded. "He's even getting me some fresh goat cheese. He's got a supplier in Antero."

I took a final bite of pasta salad. "I hope this whole thing is settled soon. Marcus needs to be cleared so he can be up and running full steam again. I don't want to lose him."

"Me, either. He's made our business better."

To say nothing of making Bianca happier. His mom would be devastated if Marcus had to go to the Front Range because he couldn't keep his shop open. She might even go with him, which would be devastating for Shavano given that everybody bought her bread.

And then there was Coco. I doubted if she'd be devastated if Marcus moved elsewhere, but she wouldn't be happy.

The next day I worked on my apricot preserves with thyme. It was a relatively easy recipe, although the ingredients had to sit for a while and macerate. The result was a lovely jar of preserves, though—a beautiful pinkish orange with flecks of green, and a taste like sunshine with a slight tang of lemon.

I decided to take a jar along for Bianca, although it needed to set up a bit longer. I figured she could study it before she ate it, and maybe it would calm her soul.

I set the jar on the table in Bianca's back room after Susa and I got there. She'd told us to go on in and have a seat—she was still getting the baking set up for tomorrow morning. Susa studied the apricot preserves dolefully. "You didn't bring two?"

"It's not done yet. Bianca will have to let it sit."

"I would have let it sit."

"You'd have let what sit?" Bianca wiped her hands on a cloth. She looked a little more frazzled than usual, with a flour-dusted apron and wisps of gray hair escaping from her ballcap.

"I brought you some apricot thyme preserves, but I just finished it this afternoon. You need to let it sit for a day or so before you try it."

Bianca squinted at the jar. "Luscious. Thanks." She turned away to pick up a teapot and set it on the table along with three mugs.

That lukewarm response wasn't like her. She was one of my biggest boosters normally. But I guessed she had other things on her mind just then.

"How's Marcus?" Susa asked. Apparently, she'd reached the same conclusion I had.

"Okay. Worried about his business, which is definitely down by a bit. I don't think he's hurting yet, but he may be soon."

She sat down at the table with us, pushing a stainless-steel bowl to the middle of the table along with some napkins. "The tea's brewing. Help yourselves. Dinner rolls that didn't make the cut."

They looked great to me, but they weren't up to Bianca's standards. Susa tore one into pieces and popped one into her mouth. "Terrific," she mumbled around the bite.

"Like I said on the phone, we need to talk to you about Sara. About her background, what kind of person she was. I knew her a little, but Susa didn't know her at all. And neither of us know anything about her life before she landed in Shavano." I munched on a bite of dinner roll. It was lovely—buttery and light—but maybe a little overdone on the bottom.

Bianca rubbed her eyes. She looked tired, also older than she had before this mess had landed on her doorstep. "I don't know much about her family myself. Her parents were divorced; I know that much. She's from western Nebraska, but I'm not sure where. She took off for Denver as soon as she graduated from high school. I guess her hometown didn't meet her exacting standards for excitement."

"What did she do when she got here? Go to school?"

Bianca shook her head. "She may have picked up some community college courses, but she wasn't interested in getting a degree. She was going for bright lights and fast times."

Susa raised an eyebrow. "In Denver?"

Bianca sighed. "She'd probably have been better off in Los Angeles or Chicago. Denver's got lots of bright lights, but it's not the wicked city. Everybody's too busy buying hiking gear."

"What did Marcus do on the Front Range?" Susa leaned forward to pour the three of us some tea.

"He had a job in Boulder, working for Damon Sundell at his place."

Susa and I exchanged glances. "The guy who was on that chef competition show?"

Bianca nodded. "Marcus got his start as a butcher at his restaurant. They've got a small deli on the side, and Marcus made a lot of the meats they sold. It was a great beginning. Took him well beyond what he'd learned apprenticing."

"Was Sara working in the kitchen, too?" I couldn't envision Sara working for someone as high powered as Damon Sundell. Actually, so far as I knew, Sara had never done anything at Jordan's Meats beyond running the front counter.

"She waited tables there for a while. She worked at a lot of restaurants in the Boulder area. She and Marcus were both part of the restaurant scene in Boulder—that's how they met."

"How long had they been married?" Susa asked.

Bianca paused, thinking. "Three years? Thereabouts anyway."

"Marcus opened his store last year, didn't he?" I knew I'd started buying stuff there within a year or so. It was new enough to still get a lot of word of mouth from people like me.

"He opened it a year or so after they got married. Which didn't make Sara happy. She wanted him to go on working at Sundell's place. It was a bigger splash—Sundell gets a lot of publicity. Whenever celebrities show up in Boulder, they go to Sundell's."

"But he'd just be an employee there. Coming here and opening his shop meant he was in charge." That seemed pretty straightforward to me. Why wouldn't Sara understand?

"It did. But he took on a lot of debt to do it, even with backers. They moved into my old place where I lived when I was married to Pat. It's pretty small, and not what you'd call upscale. Sara wasn't happy."

Sara wasn't happy most of the time I'd been around her. "Why did she come here if she was so bitter about it?"

"She loved him. Or anyway, she said she loved him. That may have been true at the beginning. But she didn't know then how long it would take for them to get on a solid footing financially. Marcus was putting everything into the shop, the way you do when you're starting out, and he was spending most of his time working there. Sara began to get fed up."

"Did they try any counseling?" Susa asked.

"Not that I know of. Probably should have—that might have gotten Sara to back off. But I guess she decided to find someone else to get attached to. Someone who'd be her ticket out of Shavano. She chose Alan Adamo, which shows how faulty her judgment was."

The results of Sara's affair with Adamo had been far-reaching and included sending Nate to the hospital and almost getting me killed. I wasn't inclined to be too forgiving. "I'd say her judgment was really, really faulty on that one."

"So did she ever settle into Shavano? Make friends? Get a support network going?" Susa was more generous than I was, or more willing to ask about Sara's day-to-day life.

"If she had friends, I didn't know them," Bianca said. "She never found much about the town that made her happy, not even Marcus. It's a lot of work, getting a new business up and running. I don't think she ever wanted to put in the time. To tell you the truth, I think she came up here hoping Marcus would fail so that she could convince him to go back to the Front Range. Then when he started to make it, when his hard work paid off, she was pissed. She knew she'd never get him to leave if the shop was succeeding. And it was, bit by bit."

"The success didn't bring her around?"

"Not really. Even if she hadn't gotten mixed up with Adamo, I think she'd still have left. This just wasn't her dream. And she wasn't interested in Marcus's."

We all sat staring off into the gathering dusk outside the bakery windows. Sara had been tough to like, and she'd come here for all the wrong reasons. But she still didn't deserve to get killed, particularly not in a way that was designed to hurt Marcus.

"Anything else?" Bianca asked.

"What about the divorce? Were they any closer to figuring out how to divide everything?" I'd heard bits and pieces about their fights over property settlement, but I didn't know how accurate they were.

Bianca grimaced. "Sara wanted to wipe everything out. She wanted Marcus to sell the business so she could take half. He wasn't about to do that. They were negotiating on how much she was owed, how much he'd have to pay her. She'd done some work on the business, and she had some investment that he was willing to pay back. They were arguing over just how much that would be."

"Would she have been trying to hook up with someone else, get a bigger payout?" Susa raised her eyebrows. I wouldn't have put it quite that flatly, but it was something I wondered about.

Bianca looked like she'd tasted something sour.

"You're probably asking the wrong person about that. I didn't like her. I didn't have a high opinion of her ethics or what she was likely to do. So yeah, I could believe she'd be searching for another sucker to take her on. I have no idea whether she found anybody, but I can believe she was searching."

I thought about asking Bianca if she knew the owner of Sylvano's, but I couldn't see any point in starting rumors. Or rather, treating Bridget's rumors as if they were fact. "Thanks, Bianca. If you think of anybody else we should talk to about Sara, give me a call."

Bianca stared down at her hands. "There's Marcus, but I'd rather you didn't talk to him. He's had it with the police. They've got no proof he did anything, but they keep questioning him. I guess he's the only person who seems like a logical suspect."

"We won't talk to him. I promise." Among other things, I couldn't think of anything I could ask Marcus without feeling like a complete shit. I started to stand.

"Have you turned up anything yet?" Bianca asked.

I dropped my butt into the chair. "Just bits and pieces. There were rumors that Sara was dating the manager at Sylvano's, but I guess they broke up. She claimed she was their meat buyer, but that wasn't true. She was counter help, like she was at the shop."

"Other people confirmed what you said," Susa added. "She didn't have many friends, and she had a reputation for being cranky."

"Did she still have the job at Sylvano's even if she wasn't dating the manager?"

I thought about what Katie had said. "I think so. I talked to someone who worked with her, and she didn't mention anything about Sara quitting. Or being fired."

"Was she working that Saturday?"

Now there was an interesting question, and one I had no idea how to answer. Fowler would probably know, but there was no way he'd share. "I don't know. All I know is she was killed somewhere else and dumped in the trees below Sawmill. If she was working, she must have left for some reason."

"Who is the manager at Sylvano's anyway?" Susa asked.

"I'm guessing it's the owner, another Sylvano."

"Ted Sylvano, probably. He used to run the Coffee Spot before they opened Sylvano's." Bianca shrugged. "Pat used to hang out there. I'd bring Marcus over to spend time with his dad, so Marcus knows them, too."

That served to remind me just how long Bianca and her family had lived in Shavano. They were pioneers, and the rest of us were late comers.

"I'll let you know if anything else turns up," I said. But deep down I figured Fowler had a better chance of coming up with something significant than we did.

Out on the street again, Susa bit her lip. "This really stinks. I don't believe Marcus had anything to do with what happened to Sara, but if they don't find her killer, he'll be stuck with everybody's suspicions."

"Maybe we'll find something," I said, but even I didn't believe that.

"We'll try," Susa said. "I'll do my best to turn up whatever I can on Sara. But I don't believe we're going to be able to crack this one. Which pisses me off."

It pissed me off, too. But that didn't make it any easier. "Have you got a minute to talk about what we've got so far?"

"Sure. Let's go over to Dirty Pete's and have some nachos or something."

I wasn't really hungry after Bianca's dinner rolls, but Dirty Pete's was a good place to sit and ruminate. Susa ordered a beer, but I stuck to iced tea since I had to drive to the farm. "So what's your sense of Sara after all we've dug up?" Which admittedly wasn't much.

"I didn't know her, but to know her definitely wasn't to love her." Susa settled back in her chair. "She strikes me as one of those people who always feels like the universe owes her something. Like she should succeed at whatever it is she's trying just because she's Sara."

"I'd say that's true. But she also comes across as someone who's willing to go out and get what she wants regardless. If the universe doesn't pony up, she'll find another way to get ahead."

"So if that's the kind of person she was, what was she up to?"

That was the million-dollar question. "She couldn't rely on the divorce to get her where she wanted to go, that's for sure. No judge in her right mind would require Marcus to sell out so that Sara could have a payday. And frankly, I don't think the shop would bring all that much money even if he sold out. They'd have to pay off their debts, and there might not be much after that. She'd get something out of it, but probably not the payout she'd be hoping for."

"So she'd be searching for something else, some other way to cash out. A man, maybe?"

"She tried that with Adamo, so she might have tried it again. Of course, it didn't work out that well with him."

"Still, she might see it as the easiest way out."

"Maybe. She dated her boss, so maybe that was one route she was pursuing."

"Unsuccessfully." Susa dipped a chip in the bowl of salsa. "What do you mean *one route*? What else was she doing?"

"I don't know. But she'd been involved in a blackmail scheme before. Maybe she thought that might be another possibility." Sara had been one of the people being blackmailed in that scheme, but she'd also connected with the person who'd murdered the blackmailer, my cousin as it turned out.

Susa narrowed her eyes. "You've got nothing in the way of proof here, do you?"

"Nope. Not even anybody to nominate as the blackmailee. But if there's one thing we know about Sara, it's that she wasn't shy about going after what she wanted. And something she did pissed off someone so much they killed her." I munched on a tortilla chip.

"There is that," Susa said slowly. "It would make sense that Sara was pressing somebody about something. And I guess, given that she was trying to get some kind of payoff that would get her out of Shavano, blackmail also makes a certain amount of sense. Somebody wanted to get rid of her, and blackmail would make her expendable from the point of view of the guy she was blackmailing. So you're ruling out a sudden fit of passion here?"

I shrugged. "Somebody went to the trouble of killing her elsewhere and then transporting the body to the woods below Sawmill, where she'd be more likely to be connected to Marcus. That's not passion. That's calculation."

Susa shivered. "That's creepy. Believable, but creepy. It's also way out of our competence to find."

"True. Fowler can track down the people Sara had relationships with, but nobody's going to share information with a couple of random nosy women. I just hope Fowler's doing that instead of focusing exclusively on Marcus."

Susa looked uncomfortable, and I felt a little bad about casting even random aspersions on Fowler. "He's smart. And he's good at his job. If the murderer can be found, I believe Ethan will find him."

"I agree with you," I said. Judging from her expression, that idea caught Susa by surprise. "The problem comes with the first part of that statement. 'If the murderer can be found.' I hope he can be, but I worry he might get lucky and slip away."

"Always possible," Susa said glumly. "But I might drop the blackmailer theory in front of Ethan sometime, just to see how he reacts."

I'd guess Fowler's reaction would be to tell us to butt out of his investigation, something he'd told us about other investigations in the past. But floating the idea by him couldn't hurt.

In fact, for once I felt like leaving things to Fowler and crossing my fingers.

Chapter 19

Of all the events we worked at Robicheaux Catering, birthday parties ranked near the top for me in terms of enjoyment. We didn't do kids' parties, since they tended to be nightmares. But we did a good business in family parties, the kind of parties where everybody from matriarchs to newborns showed up, and where people were most likely happy they'd come.

The birthday party we were doing this Friday was at one of the farms outside town, although I didn't know the family who lived there. They were relative newcomers, and they specialized in growing hops for the artisan brewers in the state and surrounding areas. I knew squat about hops farming, but I knew it was in demand. I was curious to see what kind of place they had.

By the time we got there, though, it was moving toward evening. All I could see were the curving poles and wires stretching along the hop vines, of which there were quite a few. The house at the end of the drive was a spacious single-story that sprawled across the yard. It didn't have a log façade, but the weathered wood trim along the fieldstone walls screamed *western ranch style.*

Also money. Apparently hops paid well. Or maybe they'd started out rich and moved into farming, a business almost guaranteed to reduce any size fortune.

"How many people tonight?" I asked.

"Orders for thirty-five," Nate said. "I don't know if that many will show up, though. We're doing it buffet, except for the cake that we'll bring in at the end."

"Who's the wait staff?"

"Donnell. And Dave Tresher, who's also tending bar. We'll be hopping."

"Is Dan here?" He'd offered to help out in the kitchen sometimes with the bigger events.

Nate shook his head. "He was booked. Just you and me, babe." It might have been my imagination, but he seemed a little annoyed about Dan not being around. On the other hand, he'd known going in that Dan's time was limited.

"We can do it," I said, slipping into cheerleader mode. We could, but it was going to be a push. I sneezed a couple of times, then dug a tissue out of my purse.

"You okay?" Nate asked.

"Sure. Just a little cold." Knock wood.

A push was exactly what the evening turned out to be. The crowd fulfilled all my requirements—matriarchs to newborns and their sibs. The matriarch was actually the birthday girl, but she looked like she'd very much prefer to be in the kitchen rather than seated at the dining room table. She kept trying to buttonhole Nate to ask him about recipes and prep time. He kept his polite smile in place, but when he came to the kitchen he seemed harried.

The family had set up multiple tables around the living room and dining room, which kept Donnell and Dave hopping to clear dishes and bring refills. We were hopping in the kitchen, too. The buffet table used hot trays, which meant warming the food in the kitchen and then refilling the trays as they began to empty. The primavera sauce wasn't that tough to keep going, but the spaghetti took careful planning. We didn't want it to be soggy, but we also didn't want the trays to run empty. We were cooking the pasta a little short of al dente, then keeping it warm in the oven with a generous serving of pasta water in hopes it wouldn't go much beyond the ideal point of doneness.

All in all, it was one of those evenings where we were way too busy to worry about anything except keeping everybody fed. I felt a little stopped up and headachy, but I ignored it. When it was finally time for Nate and Dave to carry the cake into the dining room, I didn't even try to follow them. It was Coco's cake. It would be a smash. And I desperately wanted to sit down for a few minutes before I started cleanup.

As the evening had worn on, I'd begun to suspect that my *little cold* was bigger than that. My throat felt scratchy now and my sinuses had begun to ache. I'd been working too hard to let myself feel it, but once I sat down my head began to throb, and the party noise came and went.

This was definitely not good. I couldn't be sick when the farmers market was tomorrow. I had jam to sell, dammit.

Finally, I pushed myself to my feet and started cleaning up. We'd already run a couple of loads through the dishwasher, but I loaded one more then started rinsing our pots and the warming trays. We'd take them back to the café and Tres, the café's dishwasher and janitor, could do the final wash, but it made things easier if I got the first layer of gunk out before we left.

Nate returned a few minutes later, smiling. "Cake was a hit. Donnell's doing the last coffee run. Dessert plates should be coming down in a few minutes."

"Great. We're close to done down here." I took a minute to lean on the sink, closing my eyes as my head throbbed again. I'd be taking some cold medicine as soon as we got to the cabin.

"You don't look so good. Is it still that 'little cold'?" Nate stepped closer and rested his hand on my arm.

"I think I'm coming down with something a bit bigger," I mumbled. "But I'll make it until we're done here."

"Why don't you sit down for a while? I can take care of the trays."

I shook my head, which turned out to be a bad idea, given how stopped up I was. "I can do it. It's better if I keep working." Largely because if I stopped, I might not be able to start again.

Somehow I managed to get all the trays rinsed and into the boxes we used to carry them. Nate and Donnell loaded the dessert dishes into the dishwasher and got it going. The owner of the house, who looked about as much like a farmer as I look like Lady Gaga, gave us a bonus that Nate divided with Donnell and Dave.

And we started down the road. I settled back against the seat, closing my eyes for a moment, only to discover I'd slept through our stop at the café. "Sorry," I said when Nate returned. Then I sneezed a couple of times for emphasis.

"Not your fault," he said. "I took care of it. Go to sleep. You probably need it."

I did need it, although my occasional sneezing kept me awake most of the way back. When we got to the farm, Nate helped me out of the SUV and into the cabin. I sank down on the couch, gathering my energy together to get ready for bed, but then Nate leaned over me, handing me something warm in a glass.

"What is it?"

"Whiskey and lemon and hot water. It'll help clear your sinuses." He took a breath as I swallowed warm whiskey and lemon—heaven. "You can't do the farmers market tomorrow, babe."

I stared up at him. "I have to. I've got a whole bunch of jam to sell."

"I'll do it. I know the prices and the jams. Anything I don't know, Beck can show me."

I started to shake my head then remembered it wasn't a good thing to do. "I can do it. Maybe I'll be able to sleep this off. I could be recovered by tomorrow."

Nate sighed. "You shouldn't have to sleep it off. You need to get some rest so you can be on your feet next week. I'll call Mike to let him know what's up. Maybe Dolce could come along with Carmen and Donnie to help out."

He looked very determined, and as I thought about it, I was inclined to let him have his way. I felt wretched, even after the whiskey and lemon, and I doubted I'd feel that much better by tomorrow morning. "Aren't you supposed to work lunch at the café?"

"Bobby and Marigold can handle it. I was just going to sleep in tomorrow, but I can catch up on Sunday."

I tried to think of any other arguments that might

make a difference, but my brain was too fuzzy to come up with much. "Okay. If you're sure. You can always call me if there are any problems."

"I'm sure. And there won't be any problems. Now go take a bunch of ibuprofen and cold meds. And get some sleep."

And so I did. As I was brushing my teeth, I heard Nate's voice as he talked to someone, probably Uncle Mike. I hoped Uncle Mike didn't take over the booth since he spent more time policing the sample bowls than selling jam, but I was in the *beggars can't be choosers* category by that point.

I washed my face and swallowed down a major slug of nighttime cold medicine then limped toward the bedroom, pausing long enough to check in with Nate in the living room. "Everything okay?"

He nodded. "Mike and I will switch off in the booth and Dolce's coming in to help. We should have more than enough people working." He gestured toward the boxes stacked next to the front door. "Is this everything to go tomorrow?"

"Yeah, along with what I already loaded into the truck." I'd started feeling tired while I'd been lifting boxes. Probably an early sign that I was fading.

"Okay, I'll get it all loaded tomorrow." Nate stepped up to kiss my forehead. "I'll sleep in the guest room tonight so you can stretch out. Don't set your alarm."

"Don't worry," I said. "I'm going to go lose consciousness."

Nate didn't need to sleep in a separate room, but I was glad he did. I didn't know how much thrashing about I'd do, plus I might be contagious. Of course, if I was, he'd probably already been thoroughly exposed. I only hoped I hadn't been Typhoid Mary to the birthday party.

The cold medicine worked pretty well, although I was up and down during the night. I had some feverish dreams, and by the time I woke up for good, my chest was hurting, too. All in all, I wasn't in good shape, and I was more than grateful that Nate and crew had taken over for me. The idea of standing up in my booth for four hours was close to torture.

When I finally dragged myself out of bed, I was too late to say goodbye to Nate and Uncle Mike. I tottered into the kitchen, checking out the window to see if anyone was still around, but I didn't see a soul. Nate had taken my truck, and Uncle Mike's van was missing, which meant Donnie and Carmen had taken a load of peaches and raspberries into town. I turned toward their house, but I didn't see any signs of people. Probably Dolce had gone with them to help out either with her parents' booth or mine.

There weren't many people around the farm on Saturdays during farmers market season. Sometimes Uncle Mike stayed home, but more often he came in with Carmen and Donnie to keep an eye on what was selling best. I knew that week he'd had orders for several flats of peaches, and he liked to be on hand when the customers showed up to make sure they were happy. The boxes I'd stacked next to the door were all gone, and I trusted Nate to know how to set things up in the booth. He'd seen me do it often enough, and even if he forgot some of the details, Beck and probably Dolce would be there to straighten him out.

The only sign of life at the main house was

Herman wandering around the yard behind the fence. He looked bored and a little doleful. I figured I could go up and bring him to the cabin after I finished breakfast.

I considered spending the morning in bed, but that had less appeal than you might think. What I actually wanted to do was pour myself a cup of tea and sit down to read the morning news. I figured I'd spend the day gobbling cold medicine and hot lemon tea in the probably vain hope that my condition wouldn't get any worse. But I preferred to do that in sweatpants and a T-shirt rather than pajamas. Granted, it wasn't much of a step up, but it felt like I was making an effort.

I'd just settled in with my first cup of tea and a bowl of oatmeal, which was a good thing for a scratchy throat, when I heard barking. At first, I didn't recognize the dog. It definitely wasn't Herman, and I didn't think it was Lulabelle either. It took me a minute to remember—Duke, of course. It was his kind of yapping.

Normally, I might have stepped out the door and yelled for Duke to quiet down, but I knew my voice wasn't up to it right then. I figured he'd quiet down on his own soon, but I was wrong about that. The more Duke yapped, the more the other dogs became unhappy, too. I heard Lulabelle's unmistakable bay and Herman's unhappy *woof.* That struck me as unusual. Normally, Duke could bark himself into a coma and the other dogs would ignore him.

Something was stirring them up.

My first thought was a bear. We do get them out here, and this had been a particularly bad year for bear invasions. Just the previous week a bear had managed to open the door to one of the suburban homes near Mt.

Oxford and done several hundred dollars' worth of damage while searching for a little snack. Besides bears, we also got the inevitable coyotes and even the occasional moose. Of the three, the moose was probably the most problematic, considering their perpetual bad attitude, but all of them could do some damage to the dogs.

I pushed myself up from the breakfast table, much as I wanted to stay right where I was, and found my running shoes. Then I grabbed my rifle.

Yeah, I have a rifle. Not that I know all that much about shooting. It was my dad's single-shot .22 that he used mostly for target practice. I'd shot a few beer cans with it over the years, but I've never done much more than that. Uncle Mike referred to it as "one step up from a BB gun," and it wasn't much in the way of protection. But I knew how to load and unload it, and I kept it cleaned and oiled, just as my dad had done. It wouldn't be much defense against a bear or a moose, but it would make some noise and maybe encourage them to do some thinking before they decided to charge me or the dogs.

I made sure the rifle was loaded before I started out and put a few bullets in my pocket. That's the thing about a single-shot: you have to reload it each time you shoot, but I hoped it wouldn't come to that. I stepped out on the front porch, scanning the immediate area around the cabin. No bears or moose that I could see, but Herman redoubled his barking when he saw me.

"Settle down," I croaked, not that he could hear me say anything at all with my voice mostly missing.

Herman added hopping up against the fence in his efforts to get my attention. I thought about letting him out but decided against it. If it really was a bear, I'd be so worried about what Herman might do that I might not keep my attention on the bear, where it would very much need to be concentrated.

There didn't seem to be anything threatening around the main house or the cabin, so I started walking toward Carmen and Donnie's house. Given Duke's almost hysterical yapping and Lulabelle's regular baying, it was a better bet than our place.

My head was throbbing lightly in time with my footsteps, reminding me that I wasn't in shape to take this on. But whether I was or not, I was committed. Even if I ended up running to my cabin and calling the cops for help, I'd at least have some idea of what was out there causing all this ruckus.

As I neared the house, Lulabelle trotted toward the gate, clearly glad to see somebody she recognized even if I wasn't one of her main sources of reassurance. Duke was nowhere to be seen, although I could certainly hear him clearly. Both of them had been shut into the small yard near the house rather than being free to wander the whole area.

I stepped to the gate, scanning the yard for wildlife, but all I could see was Lulabelle. Somewhere closer to the house Duke was still yapping hysterically. I guessed he didn't have enough sense to stay away from whatever was causing his excitement, which meant sooner or later he was going to have a very grievous accident.

And then I heard a man yell, "For Christ's sake shut up, you little runt!"

It wasn't Donnie, and it wasn't Uncle Mike, which eliminated the only two men who could be there legitimately. The rifle felt suddenly heavy in my hands. It was one thing to fire in the air to get a bear to run, and another thing to point a gun at somebody and threaten them with dire consequences.

I took a breath and started moving again toward the sound of Duke's yapping. When I was close enough to see the first beehive, I braced the rifle on my shoulder in firing position. As if I was capable of firing that rifle at another human being.

Maybe I wasn't, but whoever had just yelled at Duke didn't know that. I took a deep breath and stepped forward as quietly as I could. Duke was still yapping, but then I heard a heavy thud and his barks turned to high-pitched whining. *Okay, that's it, that's enough.* Duke might be thoroughly aggravating, but you didn't kick animals, even if they annoyed the hell out of you.

"Hold it," I said flatly and stepped forward toward the line of hives.

And saw Dan Griffin standing next to a partially disassembled beehive that had been knocked over.

Chapter 20

"What the fuck are you doing here?" Dan blurted. He was wearing long leather gloves that were like the ones Uncle Mike used when he was grilling. He had a utility cart pulled up beside him.

"I was about to ask you the same thing." I kept my rifle on my shoulder, although the chances of me shooting Dan on purpose were vanishingly small. I was hoping he didn't know that, though. "Put your hands up."

Dan put his hands in the air, squinting at me. "You're supposed to be at the farmers market with everybody else."

"And you're supposed to be cooking for somebody not us. Yet here we are." I took a breath, taking a tighter grip on the rifle. "Did you steal all the other hives, too?"

Dan's jaw firmed. "We're not having this conversation."

We stared at each other for another moment while I tried to figure out what the hell to do next. I needed to tie him up or something, but if I tried to do that, I'd have to put down the rifle, which was currently my only means of keeping him around.

Apparently, Dan had also figured out my dilemma. He began backing away from me slowly, hands still raised in the air. "I'm leaving now. No harm done. I don't think you'll shoot me, Roxy. That's not your style."

"You broke into Carmen's beehives, you son of a bitch. You expect me to just let you walk off?" Anger was replacing shock, and the reality that Dan was a crook and the fact that his crookedness might hurt Nate by association was making that anger a lot hotter than it could have been.

Dan's lips edged up in a sort of smile. "You know, I think you really do want to shoot me, Rox. But I don't think you will. I may be wrong about that. I guess we'll see." One more smirk, and he took off, sprinting toward the fence a lot faster than I'd anticipated.

I fired the rifle. It sort of took me by surprise since I hadn't intended to. I hadn't aimed, and the rifle wasn't pointing at him. The bullet whizzed through the branches of a blue spruce. Dan didn't pause. When he got to the fence, he took off over it, half-climbing and half-jumping. He was gone before I could get another bullet out of my pocket and loaded into the rifle, not that I would have had any better luck with a second bullet. A minute later I heard the sound of his truck rattling down the dirt road that led to the county highway.

I wanted to scream. I wanted to yell. I wanted to jump up and down in frustration. But I had a bad cold and I was standing next to a disassembled beehive where the bees were not happy. If ever there was a time for a strategic retreat, this was it.

I turned to my cabin at a slow trot, holding the rifle carefully at my side. It was supposed to be empty, but it would be just my luck to trip and shoot myself. Inside, I tried to decide who to call first, but the cops had priority. I could have called 911, but I decided to go with Fowler first since it was kind of an involved story and the 911 operator might think I was nuts. Fortunately for me, he was in his office even though it was Saturday.

"What's the problem, Roxy?" He sounded a little annoyed and more than a little tired of hearing from me.

"I'm here by myself today because I've got a bad cold. About fifteen minutes ago the dogs started making a racket and I went to see what was bothering them. I found Dan Griffin trying to steal one of Carmen's beehives. He ran off before I could do anything." I paused to take a breath. I'd probably have to explain about the rifle at some point, but it didn't seem like something I needed to include in my first report.

There was a beat of silence on Fowler's end, and then he came back again. "All right. Don't touch anything. We'll be there in twenty minutes or so."

I wasn't sure why he didn't want things touched, but I wasn't about to do anything like that myself, particularly when the bees had sounded very irritated the last time I'd been out there. "Can I call Carmen and Donnie? They're at the farmers market, but they might like to be here, too."

Fowler sounded resigned. "Yeah, sure. As long as nobody disturbs anything, you can call them."

There was a slight problem with that since I didn't have Carmen's cell number, although I had Dolce's. I figured I'd call Uncle Mike first and let him pass on the message.

Uncle Mike was, predictably, outraged. And when he's outraged, he tends to take it out on anyone within range. "You went running out there without knowing what the problem was? Hell, Roxy, it could have been a bear or something."

"I did think of that," I said mildly. "I took the rifle."

"Terrific," Uncle Mike growled. "Why not take the super-spraying water gun while you're at it?"

"Will you just tell Carmen and Donnie? They might like to be around when Fowler gets here. Plus somebody's going to need to put that beehive back together. For all I know the bees are getting ready to leave."

"All right, all right." Uncle Mike paused. "Are you okay? That cold any worse?"

I took a quick inventory. I still had a scratchy throat and headache, but overall I was no worse for wear. "I'm okay. But I'm going to bed when this is all over."

Uncle Mike sighed. "Do you want me to tell Nate, or are you going to call him?"

"I'll call him. You tell Carmen and Donnie."

Telling Nate was going to be tough, since it meant we were out an assistant before our big corporate do next week, and that former assistant might actually bring down some crap on Robicheaux Catering. I decided to chicken out for the moment. Instead, I texted him:

—*Call me when you get a chance. Something big has happened.*—

That seemed suitably mysterious. I went to the cabin and ran a brush through my hair. I didn't bother with makeup because I figured I might as well look as lousy as I felt. Maybe Fowler would take pity on me.

But probably not. As good as his word, Fowler and

another cop arrived a few minutes later. I showed them the place where I'd seen Dan. There were a lot more angry bees around the knocked over beehive now. I was pretty sure they were more interested in the hive than in us, but I wasn't ready to get any closer to see. Neither were Fowler and his helper.

"Donnie and Carmen should be on their way back," I explained. "They can probably put the hive back together so the bees settle down."

"Sounds like a good plan." Dan had left his utility cart behind along with some tools, maybe for transporting the beehive. Fowler gestured toward the area beyond the fence where his truck had been parked. "Go out there and see if he left anything else around here," he told the other cop.

I put a hand out to brace myself against a fencepost. Fowler peered at me and grimaced. "You look like death warmed over. Let's go to your place. You can tell me all of what happened."

I wasn't sure I'd tell him *all of what happened,* but sitting down sounded like a good idea. I slumped into one of the rockers on my front porch to watch for Carmen and Donnie while Fowler rested against the porch railing. "So you stayed home today."

I nodded. "I've got a bad cold." I sneezed by way of demonstration.

Fowler moved a couple of inches away from me. "What happened?"

"I was sort of dozing on the couch when I heard the dogs barking. Carmen's dogs started and then Herman picked it up. I figured something was getting them all stirred up, maybe a bear or a moose. So I grabbed my dad's rifle and went over there."

Fowler's eyes narrowed. "You own a rifle?"

"It was my dad's," I repeated. "I don't hunt." I reached inside the door and picked up the rifle where I'd leaned it against the wall. I'd figured Fowler would need to see it.

He took it from me and stared down at it for a long moment. "Single-shot .22."

"Yep."

"Pre-war." I noticed he didn't specify which war.

"I guess."

"Not much fire power."

I shrugged. "It is what it is. I figured it was better than nothing."

Fowler muttered something that sounded like "Barely."

I decided to ignore comments on my rifle. "Anyway, I walked over to Carmen and Donnie's place. The dogs were still making a racket and I heard somebody tell them to shut up. I went inside the fence and I saw Dan when I got to the beehives. He had on gloves and it looked like he'd started to take apart one of the hives. He had that utility cart there, too, maybe to haul the hive to his truck. I guess it's still there. The cart, I mean."

Fowler wrote a couple of notes. "Did he say anything?"

"He asked me what I was doing there because I was supposed to be at the farmers market. I asked him if he was the beehive thief, but he wouldn't tell me. He turned around after a minute and ran for the fence. I fired the rifle, but I wasn't aiming and the shot went into the trees."

Fowler paused. "Did you mean to hit him?"

I rubbed a hand across my feverish forehead. "I don't know. Probably not. I've never shot anything livelier than a beer can. But I was pissed that he got away so easy."

Fowler's cell phone rang. He pulled it from his pocket and turned away from me to have a very short conversation then put his phone in his pocket. "Griffin wasn't at his place when we got there to check."

"He'd have to be an idiot to go there." Dan was infuriating, but he wasn't an idiot.

"You never know. People don't always think things through."

Just then Donnie's pickup truck rolled down the drive, and Fowler pushed himself upright again. He turned to me one more time before he walked over to them. "Dan Griffin was at that barbecue at Sawmill Brewing, wasn't he?"

"He was grilling, along with Nate and Marcus. Why?"

"Just additional information. Go on inside and get some tea. We'll come get you if we need you."

I did as he suggested, settling down at the kitchen table with another cup of tea. And then I called Nate.

It was a tough conversation for more reasons than one. He was in my booth selling jam with Beck and Dolce, and he kept getting interrupted. "All right," I said finally, "give me a call when things slow down, and I can explain it more."

"Okay." He paused. "But you're all right?"

"I'm as well as I was when you left." I sighed. "Which means I still have this rotten cold, but nothing else."

"Go to bed," Nate said flatly. "We'll figure it all

out later."

"Yeah, okay." That sounded like very good advice, but I didn't think I could go to bed until Fowler was finished. I grabbed my tea and a book and curled up on the sofa where I'd hear anyone knocking.

Of course I fell asleep almost immediately, but I woke when someone hammered on the door. "Roxanne?" Carmen called. "You awake?"

"I am now." I stumbled to the door and let her in.

She put her hands on my shoulders and stared up at me. "You look awful."

"I feel worse," I said. "Did you get the bees back in their hive?"

Carmen pushed past me, turning toward the kitchen. "We got everything put together again. It'll be a while before we know if the hive will make it, but it probably will. The weather was warm and dry, and that makes a difference." She paused, surveying my kitchen. "You got any chicken broth?"

"In the freezer," I said. I don't make chicken broth because they make lots at the café, and Nate brings it home. Fortunately, he'd just restocked our supply.

"I'll make you some chicken soup," Carmen said. "You eat it for lunch and then have some more midafternoon. It'll help clear out your sinuses."

That sounded amazingly good. "Thanks."

She nodded at me. "Least I can do. If you hadn't gone up there, that pissant would probably have cleaned us out. Thanks for that."

"I heard Dan kick Duke. Is he okay?" I felt a little guilty for not checking on him, but too much had been happening.

Carmen shrugged. "Seemed okay to me. I gave him

a doggy treat for raising the alarm." She started pulling vegetables out of the refrigerator and got the broth from the freezer. Her thanks was the equivalent of getting a medal from Carmen, and I decided it was enough. Especially if it came with chicken soup.

I ate my soup after Carmen left, thankful that she hadn't decided to stick around and make sure I finished my bowl. I watched the police cars leave a few minutes later. Then I did what everybody had been telling me to do—I went into the bedroom and fell asleep almost as soon as my head hit the pillow.

I slept until I felt the bed dip slightly and opened my eyes to see Nate gazing down at me. He brushed the hair from my forehead and left his hand there for a moment. "No fever, at least not that I can feel."

"I don't think I've had much of one. Just a scratchy throat and a headache. Carmen made me some chicken soup for lunch."

"Probably better than cold medicine." He stroked my hair again. "We had a good day at the market. By which I mean you had a good day at the market."

"Thanks. For everything. I don't think I could have done it on my own."

"Probably not. And if you'd been there, you wouldn't have been around to stop Dan." He glanced out the window. "If I'd known that asshole was moonlighting as a hive thief, I'd have bounced him a long time ago instead of thinking I'd give him a chance to see if he could pull himself together."

"You were going to fire him?" That was news to me.

"I was thinking about it. When he was on his game, he was a decent cook. But when he felt like screwing off, he messed up a lot. I was thinking maybe I'd try to find somebody else. But I sure as hell wouldn't have fired him when we had a big cocktail party coming up in three days."

I closed my eyes. "That's going to be a mess. You'll need me to help you get everything ready."

"I'll need everybody to help get things ready. Definitely all hands on deck time. Here's hoping you're on your feet before Tuesday."

Right. I figured neither of us were excited about having me sneezing all over the meal prep before then.

"You should get some more sleep," Nate said. "I'm going into town to fill Mom in and do some prep for the party and for brunch tomorrow. I'll bring you some soup for supper."

"That sounds good," I mumbled, although my intake of liquids would probably keep me up all night peeing.

Nate kissed my forehead, then started toward the door.

"Fowler asked me if Dan had been around the barbecue the night Sara was killed." I'd just remembered that and the fact that it seemed sort of strange.

Nate paused. "Yeah? Did he say why?"

"Nope. Just wanted to know if he was at Sawmill Brewing with the rest of us. Did you get the idea the murder was connected to the beehive thefts?"

"Not until now," Nate said slowly. "I guess it figures that a town like Shavano doesn't get a lot of serious crime. If you have two major problems at around the same time, maybe it makes sense to think they're related."

"Maybe. But I don't think Dan had any better opportunity to kill Sara than Marcus did. They were both pretty busy at their grills."

"Yeah. Of course, Dan wasn't as busy as Marcus was. The plant-based burgers and sausage weren't moving as fast as the meat."

"And Dan came late, didn't he?" I bit my lip. The idea that Dan might be a murderer hadn't occurred to me before. And I wasn't sure I accepted it even now. I didn't want to think about it.

"Yeah." Nate looked troubled. "I don't know if he even knew Sara. I never saw them together."

"I imagine Fowler's going to check that out. If he's switched his focus to Dan, he'll need to find out how much contact the two had."

Nate stared down at the floor again. "Crap," he said, finally. "I don't want it to be Marcus, but I don't want it to be Dan either."

"It's not Marcus. But you're right. Dan doesn't strike me as much of a possibility as a murderer. He's more a minor thief type."

Nate sighed. "I still need to go to town. Take it easy. We'll figure stuff out when you're on your feet again." He walked down the hall, and a few moments later I heard the front door close.

I wasn't sure what we were going to be figuring out exactly. Probably how we were going to get all the food ready for the corporate cocktail party on Tuesday. I felt like that would be fairly easy to work out. It just meant a lot of work for a lot of people between now and then, including me. I'd probably turn Dolce loose on making jam at the beginning of the week, then catch up when the party was over.

Always assuming I was back to vertical again, preferably by tomorrow.

Figuring out whether Dan was a suspect in Sara's murder would be a lot tougher. Chances were he had means and opportunity. But I still couldn't see motive, unless both Dan and Sara had hidden lives none of us was aware of.

I was all for getting Marcus out of Fowler's sights as a prime suspect. But I wasn't sure how good a substitute Dan would be.

Mainly what I wanted to do was go to sleep. So that's what I did.

Chapter 21

On Sunday morning I woke up marginally better. I'd slept a lot more than I usually did, and I'd slurped up several bowls of nourishing soup. I'd also had a chocolate cupcake from Coco, which made me feel even better than the chicken soup.

Nate left early so he could work brunch and then shift over to prep for the party. Coco had agreed to stick around and help him with prep—even Marigold had agreed to come in on her day off. Surprisingly enough, Bobby said he'd help out too. Which meant they didn't need me, probably a good thing since I was still sneezing and wheezing and probably contagious.

Nate called me around one. "How are you?"

"Better. I think I'm through the worst of it. How's the prep coming?"

"It has its highs and lows," he said. "I've got lots of hands. Even Mom is pitching in when she's got a minute."

"What's the low?"

"I'm missing the halloumi that was supposed to be in yesterday's shipment from the cheese supplier. I'm going to have to scare some up somewhere, and maybe pay special shipping costs."

Halloumi is this funky Greek cheese that can be grilled or baked without melting away. It's sort of tangy and nutty and tasty on a cheese tray. We'd been adding it to charcuterie and cheese board apps for a while now. "They've got it at Sylvano's. I remember seeing it in the cheese case when we were there."

"No kidding? That's great. I'll go over there when I get a break. It'll save us a mint on shipping."

"I'll do it," I said quickly. I was, by then, going slightly nuts sitting around and doing nothing. I figured if worse came to worst I could always wear a facemask.

"Really?" Nate said. "You feel well enough for that?"

"Absolutely. And that way you won't have to leave until you're ready." And I'd feel like I'd done something for the cause. "How much do you want?"

"As much as you can get. Try for a couple of pounds, and if they don't have that much, take what they've got."

"Right. I'll go over there as soon as I get cleaned up."

It occurred to me after I hung up that I wasn't absolutely sure Sylvano's was open on Sundays, but I was betting they were. In places like Geary, Sunday was a prime time for people to wander around and buy scrumptious things for dinner. Sylvano's catered to that kind of impulse buy.

Still, I was happy to see the *Open* sign in the window when I pulled up, although it was a pleasant day for a drive whether they were open or not.

There were more customers this time than the last time we'd come to Sylvano's, along with several people scattered at the tables on the side patio having sandwiches and beer. Inside, I saw Katie Sylvano ringing up a sale at the front. A solid-looking middle-aged man was behind the meat counter. I wondered if he was the Ted Sylvano Bianca had mentioned. If so, he was probably the guy who'd been dating Sara.

Before they'd broken up and she'd gotten killed.

I headed for the cheese case and found the halloumi. Unfortunately, all I saw was a piece that was around a third of a pound—not nearly enough for a respectable cheese board. I turned toward the guy who was probably Ted Sylvano whose customer had just left.

Sylvano narrowed his eyes at my single small piece of cheese. "Can I help you with that?"

"I hope so," I said. "Do you have any more halloumi?"

"How much do you need?" His eyes stayed narrow.

"A couple of pounds if you have it. But we'll take any amount."

That got me raised eyebrows. Given the price per pound, two pounds was a substantial purchase. "I'll see what we've got. Hang on a minute." Sylvano disappeared behind a door at the side. He reappeared a few minutes later with a substantial block. "Pound and a half is all I have. I'll get a delivery in a couple of days if you can wait that long."

"I'll take the pound and a half. We've got a party to cater Tuesday evening."

"Okay, let me wrap it up for you." He paused. "Are you with St. George?"

I shook my head. "Robicheaux Catering in Shavano."

"Like Robicheaux's Café?"

"Yep. Their catering service."

"Interesting. I didn't know they had a catering service." Sylvano fumbled in his pocket then handed me his business card. "Pass that on to the manager, would you? We can work some pricing for special orders."

I decided I wasn't insulted that he figured I wasn't the manager. Anyone who knew what the Robicheaux kids looked like would know I wasn't one of them.

I watched him wrap the block of cheese in plastic wrap, trying to figure out a way to bring the conversation around to Sara and coming up with nothing. "I was curious about your honey," I said finally. "The Mt. Oxford stuff. Is it from one of the Shavano honey producers?"

Sylvano sighed as he handed me the cheese. "I don't know where it's from. A former employee bought it for the store. I never knew who she dealt with."

I felt a chill along the back of my neck. "Sara Jordan?"

Sylvano's eyebrows went up. "You knew Sara?"

I nodded. "I'm friends with her former mother-in-law."

"Bianca." Sylvano gave me a smile. "I'm friends with Pat."

Pat was Bianca's ex, but they were still on good terms. Knowing one didn't mean you couldn't hang out with the other.

"So Sara bought the honey?" I figured I might as well get as much information as I could before I took my halloumi to Shavano.

Sylvano's expression cooled. "It's good stuff. Well, good enough. But I don't know where she got it. I just figured it was Shavano."

"Yeah, the name sort of implies that." I'd have to ask around. Maybe Carmen or Aram had heard of the label. I picked up a jar of Mt. Oxford honey and added it to my order. Then I dug my credit card out of my purse and handed it to Sylvano.

He started to run it, but then he paused, frowning down as he studied it. "Roxanne Constantine?"

"That's me." I wondered if Sara had told him something nasty about me. Surely he'd still sell me the halloumi.

He looked up at me. "Luscious Delights."

I nodded. "That's my brand."

"I've tasted your pepper peach. Good stuff."

"Thanks."

"You ever sell out of other stores besides your own?"

I took a breath. "Sure. I sell some at Bianca's bakery and a few at the Made In Colorado place in Shavano."

"I'd be interested in seeing what you've got. Maybe we can set up a tasting."

"I'm sure we can," I said. "Count on it."

I traveled home with a warm glow. I'd found Nate's halloumi and I'd gotten a potential customer. And I'd learned a little more about Mt. Oxford honey—I now knew there was a definite connection with Sara, although I wasn't sure what that meant.

Nate hadn't gotten home yet, which wasn't surprising. I texted him about the halloumi then put it in the refrigerator. Then, since I had a little extra time, I decided to go find Carmen.

Predictably, she was with the beehives. She and Donnie had gotten the broken hive together again, and I noticed they'd added straps to all the hives, securing them to some solid rings they'd sunk into the ground next to them.

I gestured at the straps. "Smart. I've never seen that before."

"Supposed to keep bears out and keep the hives from being blown over in windstorms. I kept meaning to do this, but I never got around to it until we almost lost them." She gave me a slightly sour smile. "Won't keep assholes like Dan Griffin out, but it's a start."

"How's the hive?"

"Seems okay. We'll keep checking over the next few days."

"You ever hear of Mt. Oxford Honey Company?" The label had the name of the manufacturer, although not the location.

Carmen tightened down another strap on one of the hives. "Nope. Are they supposed to be from around here?"

I handed her the jar. She turned it over in her hand, frowning. "No address."

"Nope. Just 'Made In Colorado'."

"Which could mean damn near anywhere. Hell, they could be out on the plains or someplace like that. No connection to Mt. Oxford."

"True. I just thought it might be local."

"Have you tasted it?"

"Not yet. I just bought it. At Sylvano's over in Geary. Apparently, Sara Jordan set up the order, but Ted Sylvano didn't know where it came from."

"Come on to the house." Carmen marched toward her back door, and I followed.

Dolce was stirring something on the stove when we came in. She gave me one of her seraphic grins. "I was just about to call you. I'm trying some orange marmalade, and I need some guidance."

Orange marmalade is a pain in the butt, but I wasn't about to dampen Dolce's enthusiasm. "Hang on a minute. I want to taste this honey. Then I'll do what I can."

Carmen cracked open the Mt. Oxford jar, then handed me a tasting spoon while she grabbed one of her own. We each took a spoonful and tasted.

Honey on its own is pretty intense—so sweet it can make your teeth ache. But sometimes you can pick up overtones of the plants the bees had visited, particularly if it's something strong like sage. I didn't get anything from the Mt. Oxford honey, though. It tasted like…honey.

"Is it anything you've tasted before?" I asked Carmen.

She shrugged. "Hard to say. It's regular honey, which means it's been pasteurized. That takes out a lot of the flavors you get in raw honey. To me, all regular honey tastes the same."

"Do they claim that it's raw?"

Carmen checked the jar then shook her head. "Nope—not on the label. And they would if it was raw since that's a selling point. It is what it is."

"Does pasteurization take a lot of equipment?"

"You can do it on a stove top, but it's an extra step. Most of the honey farmers I know produce raw honey like we do. Besides, it tastes better, and it's better for you. Pasteurization kills the micronutrients."

I knew there was a big fight over honey's healthy properties, but I wasn't about to get into it. "This doesn't taste like much, I'll grant you that. So all the Shavano farmers do raw honey?"

Carmen nodded. "All the ones I know. Which is all the ones who sell their honey at the farmers market. There may be a few people with one or two hives who pasteurize their stuff, but they don't sell it like we do."

I squinted down at the jar of Mt. Oxford Honey again. Definitely not raw honey. Definitely generic. I wondered if Ted Sylvano had ever tasted the stuff, or if he'd relied on Sara's judgment. Judging from the shelves, he hadn't bought a lot of jars.

"Maybe I'll check at the market next week," I said. "Maybe somebody else knows who makes this stuff."

"Maybe." Carmen didn't sound optimistic.

I turned to Dolce. "Okay, about orange marmalade."

I spent the rest of the afternoon cutting orange rinds into ultra-thin ribbons and getting my hands thoroughly sticky in the process. The thing about marmalade is that you have to boil both the rinds and the fruit pulp, along with sugar and pectin. And you need to cut the ribbons really, really thin and then slice them across the middle, too. You don't want big pieces of orange rind plopping down on your morning toast.

It's a painstaking process, as Dolce discovered when we'd made tangerine marmalade a few months ago. But all budding jam makers need to try it once or twice. I could duck it for the most part because I tried to use Colorado fruit for my jams and, needless to say, we didn't have much of an orange crop. But I'd done the tangerine marmalade for a winter monthly special when there wasn't any fresh Colorado fruit available.

In the end, Dolce gave me a jar of our joint production and I took it home for Uncle Mike, who's a bigger orange marmalade fan than I am.

Nate was finally back at the cabin, stretched out on the couch with a beer. He smiled when I walked in. "You must be doing better. You're on your feet."

"I am," I agreed. "I can probably help you out tomorrow."

"Great." He squinted at the jar of honey I held along with the jar of Dolce's marmalade. "What's that?"

"I got some of the Mt. Oxford stuff to show Carmen. But she's never heard of it."

"Any good?"

"Not really. Tastes like all the commercial honey you see at City Market."

"Carmen sneered?"

"Carmen definitely sneered."

"What did Sylvano say about it?"

"Sara bought it. He doesn't know the seller."

"Sara?" Nate raised his eyebrows. "I didn't realize Sara was a buyer for Sylvano's. I thought she just worked the counter."

"She may have had more clout than we realized. But Sylvano didn't appear to be too broken up about her memory."

"Does anybody?"

I shook my head, suddenly melancholy. Nobody much missed Sara because nobody had known her when she was alive except those close to her. And she irritated the people who were close to her. Nobody seemed to remember her fondly, not even me.

At this point her death was more an irritant than something that made people sad.

I took a deep breath. I probably couldn't do much to make Sara's death provoke a more sympathetic response, but I could do my part in finding out who killed her.

Maybe no one liked her, but that didn't mean her killer deserved to get away with murder.

Chapter 22

Nate and I worked steadily through Monday to get everything ready to go. The event we were preparing for was billed as a cocktail party, which meant we didn't need to make any main dishes. But it was a cocktail party with lots of appetizers of various weights.

We had our usual filo pockets for the vegans. I could do the filling, but I'd wait to actually put the packets together until the day of the party, since I didn't want to leave them sitting in the refrigerator and becoming soggy. We had a large charcuterie tray and cheese board that would go out early so that people could have something to munch on as they got their drinks. Neither of the trays would take much beyond assembly, although Nate would grill the halloumi shortly before we set it out. And then there were meatballs and crostini and cheese-stuffed jalapenos and chicken skewers and mixed crudités and crackers and sauteed vegetables with two kinds of dips.

It was a lot.

Most of it we'd put out on tables, but some of it, like the chicken skewers and the crostini, would be served by the wait staff to people standing around. We'd done all of this before in various combinations, but this was one of the biggest parties we'd handled. And it hadn't helped that we'd had a party on Friday that had required a lot of prep, too. Nate had been relying on Dan to work on prep Sunday and Monday. Now he had to rely on me and whoever was around the café with some free time.

The all hands on deck afternoon after Sunday brunch had helped a lot. The meatballs and cheese-stuffed jalapenos were ready to be cooked, and Nate was busy getting them into the oven. About half of the crudités and veggies to be roasted had been taken care of, and I figured I'd get the rest of it once I had the filo filling done and refrigerating. We were going to make it, but it was already a bit of a crunch. Once again I cursed Dan in my mind. Why couldn't he have waited to pursue his crooked lifestyle until after the party was finished?

The café was closed on Mondays, so we were the only ones around. But Coco showed up mid-morning with brownies and gossip. Nate put her to work toasting crostini. "Fowler says Marcus is off the hook," she announced as she applied olive oil to a sheet pan full of baguette slices.

"Oh, yeah? Why?" I was slicing carrots for the crudités.

Coco raised an eyebrow at me. "Because he's innocent?"

"You know that and I know that, but Fowler's a hard sell. Why did he take Marcus off the suspect list?" I did a quick check of my carrot pile, which I needed to maximize before switching to the broccoli that needed to be roasted.

"Apparently, they got a better estimate on when Sara was killed. Marcus was working in his shop at the time in question. Two or three people bought stuff from him, ergo he's in the clear. More or less."

That *more or less* sounded like Fowler. He'd never rule someone out completely until he had the actual murderer in hand. "That's good for Marcus."

"Bad for Dan Griffin, though." Coco slid the sheet pan under the broiler to toast the crostini.

"Fowler suspects Dan?" It wasn't entirely a surprise, given that Fowler had asked me if Dan was around at Sawmill when Sara had been killed. But it was still a little jarring.

"Those beehive thefts put Dan in Fowler's sights. I think he figures anyone who was responsible for several hundred dollars in losses could also have committed murder."

"Maybe," I said slowly. "But I never saw Dan with Sara. Is there any evidence they even knew each other?"

Coco shrugged. "Maybe he was working for someone else."

"You mean like a killer for hire?"

"Why not? He needed money, right?"

"Right." Only somehow that didn't sit right with me. I couldn't see Dan agreeing to kill someone for money. That just didn't strike me as something he'd do. But now that I thought about it, I could believe Dan would steal beehives for somebody else. Dan had never struck me as a criminal mastermind, the type who'd come up with this elaborate plot to steal beehives and sell them to farmers who needed pollinators. But he was the type who'd take on the job of stealing the hives for the mastermind if the pay was good enough. He'd probably see it as a quick and easy way to make some extra cash.

Which left open the question: who was the

mastermind? Who had come up with the idea of stealing beehives in the first place? And was that person also involved in Sara's death?

Tuesday was hectic by any standards. We had to finish cooking everything that hadn't been cooked yet, like the filo packets, and then get set up to transport everything to the event center where the party was happening.

Everything was supposed to start at five, which meant we had to be there by four at the latest. We took time to swing by the cabin and pick up our chef's clothes: coats and Robicheaux ballcaps for the two of us. On some of the jobs, like the family birthday party, we worked in jeans and Robicheaux's Café T-shirts. But on this one, we were going full-out chef, complete with checked pants and black jackets.

The event center was blessedly well equipped with ovens, counter space, a large refrigerator, and a functioning dishwasher. By now we'd worked in some marginal kitchens, so it was always nice to be able to spread out and do justice to our creations.

I got to work warming all the food that needed to be hot, while Nate set up the charcuterie and cheese tray that would go out first. "Are we assuming this thing will start on time?" I asked.

"Probably. Vendome runs a tight ship." Vendome was the company running the show. They did something connected with big agriculture, but I wasn't sure what. Uncle Mike had tried to explain, but it was largely financial. Whatever it was they did, they made enough money to pay for the spread we were going to be putting out.

Nate grilled the halloumi slices, then got the

charcuterie and cheese trays out. Our servers were busy setting up the plates and napkins. We had three waitresses from the café, all veterans. Making good money moonlighting for the catering company was considered a perk, and Madge was careful to spread the jobs around.

All in all, it would be a pretty routine gig. Big and busy, but not complicated. I started loading up the platters with the first round of broiled jalapenos and meatballs, with a separate tray of filo packets so the vegans didn't have to worry about their proximity to ground pork.

I worked steadily for the next hour or so, warming food and pulling it from the oven and loading it on trays and platters. Nate and the servers carried the various plates to the party and brought dirty dishes and platters to be loaded into the dishwasher.

At the end of the second hour, things began to slow down a bit. Nate leaned against the counter. "You want to go up and take a look? I can keep up with what's happening down here."

I hadn't seen the actual space where the party was going on. "Sure. Let me take the platter of vegetables and the bowl of dip."

The kitchen opened onto the event space, which was another thing that was helpful. We'd worked in places where there was a flight of stairs to be navigated with trays of food. Being able to walk straight through a swinging door was a big plus.

I stepped out into the party carrying food, which immediately made me popular. I put the platter of roasted veggies down on the serving table and refilled one of the dip bowls. We must have had a large contingent of vegetarians that night, given the rate at which the crudités and roasted vegetables were disappearing.

I paused then to survey the people around me. I saw a few familiar faces—some of the commercial customers who bought fruit and arugula from Uncle Mike, movers and shakers from town, even some of my jam customers, although it was hard to recognize them in business wear. Then again, I was probably fairly hard to recognize in my black chef's coat and ball cap. We were all more used to our farmers market selves.

And then I saw someone I sort of recognized but couldn't place. A man who was probably in his fifties in a handsome suit, talking to one of the Vendome managers who'd come down to make sure everything was okay in the kitchen. He was high-end—his clothes cost a chunk of cash, although he didn't look like a man who spent a lot of his time in Italian couture. I ransacked my memory trying to place him. Obviously, I'd met him under different circumstances, but I couldn't remember where. His thinning brown hair was brushed to the side, and he had the remains of a farmer's sunburn. Normally, he must have worn a hat.

And then the penny dropped. Fred Hutchinson. The guy who'd sold me expensive honey when I was making my honey jam. He wasn't that different, now that I'd placed him, but he looked richer than he had when I'd seen him before in his threadbare farm stand. Then again, I'd never seen a working farmer who appeared to be wealthy.

The Vendome manager patted him on the shoulder and then turned away, obviously searching for yet another customer to schmooze. On impulse, I walked toward him. "Mr. Hutchinson?"

He turned, frowning.

"I'm Roxy Constantine. You sold me some honey for my jam."

His expression cleared slightly. "Oh, yeah, I remember."

"I've got a question for you. Do you know who makes Mt. Oxford Honey?"

He stared at me blankly. "Mt. Oxford Honey?"

"Yes, I saw it at Sylvano's in Geary, but the jars don't have a location other than Colorado. I just wondered if it came from somebody here in town. One of the honey farmers."

Hutchinson's face stayed blank. "Doesn't ring a bell. I'll think about it."

"Oh, okay. Well, thanks." I turned toward the kitchen, hoping that hadn't constituted an intrusion. I'd sort of accosted Hutchinson in the middle of a big industrial party, asking him about an almost mythical honey that nobody had ever heard of. Except it was real. Why would I expect him to know anything about it? I'd probably just convinced him I was some kind of nut myself. I sighed and opened the kitchen door, ready to start winding down our contributions to the evening.

After another thirty minutes or so, Nate brought a tray of dirty dishes to the kitchen and checked our supplies. "That's it, more or less. We've got everything out there except the filo packets. I'll put the last few on the table in hopes a few people will ignore the vegan label and give them a try."

"They're delicious," I said loyally.

"Yeah, they are. Which you and I both know, but this is Shavano, so the suspicion of vegetarianism in general is high. On the other hand, they've been moving pretty well tonight." He grabbed the final tray, and I set about loading the dishwasher one more time. The dishes belonged to the event center, but the pots and pans, along with some of the platters, belonged to us. I started doing the usual rinsing we always did at the end of the evening before we took everything to the café to be loaded into the dishwasher there.

Nate stepped back in the kitchen a few minutes later. "I've got something for you."

"For me?" I put down the sheet pan I was rinsing. "What?"

"This note. One of the managers handed it to me and said it was for you."

I stared at the piece of paper in his hand. For the life of me, I couldn't figure out why someone from Vendome would be sending me a message. I didn't even know these people. And I'd only been out of the kitchen once.

Then I opened the folded paper and saw the signature: *Fred Hutchinson.*

"Oh," I said. "Maybe he remembered something."

"Remembered something?" Nate narrowed his eyes, but I was already reading the note.

Ms. Constantine:

I think I remember hearing about Mt. Oxford Honey, but I need to check on something at home to be sure. Could you drop by my farm stand around two tomorrow afternoon? I might be able to pass some information along.

Fred Hutchinson

I handed it to Nate. "I talked to him for a couple of minutes and asked him about Mt. Oxford Honey.

Maybe he's remembered something. Maybe." It did seem a little strange that he'd be so helpful now, given how reserved Hutchinson had been when I'd talked to him.

Nate was still dubious. "Why can't he just phone you?"

"I don't know. Maybe he needs to show me something." And after I'd visited Hutchinson, I might have some information I could carry to Aram and Lynn Bridger. I'd been planning to go to the honey farmers again. Among the three of them, I might be able to figure something out, although I still wasn't entirely sure what I expected to find. Or why I needed to find it. Did I think Mt. Oxford Honey was the key to the honey thefts? Not likely. Maybe it was just Constantine curiosity raising its nasty head again.

Curiosity killed the cat, Roxy. I decided to ignore untimely mottoes, even though it did give me a slight chill.

Nate paused, frowning. "Do you want me to come with you?"

"Why? It's not like I'm going into his house or anything. His farm stand is right out on the county road like the others. And I'll be there in daylight." The more we talked about it, the less threatening it seemed. Plus, it would give me a chance to talk to the other honey farmers. It was just another chore to perform. Nothing big.

"Okay, if you say so. Is everything ready to go here?"

"It's ready to be loaded." I ran a dishtowel over the last sheet pan then added it to the stack.

"Let me do one more circuit of the dining room to

make sure we're set."

"Right."

Sometimes that last circuit would include a bonus from whoever booked us. With parties in private homes, it usually did. But I wasn't expecting much from Vendome—corporate customers didn't usually go beyond whatever they'd contracted to pay us.

Still, it had been a big party with several pre-party glitches, and we'd gotten through it successfully. We could add another accomplishment to our list.

And maybe, just maybe, I was one step closer to solving the riddle of Mt. Oxford Honey. Whether that brought me any closer to solving the question of who was behind the honey thefts, to say nothing of Sara Jordan's murder, remained to be seen.

Chapter 23

I took time on Wednesday morning to check in with Dolce and Bridget. I hadn't had a chance before that to do much more than wave as I headed out to work on meal prep. I figured by now they could probably take care of themselves for a couple of days, and of course they had. Bridget had packaged all the mail orders and gotten them picked up. Dolce had whipped up enough strawberry jam to carry us through a couple of weeks, and she'd done a small batch of peach preserves, which were excellent.

I dismissed the passing thought that I might not be as necessary to Luscious Delights as I'd always assumed. We were still hand-making all our jams, and my hands were still the ones that did most of the work.

I got a couple dozen jars of peach preserves done along with another couple dozen of pepper peach. Dolce worked on raspberry, which is a relatively low-stress jam, so the learning curve was small. Once again, I rejoiced that Uncle Mike had talked me into buying a commercial-sized stove since it gave us a multitude of burners to use at once. Dolce took one side, and I took the other.

Bridget helped get the finished jars onto the rack to cool and seal, all the while sharing the newest gossip. "So nobody knows where Dan Griffin was stashing the hives he stole since he lived in one of those apartments over on Spruce," she said.

"Nobody thought he was stashing them at his house, surely." Although the question of where the stolen hives had been stored was interesting. It just reinforced my theory that Dan was working for somebody else—maybe somebody with more space or a ready buyer.

"Maybe not, but what did he do with them? I mean, how did he get them out of town with nobody noticing? And what was he using to carry them around? From what I heard, he stole dozens of hives, assuming he was the one who did all the thefts here and in Geary. He couldn't have hauled them around in that old pickup of his. That thing wouldn't hold more than a half dozen hives at most. You think he stored them in the hills somewhere?"

All very good questions, for which I had no answers at all. "Maybe he had a partner, and the partner had a way to transport the hives wherever they needed to go."

Bridget nodded. "Makes sense. You think he killed Sara Jordan?"

That one pulled me up short. I wasn't aware the speculation about Sara had gone any farther than Fowler's office. "I don't know," I hedged. "I don't think they knew each other. If they did, I never heard anything about it."

"Well, Dan always had a way with the ladies," Bridget said.

I worked hard on not looking at her. So far as I knew, my one-month relationship with Dan back in the day wasn't common knowledge, and I didn't want it to be. "I thought Sara was dating Ted Sylvano."

"She dated him for a while," Bridget mused. "But he wasn't her type. Hard-working shop owner trying to make a buck. Must have been a lot like dating Marcus."

And based on what Bianca had told us, Sara had been searching for a quick score, preferably something to get her out of Shavano and environs. If she couldn't force Marcus to sell his butcher shop, maybe she'd tried her hand at something else.

Like blackmail.

Bridget seemed to be thinking along the same lines. "Maybe she found out what Dan was up to and tried to get him to share his profits or she'd tell Fowler. That's the kind of thing that would piss off a thief."

"True," I said. "It would piss off anybody." Unfortunately, that made a lot more sense than some of the other possibilities I'd heard. Dan wasn't the type to murder someone in cold blood, but he might murder someone who was threatening him. Sara might have misjudged just how dangerous Dan could be if pushed.

Dolce took off around one, but we'd made a respectable amount of jam between the two of us. Bridget left soon afterward, promising to drop off the last of the mail orders at the post office on her way home. That left me with an empty kitchen and a powerful load of curiosity. I still considered the idea that Mt. Oxford Honey had anything to do with the honey thefts pretty shaky. And I was even more certain it had nothing to do with Sara's murder. But I still wanted to know who ran the company and where they were based. Just random curiosity more than anything else.

Which meant a quick trip to Fred Hutchinson's farmstand.

I made sure all the jam we'd made was racked and cooling. When I got back I could do a couple more rounds of jam, which would give us a bit of a surplus going into the weekend. I figured I could take off an hour or so without giving up too much. Talking to Hutchinson shouldn't take much time.

I drove out the county road where most of the farmstands were located. Not many of them were open during the week—they got most of their customers from Friday through Sunday, although a few of them had afternoon hours on other days. Apparently, Hutchinson was one of this group.

When I got to his farmstand, though, it was a replay of my last visit. I wondered if he was actually open. I didn't see any customers, and the shelves that usually held produce were empty. I parked in front and walked slowly toward the stand, trying to see if anyone was around. Hutchinson had told me to come by around two and it was just five past, so I hadn't considered calling ahead. I stepped into the stand and stood in the midst of the empty shelves. "Hello?"

A moment later, a door opened in the storage building behind the stand, and Hutchinson stuck his head out. "Oh, Ms. Constantine. I forgot all about you. Hang on a minute."

He ducked inside, then stepped out, leaving the door open behind him. "What were we talking about? Oh, yeah, Mt. Oxford Honey."

"That's right. You said you'd remembered something."

He nodded. "I did. They sent me a letter a while back to see if I'd be interested in selling them honey. I guess they're some kind of corporate honey producer.

I've still got that letter somewhere. Come on in my office, and I'll see if I can dig it up." He turned toward the building he'd just left.

I followed him in the door, glancing around as I did. For an office it was pretty spartan—a desk in the corner with a filing cabinet next to it, a table near the door. No computer, not even a chair for visitors. And the cement block building didn't even have a window. I figured it must get pretty stuffy in summer, to say nothing of freezing in winter. And it was dim. The only light came from a desk lamp on the table at the side.

Hutchinson started flipping through some papers in a cardboard box on the table with the lamp as I surveyed the room. "Now where did I see that thing?" he muttered. He stepped away toward another filing cabinet deeper in the shadows at the side of the room.

I took another survey of the area, noting a hanging lightbulb over the desk, and wondered why Hutchinson hadn't turned it on for more light. I wondered how he had enough light to see in the filing cabinets and started to turn toward him.

And then the world exploded.

I felt a sharp pain at the back of my head as I staggered forward, my knees giving way. I tried to find Hutchinson, although my vision was getting darker in the already dim room. "What…what's…"

Hutchinson had become a shadowy figure somewhere behind me, and that shadowy figure was swinging something in my direction. It looked like a garden spade.

I ducked enough that time to keep him from hitting me full on, but the blow caught my shoulder and threw me forward onto my hands and knees. My ears were ringing, and the world was going dark. I fought to keep from blacking out because I had enough sense to know that blacking out just then would be a very bad idea.

I heard a sound like the door opening somewhere in front of me, but I didn't try to see where it was. I wanted to get away from Hutchinson before he tried to hit me again, so I began crawling toward the door as best I could. My arms and legs weren't working right. I ducked down farther, struggling to protect my head while I scrabbled to the side like a crab. I felt something whiz through the air near my ear, and figured it was probably Hutchinson's garden spade again.

The table loomed out of the darkness in front of me and I managed to drag myself underneath. At least that should slow Hutchinson down a little, maybe even give me a chance to crawl to the door.

Then I heard a man's voice shout, "What the fuck?" It didn't sound like Hutchinson.

I could hear noises coming from behind me, the sounds of a scuffle and men grunting at each other, but I couldn't really see in the dimness of the building. Whatever was happening seemed to have distracted Hutchinson from swinging the spade at me again. I put all my strength into staying conscious and moving out of range as I crawled a few feet closer to the door. I heard someone yelp in pain and someone—maybe someone else—curse. And then there was the thump of someone or something hitting the ground somewhere on the far side of the room.

I held still a few feet from the door, wondering if it would be better to close my eyes and pretend to be unconscious or keep them open so I could make an attempt to get away. Then someone stepped beside me and placed a hand lightly on my shoulder. I caught my breath on a sob and tried to look up again.

"Don't worry, Rox," the shadowy figure next to me said. "I took care of him for you. I can't stick around to help you any more, but I'll call Nate on my way out."

I tried to reach up and made it halfway. "Dan?"

The person beside me walked to the doorway, then paused, sunlight streaming behind him. "Somebody will get here soon, Roxy. They'll take care of you, I promise." And then he was gone.

I stayed hunched on my hands and knees, trying to figure out what had happened or was still happening. I was pretty sure Dan hadn't been around the stand when I drove up, and I didn't think he'd been in the office when we'd stepped inside. Surely Hutchinson wouldn't have hit me with the spade if Dan had been there. But that meant he'd gotten there after Hutchinson had started swinging. And he'd done something to Hutchinson that kept him from coming after me again.

I was having a hard time keeping my eyes open by then. The idea of letting go and sliding into the darkness that was hovering around the edges of my vision was seductive. But the remnants of my consciousness were screaming at me. *Get up! Get out! Get away from here!*

I grabbed hold of the edge of the table, pushing myself away from it a bit, and then I used it to pull myself to my feet. It took forever to get up because every effort set off a wave of bright red pain in my head, but I got there. And then I checked around the room, very, very slowly. Obviously, quick movements were not advisable. Finally, I saw Fred Hutchinson lying in a heap on the floor near the desk. The garden spade lay next to him.

I had no desire to find out if he was dead or alive. I figured that was who Dan had been talking about when he said *I took care of him for you.* I also knew Hutchinson had been the one who'd hit me, although my foggy brain could supply no reason why he'd done that.

I turned toward the door and got there by holding on to the wall and then the side of the doorjamb. Then I faced the problem of how I was going to get across the three feet or so of open ground before I made it to the farmstand. I was pretty sure I couldn't walk there. I might have to crawl through the dirt.

Something started making noise close to me. It took me a moment to identify it as my phone, which was still in the pocket of my jeans. I dug it out and hit the connect button.

"Roxy," somebody called. "Rox, are you okay?"

"Nate?" I said groggily. "No, I'm not. I need some help. Hutchinson's farmstand. That's where I am."

"Stay where you are. I'm almost there."

I thought about telling him I didn't have much choice. I was pretty sure I couldn't walk to the stand without falling on my face, and I didn't want to try. I pulled the door shut behind me to make it harder for Hutchinson to sneak up, assuming he was still alive and able to stand on his own. And then I stood very still, hoping that Nate's SUV would be the next vehicle I saw.

It was. He pulled up in front of the stand and jumped out, running toward me. "Roxy," he called, "what happened? Are you okay?"

I managed to stay upright until he was next to me,

and then I let myself slump against him. "He hit me. On the back of my head. Fred Hutchinson hit me."

Nate leaned around to look at the place where I'd been struck. He didn't gasp, but his expression told me it wasn't good. "Come sit in the SUV. The cops are on their way. I'll get you to the hospital as soon as they get here." He glanced around the farmstand as we limped toward his SUV. "Where's Hutchinson now?"

"He's in the building where I was standing. Dan hit him to keep him from hitting me again. I don't know how badly he's hurt." And I didn't care.

"Dan hit him?" Nate got the door of the SUV open. "Dan was here?"

But by then we both heard sirens. Two police cruisers pulled up, and Fowler climbed out of the first one. He stopped next to me. "What happened?"

"Fred Hutchinson hit me. On the back of my head. With a shovel. I don't know why."

Fowler looked at my head then at Nate. "You said Dan Griffin called you."

"He did. He said Roxy was at Hutchinson's farmstand and that she'd been hurt."

"Was Griffin here?" Fowler asked me.

"Yeah. He hit Hutchinson after Hutchinson hit me. Dan saved my life. I think." I was beginning to feel woozy again.

"I have to get her to the hospital. She needs a doctor," Nate said. He sounded tense.

"Wait a minute." Fowler motioned to someone. A moment later Jean Bancroft appeared at his side. Jean was a part time deputy who was also a paramedic. "Can you check her out?" Fowler asked.

Jean knelt beside me. She checked my eyes, asked

me how I felt, then touched the back of my head lightly. But even that touch hurt. I sucked in a breath. Jean stood up again. "Could be a concussion. Maybe serious. She needs to go to the hospital."

Fowler sighed. "Okay. Where's Hutchinson now?"

"He's in that building over there." I was able to turn enough to point at the office. "Dan hit him after he hit me. I don't know how hurt he is."

Fowler straightened. "Is Dan in there?"

I knew better than to shake my head. "No. He left after he took care of Hutchinson. But he promised he'd call Nate."

"Can we go now?" Nate asked. I had a feeling he was going no matter what Fowler answered.

"Go ahead," Fowler said. "I'll catch up with you later."

I thought I heard Nate mutter "Don't count on it" but he was already trotting for the driver's seat.

The hospital was sort of a blur. Jean had phoned in to let them know I was coming and that I wasn't in great shape. They took me to an examination room, and several people came in to check on me. I kept sort of going in and out of consciousness. One minute I'd be answering questions and the next I'd be staring into space. At some point Uncle Mike arrived and sat with me for a while, holding my hand. I think Madge was there, too, but I'm not entirely sure.

Finally I was in a room by myself with Nate on one side and Uncle Mike on the other. "Can I go home?" I asked.

"Not tonight," Nate said gently. "They'll let you go tomorrow if you're better."

"Okay," I said and closed my eyes.

They did let me sleep. That thing about waking concussion victims up every two hours must not be true. But the nurses kept coming in to check my vitals and make sure I hadn't developed a fever and to check the dressing on the back of my head, so they might as well have done the every-two-hour thing anyway.

The back of my head was another sore point, literally and otherwise. They'd had to shave my hair around the place Hutchinson had hit me, so I figured I'd have to get a haircut once the dressing was off. I'd had long hair for several years, and I didn't want to go short. Still, it wasn't like I was going to have much choice. And it was far from my biggest problem at the moment.

Finally, around two in the morning, I fell asleep and stayed there. I didn't even dream about Hutchinson and Dan. The drugs the hospital had pumped into me took care of that. But I was pretty sure that wouldn't be the case when I went home.

Which was one reason why, despite wanting to get home to my cabin again, I wasn't altogether delighted at the idea of sleeping in my own bed. Not unless Nate was there to hold me when I started dreaming.

Chapter 24

I woke up the next morning with a vicious headache and an empty stomach. The nurse who came in was someone I'd gone to high school with—typical small town—and she brought me a breakfast sandwich and super ibuprofen. But she couldn't give me any coffee until the doctor gave her approval.

That probably explained my crummy attitude when Fowler stepped into my room. "Unless you're bringing me coffee, you should probably go away," I said.

He paused then stepped out the door again. If I'd driven him away, that would mark a first. But a moment later he was back again with a cup of coffee from Bianca's bakery. "Will this do?"

"Oh my God, yes," I said, taking it from his hand.

"Bianca sent you a muffin, too, but the nurses confiscated it." He gave me a half-smile. "Sorry. They were too tough for me."

"This is a good start." I took a deep swallow, letting the caffeine slide into my bloodstream, then leaned back against my pillows. "So what's happening?"

"Not a hell of a lot. Yet." Fowler pulled out his notebook and dropped into one of the chairs near my bed. "I need to get a statement, now that you're fully conscious."

"The coffee helps. All right, what do you want to

know?"

"Tell me what happened yesterday, from the top."

So I did, starting with the note from Hutchinson at the party. Fowler paused. "Do you still have the note?"

"Yeah, I think so. I put it in my purse." I wasn't entirely sure where my purse was at the moment, but I figured it would turn up.

"Okay, what happened then?"

I told him about going to Hutchinson's place, the office, and Hutchinson hitting me. I paused then, trying to pull it together again. "I don't know why he did that. I still don't know. I mean, it doesn't make any sense."

"You're sure it was Hutchinson?" Fowler asked.

I blinked at him. "We were the only people in the office. Yeah, it was Hutchinson."

"Did you see him with the spade?"

"Yes," I said and paused. I closed my eyes, trying to visualize it again. The darkened office, the blow that had sent me to my knees, the man standing behind me. "It was him," I said again. "It had to be him. There was nobody else there."

Fowler lowered his notebook again, watching me carefully. "Could it have been Dan Griffin?"

"Dan? No." I started to shake my head and thought better of it. Moving my head was a bad idea. "Dan came later. Hutchinson hit me twice—once on the head and once on the shoulder. I was down on the floor, trying to crawl away from him. I heard the door open, then I heard somebody say, 'What the fuck?' It wasn't Hutchinson, I'm pretty sure. There was a struggle. I got underneath the table to hide. I heard something heavy, probably Hutchinson, hit the ground. Then Dan came over to check on me. He told me he'd taken care of

The Honey Jam Murder

Hutchinson, but he had to get out of there. And he told me he'd call Nate to come and help me."

"He said that he'd taken care of Hutchinson?"

"He did." I paused. "Is Hutchinson dead?" I hadn't thought to ask until then. Yesterday I hadn't cared if he was dead or alive. Today I sort of did but not much.

"He's alive. He's here, in fact. Getting treated for a concussion, just like you." Another half-smile. "Busy night for the concussion ward."

"If Hutchinson's here, I want to go home," I said flatly. I didn't think Hutchinson would do anything to me with all the medical staff around. But I didn't feel like sharing a floor with him.

Fowler stared down at his notebook again, then up at me. "Hutchinson says Dan hit you with the spade before he hit him. He swears he was fighting with Dan to keep him from hitting you."

"Then he's lying through his teeth. Hutchinson was the one who hit me."

"He says you're confused because he was struggling with Dan. He says he had no reason to hurt you."

"Neither did Dan," I pointed out. Of course, the last time I'd seen Dan before we met again at Hutchinson's place I'd fired a rifle in his general direction. But I hadn't come close to hitting him. And Dan had never struck me as the type to hold a grudge.

Fowler rubbed a hand across his chin. "Here's my problem, Roxy. Neither of these men had any reason to hit you with a shovel. But one of them did. You say it's Hutchinson, and I'm inclined to believe you. But I still don't have any reason why he'd do that. Unless he had some kind of psychotic break. And if he did, he's recovered. Of course, he also has a concussion."

"I don't know why he did it. Unless it's got something to do with Mt. Oxford Honey. That's why I was there in the first place. To find out about Mt. Oxford Honey." I was tired again. Also frustrated. It should have been easy to turn Hutchinson in. He'd tried to kill me. I was an eyewitness, for Pete's sake.

But then I'd always heard that eyewitnesses weren't reliable. And I had a head injury at the time I saw Hutchinson standing over me with that garden spade. A head injury he'd given me, but still. A good lawyer could probably turn my testimony into mush.

I sighed. "I'm sorry. I wish I could clear this up for you. But I still don't know why this happened. I just know that it did."

Fowler uncrossed his legs and pushed to his feet. "It's not your job to figure out why it happened—that's up to me."

"Thanks for the coffee," I said.

He nodded at me as he stepped through the door. "Take it easy now."

Uncle Mike showed up around noon to take me home after the doctor had cleared me to leave. He'd gotten my truck from Hutchinson's place the day before, and he was adamant about me staying off my feet and letting others take care of me. Those others included Carmen and Dolce and Bridget and, of course, Nate, all of whom wanted to make jam for me and feed me and generally do everything I normally did for myself. I appreciated them when they weren't driving me crazy.

I spent most of that afternoon and the next day in bed resting and taking painkillers for my queen-size headache. But predictably, I was dying to get to work by the end of that second day. Susa came to check on me and brought our friend Carolee, who owned a hair salon in town. Carolee cut my hair so that I no longer looked really weird, only sort of weird.

She refused any payment other than a few jars of peach and pepper peach. "I've wanted to cut your hair for years," she said cheerfully. "Come see me when it grows out a little and I'll shape it into something you'll love."

That didn't make up for my having been whacked on the head, but it gave me something to look forward to.

I was on my feet again in a limited way within a few more days, but I wasn't in any shape to run my booth at the market that weekend. Not that I wanted to accept that idea. "I can do it," I insisted. "I'll sit on a stool or something. I'll be fine."

"No," Nate said flatly. "You stay here and rest. On Monday, you can get back to full power again, but you rest this weekend."

Nate had had a concussion himself a little while ago, and he knew whereof he spoke. I didn't like it, but I let him run the booth with help from Dolce, Beck, and, amazingly, Susa.

But that left me with time on my hands and no immediate tasks that needed to be accomplished. As usual, there was jam to make, and I spent an hour or so doing a large batch of peach preserves. I'd decided to do blueberry for next month's special, so I tried a new recipe for blueberry jam with lime juice. It tasted okay, but I decided to let it sit for a while to see what kind of taste developed.

I'd just gotten the jars of peach jam out of the canner so that they could cool on the racks when someone knocked on my door. By then I'd learned to keep my door locked and not to throw it open to anyone who came by. Besides, everybody I knew was at the farmers market, so anyone knocking was suspicious by definition.

I stopped and peeked through the peephole. "Son of a bitch," I muttered and put the chain on the door so I could open it a couple of inches. "What the hell, Dan?" I asked.

Dan Griffin stood on my doorstep looking a lot worse for wear. Apparently, he'd spent the last few days camping out or near to it. He needed a shave and he needed to wash his hands. "Come on, Roxy, let me in. I just want to sit down for a while," he said.

"No, I'm not letting you in. Every time you come around something awful happens. I'm going to call Fowler." I started fumbling for my phone.

"Go ahead," Dan said. "Tell him I'm turning myself in. I'll wait for him here."

I took a long look at him. I couldn't see anything that was like a weapon. He could probably have a pocketknife in his jeans, but I didn't think he could use it effectively. Just then he seemed to be in worse shape than I was. After all, I'd had a couple of days off my feet. "Hang on."

Fowler picked up on the second ring. "What?"

"Dan's here at my place. He says he wants to turn himself in."

"What the hell?"

"Just what I said. You should probably get out here." I put my phone in my pocket.

Dan was still standing on my porch, swaying a little when I opened the door again. "Okay?"

"He's on his way. You can use the hose to clean up. Have a seat on one of the lawn chairs." No way was I letting him inside my house.

Dan turned on the hose and rinsed his face and hands. Then he dropped into one of the lawn chairs in my front yard. It wasn't exactly luxury, but it was a decent lawn chair. "You got a beer I could have?" he asked.

I bit back my first response, which was to slam the door again and stay inside, snarling. After a moment, I sighed. He'd probably saved my life by knocking Hutchinson out. "Okay. Stay there."

I joined Dan in the front yard a few minutes later, with a bottle of beer for him and a glass of iced tea for me. He took the beer and touched it against his forehead, closing his eyes. "Thanks. I needed that."

"So why are you turning yourself in?" I asked. "Overcome with guilt?"

Dan took a long swallow of beer. "Not so much. I finally figured out if I took off, Hutchinson could blame everything on me and get away clear. That didn't strike me as a great idea."

"How much are you guilty of?"

"I stole the hives. Well, I stole some of them. Hutchinson had more people than just me doing his scut work. He had a statewide operation."

"Hutchinson was in charge of the hive thefts?"

Dan nodded. "Oh, yeah. He has a business renting hives to people who want pollinators, plus he increased the number of hives for his own honey business. He probably figured stealing hives around the state was a lot cheaper than buying more. And it would help shaft his competitors. He's got some major honey production facilities going over near the Utah border."

"I had no idea." Which reminded me of something else I needed to know. "Why did he hit me? All I did was ask him about Mt. Oxford Honey. Has he got some kind of deal with them?"

"Hutchinson *is* Mt. Oxford Honey. Another one of his deals. He buys honey from small producers along with the stuff he gets from his own hives, pasteurizes everything so it tastes neutral, then sells it under his own label."

"Why didn't he just tell me that? It's not illegal."

"It is if a lot of the honey he uses comes from the stolen hives and from out of state. He kept his stolen hives on land he owns in Utah. People around here aren't supposed to know his production is that big. Plus Hutchinson plays everything close to the chest. Mt. Oxford Honey was supposed to stay a secret."

"That's still not a reason to hit me with a spade," I grumbled.

Dan shrugged. "It was probably enough to make him nervous. But my guess is you were a target of opportunity. He told me to come by for my share of the take on the hives, which I needed if I wanted to get out of town. I came fifteen minutes early and saw you show up, which struck me as weird. Then I slipped into the shed and saw him hit you, so I figured he was up to no good. Of course, I don't think he was ever up to good, exactly." Dan gave me a dry smile. "If I'd shown up later like he'd asked me to do, he'd probably have killed me, too, then claimed you and I took each other out. He'd take me out so I couldn't go around spreading his secrets, and he could avoid paying me at the same time."

"He'd go to that much trouble to kill you? Just because you knew about the hive thefts?" Dan was a competent cook and apparently a good part-time crook, but he wasn't a big enough threat to go to this much trouble.

"I know a lot about Hutchinson's operation—more than just the thefts. I made it my business to find out." Dan gave me a tired smile. "Knowledge is power, right?"

"Maybe. I mean, that knowledge also made you a prime target for Hutchinson to eliminate."

I could hear sirens traveling down the county road. I watched Dan as I sipped my iced tea, wondering if he'd stay put or run for daylight at the last minute. "What about Sara Jordan?"

He shook his head, smiling. "Some information I'm saving for the chief."

"Did Hutchinson do it? Why would he kill Sara?"

Dan sighed. "Sara Jordan stuck her nose in Hutchinson's business. She found out enough about Mt. Oxford Honey to know it wasn't just another honey company. I think she got a line on the stolen beehives. She thought she could blackmail Hutchinson. Bad idea. And she turned her back on him, which was worse."

I took a deep breath. "Did you put Sara's body in that meadow at Sawmill Brewing? Did Hutchinson tell you to try to frame Marcus?"

Dan stared at me in silence for a long moment. I had a feeling getting rid of Sara's body wasn't something he wanted to talk about. Or remember. But his expression told me enough.

And at that moment, Fowler's squad car pulled to a stop in front of my house and Fowler jumped out, followed by another cop in uniform. He came to a halt in front of my lawn chairs. "Well, this is cozy."

Dan put his beer down. "I'm done. And I surrender or whatever you want to call it. You want me to stand up?"

Fowler nodded, his hand resting on the butt of his gun. It struck me that I'd never seen him draw it. "In a minute. Roxy, go inside please."

I understood he wanted me out of the way in case Dan turned violent. I thought that was unlikely, but sure, why not? On the other hand, I wanted to see how this played out. I stood up and walked to my front door.

"Stand up slowly, Griffin, and keep your hands where I can see them," Fowler said.

The other cop had his gun out and moved behind Dan. That was likely a precaution since I didn't see anything like a gun around his person. Dan sighed and pushed himself slowly out of my Adirondack chair then stood with his hands up. The other cop put his gun back in the holster as Fowler grabbed his handcuffs. Dan looked up at me as they fastened his hands behind him. He gave me a half-smile. "Thanks for the beer, Roxy."

I started to say *any time* but caught myself. Dan probably wouldn't be having another beer any time soon. "Good luck, Dan," I said instead.

He winked at me as Fowler walked him to the patrol car. And then the whole caravan pulled onto the county road again. If it hadn't been for the beer bottle on the ground next to the chair, I might have believed it had never happened.

But trust me, I knew better than that.

I didn't tell Nate and Uncle Mike about Dan until they got home from the market. I figured it wasn't an emergency like it had been when Dan had tried to steal the hives. "Why the hell did he come here?" Uncle Mike asked.

"I don't know. Maybe he was hiding out around here somewhere." I hadn't seen a car, but perhaps Dan had left it with somebody.

"Good thing you called Fowler," Uncle Mike said. "Just like that bastard to come here when you were by yourself."

I let that go. I'd already told them Dan had turned himself in. All I'd done was make the call. I didn't mention the beer or the fact that I'd been sitting in the front yard with him when Fowler showed up.

Nate figured it out on his own, though, or at least he figured out I'd had some time for conversation with Dan. "What did he tell you?" he asked after Uncle Mike had gone to the main house.

I gave him a quick summary of Dan's explanation for what Hutchinson had done. Nate grimaced at the idea Hutchinson had tried to kill me to take down Dan. "That sounds sort of farfetched. But I guess it could be true. It makes as much sense as any other explanation."

"I guess it depends on how desperate Hutchinson was to get rid of Dan."

"Why would he be desperate?"

I took a deep breath. "Dan has evidence Hutchinson killed Sara. He told me enough to make me think he helped Hutchinson dispose of her body. But he obviously has more information he's going to pass on to Fowler. Maybe Hutchinson wanted to get rid of a potential witness by killing Dan."

Nate leaned back in his chair. "Well, shit. Why would Hutchinson kill Sara? Were they having an affair."

I thought of Hutchinson: short, graying, with the beginnings of a pot belly. "Not unless he's a lot richer than he seems. Which he may well have been, given the number of scams he had going. My guess is she knew he was behind the hive thefts. Dan said she knew Hutchinson owned Mt. Oxford Honey. She ordered the Mt. Oxford Honey for Sylvano's. Knowing Sara's penchant for digging up unpleasant facts on people, I'd say it's likely she found out Hutchinson was running a scam. And maybe she figured out a lot more than that."

"She did have a way of getting into things she should have left alone," Nate agreed.

"So maybe Hutchinson killed her and then had Dan dispose of the body near the barbecue so that Marcus would be implicated. After all, Dan was going to be there cooking. Maybe he was the one who dumped her in the woods where she'd be found by either the people at the barbecue or the people who worked at Sawmill Brewing."

Nate grimaced. "And make Marcus a prime suspect in the process. I'm not inclined to forgive Dan for that."

"I'm not inclined to forgive Dan for much of anything. But I'm grateful that he knocked Hutchinson out before he could kill me, too."

Nate took my hand. "Yeah," he said. "Yeah. For that, I'm truly grateful."

And we didn't talk about Dan or Hutchinson or Sara or beehive thefts for the rest of the night.

Chapter 25

A few days later, we got some confirmation for my theory about Dan and Hutchinson both being involved in what happened to Sara. Hutchinson was charged with murder for Sara's death and with grand larceny for running a beehive theft ring. They didn't charge him with assault for what he did to me, but maybe that came later. It was a big story—we even got out of town reporters who came around digging for details. They called it The Beehive Murders, and at least two budding true crime podcasts were going to be based on it. I declined to be interviewed for either of them.

It was, needless to say, a Big Deal. But most of us who live in Shavano did our best to ignore it. Fred Hutchinson was most likely going to jail, although he was wealthy enough to hire a very high-priced defense lawyer. Dan was almost certainly going to jail, but for a lesser term because he was testifying against Hutchinson.

There wasn't much information available about Sara's murder or Dan's possible part in disposing of her body. I knew from experience that Fowler would tell me squat, and the whole story might or might not come out at trial, particularly if Hutchinson made some kind of plea bargain. I still figured Sara might have found out about Hutchinson's beehive thefts, maybe when she investigated Mt. Oxford Honey. After all, Dan had said she'd tried to blackmail Hutchinson. When she did, she'd made a major mistake since Hutchinson wasn't the type to accept being blackmailed without a fight. We might find out the details at the trial, or we might not. But Hutchinson definitely struck me as the murderous type.

The bottom line was that Sara Jordan was dead and not really missed, which was a shame but also sort of predictable. Marcus's business had a tough few weeks or so, according to Bianca, and then got back on its feet again. I like to think we helped because we used Marcus's stuff for a lot of events, and people saw how good it was.

We also bought some more cheese from Sylvano's. Nate and Ted Sylvano reached an agreement about orders, which made me happy. He seemed like a nice guy, and I always like to buy local when we can.

And even better, Nate finally cracked the wedding market. An event planner in Geary added his menus to her list of caterers, possibly because of the Ted Sylvano connection, and we actually booked a small August wedding. It was, as anticipated, sort of a pain in the neck because the bride and her mom took a while to agree on what they wanted and then wanted some changes after they'd already signed the contract. But we made it work. And, also as anticipated, it was a lucrative contract.

Nate hired a couple of line cooks as temporary assistants, which was good because business picked up at the end of the summer. Neither of them could work as many hours as Dan had, and neither of them could be in the kitchen at events, so that was still on me.

I helped out with prep when I had time and went on

making jam. Dolce was a rising senior this year, which meant she'd probably be leaving for college in another year, which, in turn, meant I'd have to find somebody else. And that really did break my heart. Bridget said she'd like to try doing a little jam-making herself since she'd been watching the two of us cook for over a year now. But I needed her to do the mail orders because she had it down to a science and the mail orders continued to grow. In fact, I was coming to the realization that I probably needed full-time help both in the kitchen and on the business side of things. That was great but also kind of sad. Sometimes I missed the old days when I was a one-girl band.

Not too often, though. And particularly not when I checked my bank balance.

Nate still worked brunch at the café on Sundays when he hadn't had a Saturday catering event, although they could probably have gotten along without him. He wasn't ready to give up the café entirely, just like I wasn't ready to give up my jam making entirely. I still helped out with brunch, too, if I wasn't wiped out from the farmers market.

Thus one Sunday in early September the whole Robicheaux family except for Madge was working in the café kitchen, cleaning up from brunch service and getting ready to take off in our various directions. Nate and I were going over to the river park to watch a kayaking competition. Coco had a date with Marcus to go to the movies in Geary. Bobby was going off to do whatever he usually did on Sundays. He'd been talking about finding a puppy, and Carmen had made noises about giving him Duke.

Marigold had actually shown up in the kitchen that

Sunday, although it was usually her day off. I had no idea what she had planned for the rest of the day. As usual she looked like she was preparing to ride with a band of outlaw bikers. Her forelock was bright purple at the moment, and she'd hung her leather jacket on the rack near the door.

I'd just corked a half bottle of the exceedingly modest champagne Robicheaux's used for their Sunday mimosas when Madge breezed into the kitchen, followed by Uncle Mike. This was sort of a surprise since Uncle Mike rarely made it into town for brunch, but I figured Madge had found a way to cajole him.

"Oh good," she trilled, "you're all still here."

I blinked. I didn't think I'd ever heard Madge trill before, although it wasn't entirely out of character.

"What's up, Mom?" Nate asked.

"I have some news," Madge began, then stopped. "Well, *we* have some news." Her cheeks blushed bright pink and she grasped Uncle Mike's hand.

What the hell?

Madge took a deep breath, then gave us all a brilliant smile. "Mike has asked me to marry him, and I've accepted," she said very quickly.

There was a moment of absolute silence as the three Robicheaux kids stared at her in shock. *Oh, for Pete's sake, get a move on.*

I stepped forward and threw my arms around Uncle Mike, who looked a little dazed. "That's so great. I'm so happy for you. Congratulations." I hugged Madge then, and she hugged me back a little desperately.

Apparently, I'd broken the spell. Nate stepped up and enveloped his mom in a hug of his own. "Congratulations or best wishes or whatever it is I'm supposed to say to the bride. That's great." He turned to Uncle Mike and started to shake his hand, then gave up and hugged him, too.

Madge and Uncle Mike both relaxed a little then, and Coco handed her mom a tissue to wipe her eyes and gave her another hug. "I'm doing the cake. I absolutely am. I've already got ideas." She turned to Uncle Mike and kissed his cheek. "Welcome to the family."

"When's the wedding?" I asked. If Nate and I were going to do the catering—which we no doubt were—we'd need a little time to come up with a menu.

"Oh." Madge's eyes widened a little. "Well, I...don't know. Maybe December?"

Coco shook her head. "Lots of weddings in December. We might have trouble booking an event space this late in the year."

"Well, I wasn't thinking of an event space," Madge said a little hesitantly. "I mean, we could have the wedding here at the café, maybe on a Monday. Or we could have it at the farm—it's lovely there."

Across the room someone cleared his throat loudly, and I suddenly realized Bobby hadn't congratulated Madge and Uncle Mike yet. Bobby, who'd been closest to his dad before he died and might not be ready to see his mom get married again. Bobby, who hated changes of any kind, particularly ones that might affect the café. *Oh, hell.*

We all turned in his direction, my heart sinking. Bobby was leaning on the counter next to Marigold. They both looked a little weird—sort of flummoxed if I had to put a word on it. That made sense with Bobby, but I wasn't sure why Marigold would be perplexed. "This is really great and all," Bobby started, "but..."

Nate stiffened beside me at that *but*. I could see Coco's jaw firming for a fight.

Marigold elbowed Bobby in the side. "No *buts*, Bob," she said.

He nodded quickly. "Right. No *buts* at all. It's great, period." He took a breath. "But…"

Marigold grinned at him, fondly. "What he's trying to say is you beat us to the punch."

Madge sounded confused. "Beat you to the punch how?"

"We're getting married," Bobby said flatly. "Next Friday. At the city building. Judge Solis."

Madge blinked a few times then sat down a little heavily in the nearest chair. "I didn't even know you were dating."

Marigold grinned placidly. "He's a fast worker. Plus I'm knocked up. So we decided to get it done now."

The silence stretched a lot longer than I would have thought possible. "*Knocked up*," Madge said softly. "You mean…pregnant?"

"Yep," Marigold said. "Six weeks or so. Maybe seven."

"Pregnant." Madge took a deep breath. "A grandchild? You're giving me a grandchild?" She pushed slowly to her feet. I don't think I'd ever seen her smile like that before—pure delight. "A *grandchild*?" She hurried across the kitchen to catch the astonished Marigold in a bear hug and then the same for Bobby.

Madge grabbed another tissue to wipe her eyes again. "And you're not getting married at city hall. Absolutely not. We'll have the ceremony here, after service ends on Friday. I know Judge Solis. I'll promise him lasagna. He'll come. We can serve that for the wedding dinner. Maybe Bianca could do something for dessert. I mean she'll be a guest, but maybe she could do something, too."

Coco cleared her throat as loudly as Bobby had. "Over my dead body."

"Oh, well, do you think you'll have time, sweetheart?" Madge turned to her daughter.

Bobby and Marigold both looked slightly stunned but mostly pleased. Madge and Coco huddled together, muttering as they worked out the menu, while Uncle Mike stood with his arm around his fiancée, confused but game.

After a moment of watching the activity around us, I pulled the cork on the exceedingly modest bottle of champagne I'd just finished corking earlier, then searched for Nate. He shoved a couple of juice glasses my way. I poured and then we clinked the glasses before we each took a sip.

"Cheers," I said softly.

Nate grinned. "Big times ahead."

"True that."

"Lots of yelling."

"Yep"

"Lots of aggravation."

"That, too."

"Lots of fun."

"Undoubtedly."

He grinned as he sipped his champagne. "We'll make it."

"Yeah." I grinned back. "We will."

A word about the author…

Meg Benjamin is an award-winning author of romance and cozy mysteries. Along with her Luscious Delights series for Wild Rose Press, she's also the author of the Konigsburg, Salt Box and Brewing Love series. Her other work includes the paranormal Ramos Family trilogy and the Folk series. Meg's books have won numerous awards, including an EPIC Award, a Romantic Times Reviewers' Choice Award, the Holt Medallion, the Beanpot Award, and the Award of Excellence from Colorado Romance Writers.

Thank you for purchasing
this publication of The Wild Rose Press, Inc.

For questions or more information
contact us at
info@thewildrosepress.com.

The Wild Rose Press, Inc.
www.thewildrosepress.com